Owen rattled her.

He didn't check any—well, okay, he didn't check *many*—of the boxes on her future husband list, but Grace still wanted him. But to what end? Was he looking to settle down? In a year? In five years? Did he want kids or a dog? But these weren't the kinds of questions to ask when they hadn't even been on a real date. Talk about getting ahead of herself.

Owen leaned forward. "I think we could have some fun together."

They could. "I'm not looking for fun," Grace told him. She planned to treat her love life with the same meticulous care that she ran her business. "Dating someone is serious."

"It's supposed to be fun, too." He reached out and placed his large, warm hand over hers. "Tell me you'll think about it."

JENNIFER McKENZIE

One More Night

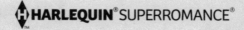
HARLEQUIN® SUPERROMANCE®

Recycling programs
for this product may
not exist in your area.

ISBN-13: 978-0-373-60909-3

One More Night

Copyright © 2015 by Jennifer McKenzie

Printed in U.S.A.

www.Harlequin.com

Jennifer McKenzie lives in Vancouver, Canada, where it rains. A lot. Which means she gets to purchase many pairs of cute boots without guilt. She spends her days writing emails, text messages, newsletters and books. When she's not writing, she's reading or eating chocolate and trying to convince her husband that it's a health food. He has yet to fall for it. Visit her on the web at jennifermckenzie.com.

Books by Jennifer McKenzie

HARLEQUIN SUPERROMANCE

That Weekend...
Not Another Wedding
This Just In...
Tempting Donovan Ford

Visit the Author Profile page
at Harlequin.com for more titles.

This book is for my uncles who have stolen my socks for fun, thrown me like a football for fun and read my books for fun. I won't name any names... oh, wait. For Brian, Ken, Rick, Dan and Jens.

CHAPTER ONE

OWEN FORD SAT in Elephants, one of his family's wine bars, enjoying the cool reprieve from the July afternoon and the opportunity to do nothing. It seemed over the past few months he'd done nothing but work, work, work. And then work some more. He'd recently taken on a larger role in the management of Elephants, trying to show that he was ready for more, ready to add one of the family's other properties to his responsibilities. But so far, Elephants was where he remained.

Owen had been surprised to find he didn't actually hate the work. Something that had shocked him as much as everyone else in the family. In fact, as he leaned back against the tufted padding of the booth in the bar he knew and loved, seeing his accomplishments filled him with a sense of pride.

Though it was only three in the afternoon, Elephants was already half full. People who'd slipped out of the office a bit early, summer tourists—anyone looking for a respite from the hot sun. And Owen knew the rest of the seats would fill up in the next hour as people got off work and looked for a little slice of relaxation after a hard day.

Owen knew he wasn't solely responsible for the bar's success, but he was part of it. It felt good knowing that his suggestions had been implemented and that they worked. He hoped to introduce similar changes at the other properties owned by the family company, the Ford Group, which included three wine bars and one fine dining establishment, but his older brother, Donovan, had been dragging his feet. Both about setting up a meeting and listening to any of Owen's suggestions other than those for Elephants.

Owen tried not to take it personally. Donovan was recently engaged and the new owner of a property he planned to turn into a gastro pub, the first in a string that would dot the Vancouver landscape. But Owen had hoped the fact that Donovan was busier than ever would encourage him to put more on Owen's plate. He'd proven he could handle it with Elephants. And yet, his brother seemed loath to allow further changes.

But he didn't need to think about that now. At this moment, all he needed to do was order something to eat and something to wash it down with.

He smiled at the pretty server when she swung

by to take his order. The old Owen would have done more than smile, would have flirted outrageously with the promise of taking it somewhere later, but the new Owen was an upstanding businessman who had learned to keep a bit of distance between himself and the staff.

Still, that didn't stop him from responding to her joke with one of his own when she returned with his meal. It was merely being friendly. Owen didn't want to become a therapist for the employees, but he'd discovered that his innate interest in people created a special bond, one that made them want to please him, want to do well.

The tension in his lower back, put there by all the nights he spent on his feet, slid away when he cracked open the water bottle—he never drank on-site, not even when he was off duty—and sucked down a long sip. Nothing like a cold drink on a hot day to make a man appreciate the good things in life. Owen sat back and sipped again. And then his phone rang.

He sighed loudly when he saw the name on the screen. Donovan. Knowing the call would be work-related, Owen wasn't comfortable letting it go to voice mail. He was still trying to prove to Donovan that he was serious about this new leaf he'd turned over and refusing to answer the phone would do little to help that, so he forced the irritation down and answered with a polite greeting. "Owen Ford."

"Owen, I need a favor."

Of course he did. And wasn't it just like Donovan to call during his downtime. Owen stifled the thought. It wasn't as if Donovan didn't work hard, too, and he couldn't possibly know that Owen had just sat down to eat. "What's up?"

"I need you to take a meeting for me. With the wedding planner."

"What?" Owen pulled his cell phone away from his ear and looked at the screen as though that would somehow explain the ridiculous request. But the screen only stared back at him, giving him the option to mute, switch to speaker mode or other useless choices. He brought the phone back to his ear. "Are you kidding? Where are you?"

"Stuck in Calgary." Donovan had gone to meet with a possible new supplier, but he was supposed to have been back this morning. "Which is why I'm calling."

Owen shook his head. He was so not the wedding type. "So call Julia and reschedule." Julia, Donovan's fiancée, wouldn't be happy but that was Donovan's problem, not his.

"Don't you think I've tried that? I can't get hold of Julia at home or the restaurant." Julia was the executive chef of the fine dining restaurant in the Ford Group, which was how she and Donovan had met. "She's not answering her cell phone."

"She probably forgot to charge it again." Owen sighed. Julia rarely answered her phone. He didn't know why she even had the stupid thing, since it was always either off or dead. "So call the planner and explain the situation." He had things to do—like eat a juicy burger and spend his afternoon relaxing.

"How well do you think that will go over with Julia?" Owen knew the answer to that, but again not his problem. "Look, if you'll just do me this one favor, I'll schedule that meeting to talk about your ideas."

Owen paused. "Really?" Because he had a lot. All of them winners in his opinion.

"Yes." Donovan sounded harried now.

"All right. Do I have to fill in on the day of, too? Or will you manage to show up?"

Donovan snorted. "As if. You're not the marrying kind."

Owen might have been insulted, except he'd had the same thought not a minute before.

Donovan rattled off directions to the wedding planner's office, which was within walking distance from the bar, and told Owen to make sure he wasn't late.

"I'm not going to have to look at color samples or anything, am I? Because I don't want to get blamed for choosing the wrong shade of pink."

"No choosing required." The relief in Donovan's voice was evident. "And tell Julia that I'm sorry and to charge her phone."

"Should I kiss her, too?" Owen and Julia had their own friendship beyond her engagement to Donovan. Not that it included kissing, but if Owen was going to be forced to attend a wedding-planning session in his brother's stead, he was going to take the opportunity to poke at said brother.

"Not if you value your life."

"I could take you," Owen said. It was an instinctual response. One borne from years of being the little brother. The second-best brother. "But I value my good looks too much." And that was instinctual, too. The desire not to fight, but to go along to get along.

Donovan laughed. "I owe you one."

"Don't worry. I'll be sure to collect."

They talked for a few more minutes, Donovan giving him instructions on how to find the wedding planner's office again as if he'd forgotten already. By the time he hung up, Owen had only a few minutes before he had to leave in order to make it to the meeting on time. He took another long swig of water and mourned that he no longer had enough time for his burger. But the promised discussion with Donovan was worth it. He'd miss a lot of burgers to get the opportunity to show Donovan that he was ready for more responsibility than simply managing Elephants.

He flagged the server and explained that he had to go and to cancel his order, then he tried calling Julia just in case she picked up. The only answer he got was the mechanical voice telling him her inbox was full.

So much for that bright idea. He wiped down the table and left a tip at the bar for the server—just because he owned the place didn't mean the servers shouldn't be compensated—then stepped out into the hot July afternoon.

He wasn't dressed for a meeting of any sort, but decided against going home to change even if he'd had the time. Why should he? This wasn't his meeting, and he didn't feel like putting on pants and a dress shirt. He'd have to change later for work, but until then Owen was content to stay in his khaki shorts and Green Lantern T-shirt. They were clean, which would have to be good enough.

The sun beat down on the back of his neck, making little beads of sweat rise up along his hairline. He was glad to reach his destination, the frosted-glass front door adorned with elegant black script. Grace Monroe Weddings.

Classy. Elegant. Boring.

Owen pushed open the door and stepped into the cool, hushed environment. He blinked as his eyes adjusted from the bright sunlight outside, smiled when he saw the young female receptionist at the long glass desk. The carpet was plush, the walls were icy blue and there was a glittery chandelier that provided a low, comforting glow.

"Hi." He strode forward, hand out. "I'm Owen Ford. I'm here for the Ford-Laurent three o'clock meeting."

"Of course, Mr. Ford." The receptionist shook his hand politely. She wore a wide fabric headband in black velvet and a pale gray dress. With her pale blond hair and light-colored eyes, she suited the style of the office. Owen couldn't help but wonder if that was why she'd been hired. It was almost as though she'd been cast in the role, the perfect front woman. "I'll let Ms. Monroe know you're here. Can I get you anything while you wait? Water? Coffee? Tea? A glass of champagne?"

Since Owen hoped to stick around no longer than it took to give Julia Donovan's regrets, he didn't see the point. "I'm fine, thanks."

He took a seat on the dark pink L-shaped sofa that stretched along two walls. It was the wildest thing in the place, which didn't say much. He drummed his fingers on his knees while the receptionist escaped through a pair of black doors into the back. He hoped Julia would show up before he had to go back there, too.

She didn't.

"Mr. Ford?" The pretty receptionist reappeared, a small, polite smile on her face. "If you'll come with me?"

He didn't see that he had a choice. He pushed himself to his feet and followed her through the doors. The back space was identical to the front. Black-and-white wedding photos lined the hall. Other clients smiling at the camera in long white gowns and black tuxes. He recognized plenty of local sites. The Hycroft mansion, Cecil Green Park House at the University of British Columbia, the VanDusen Botanical Garden. He even recognized a couple of the faces. No one he knew well, but there was an old pal from high school and a liquor distributor for the restaurant. Poor suckers.

Still, he supposed they looked happy enough in the photos and at least he wasn't the one getting married.

The receptionist showed him into a small boardroom. The table was jet-black and glossy. No sign of fingerprints, cup rings or anything to mar the smooth surface. Padded white chairs circled the table. There was a small sideboard displaying water bottles in neat lines, a small espresso maker, demitasse cups and a china teapot. An assortment of flaky pastries, small side plates and linen napkins sat beside them. "Ms. Monroe will be along in just a moment. Is there anything I can do for you?"

"I'm fine," he told her again. Or he would be as soon as he got out of here. He still had a low-level fear that he'd somehow be coerced into giving his opinion on fabric or colors or some other wedding detail that he wouldn't know was a big deal until he gave the wrong opinion. Perhaps Donovan's delayed flight wasn't wholly accidental.

"Please help yourself to anything." The receptionist gestured to the sideboard before clasping her hands in front of her. "We're a full-service boutique, so just let us know if there's anything we can do for you."

"I appreciate it." Owen remained standing after she left. No point in taking a seat as he'd be on his way soon enough. Instead, he studied the photos displayed on the walls. More locations he recognized, though he let his eyes skitter over those, uninterested in the bouquets and dresses. He stopped on a photo of a couple in front of a pond. It wasn't flashy. There was no arbor of roses above them or a brick windmill for storied ambience. It was just a pond backed by a forest of tall evergreens. The couple wasn't wearing the traditional white and black and there wasn't an explosion of roses in her hand. She wore a casual dress that reached her knees in a floral pattern, while he was in cotton pants and a loose white shirt. They were looking at each other, just a tiny upturn to their lips, as though they were sharing a secret joke. As though they were the only two people there.

Which, Owen supposed, was how it should be.

The click of the door handle interrupted his perusal and he spun, turning on his smile as he did.

"Mr. Ford." The woman who walked through the door was cool and blonde. She could have been related to the young receptionist. She wore a cream-colored suit and a lilac dress shirt and her pale hair was twisted back, not a strand out of place. Owen suspected no strand would dare to break free of the neat updo. Not if it wanted to live to tell about it. "I'm Grace Monroe."

He moved to take her proffered hand, expecting it to be as cool and stiff as everything else in this place. Like a marble statue, beautiful to look at and smooth to the touch, but lifeless.

He was wrong.

Her fingers were warm and soft as they

wrapped around his. He couldn't help stroking his thumb across them, appreciating the velvety surface. Her eyes were dark blue, like the sky just before the sun dipped below the horizon. They widened at him again when he smiled.

She pulled her hand free, quickly and crisply, like the way she walked. "Can I offer you a beverage?"

What was it with these people and the offering of beverages? Did he look dehydrated? "No, thank you." But he did take a moment to secretly drink her in. The smooth lines of her suit, hiding and covering everything beneath. He wondered if her skin beneath was as warm as her hand. He wanted to reach out and touch her again, but she moved away, stepping around him to lay a folder on the glossy table.

He caught the waft of her scent as she passed. The bright pop of grapefruit and the sharpness of mint. Clean and fresh. "Will your fiancée be joining you?" she asked.

"Oh, I'm not the one getting married." Owen realized she'd misunderstood who he was. A miscommunication from the receptionist. From him. Perhaps he should have been clearer, since he did share the groom's last name.

"I see." Her cool eyes landed on him. "Then who would you be?"

"The brother of the groom." He took a half

step toward her just to see if he could get a whiff of her perfume again.

She raised an eyebrow at him. "And you would be here because?"

"Because my brother was unable to make the meeting and he asked if I'd come in his place." Suddenly, the thought of leaving as soon as he'd arrived didn't sound quite so appealing. Owen smiled at her. "Perhaps it was fortuitous."

"How so?"

"Well, if I hadn't come, then I wouldn't be able to ask you out."

"Mr. Ford." Grace's eyes went frosty. "This is a place of business and I do not date clients."

Owen blinked. He'd been rejected before. Not often, but it had happened once or twice. "But I'm not a client. I'm the brother of a client."

"Close enough." Her fingers twitched and Owen saw her nails were painted the same pale pink as her lips. She opened her mouth, but whatever she'd been about to say was cut short by a knock at the door.

"Ms. Monroe?" The pretty receptionist entered the room. "Ms. Laurent is here."

The frosty film in Grace's eyes disappeared and was replaced by a look of polite welcome. "Thank you, Hayley." Grace greeted Julia warmly, showing a spirit of effervescence that took Owen by surprise. Not quite the cool Ice

Queen she tried to portray. The dichotomy intrigued him. It had been a long time since a woman had intrigued him.

"Owen?" Julia's brow furrowed when she spotted him standing there. "What are you doing here? Where's Donovan?"

"His flight was delayed." Owen glanced at Grace, who was watching him with no hint of that effervescence. "And he couldn't get in touch with you to let you know. He roped me into coming in his place."

"Did he?" Julia couldn't hide her grin. "How much did that cost him?"

"Just his undying gratitude." Owen included Grace in his cheerful explanation. She didn't smile back.

"Well—" Julia's voice drew his attention "—I appreciate you coming, Owen, but don't feel obligated to hang around. I'm sure you have something else to do."

Owen continued to look at Grace, who stared at him, a small pout on her lips. Clearly, his leaving would be no skin off her back. "Actually…" He sent her his most charming smile. He'd crack her facade if it killed him. "I think I'll stay."

CHAPTER TWO

GRACE COULD FEEL irritation and something else burn up the back of her neck and warm her cheeks. This man, this charming, flirty, handsome man in his casual shorts and cartoony T-shirt, with his hair mussed and flip-flops on his feet, unsettled her. She didn't like being unsettled.

Raised by a pair of unconventional hippies on Salt Spring Island, one of the Gulf Islands off the coast of BC, meant Grace was well aware of how unsettled life could be. It was something she'd fought against her whole life, longing to fit in, to be like the families she saw on TV sitcoms with parents who were married, who set rules for their kids and expected them to work toward well-paid white-collar careers. Instead of scrounging in the dirt on the family's organic farm and saving her pennies to buy the glossy magazines her mother claimed were rife with material consumerism.

Grace breathed in slowly. The room was an ideal seventy-two degrees, which felt cool in the summer season. She reminded herself that after today she wouldn't have to put up with Owen Ford again. That this wedding, like all her weddings, would find its rhythm and settle into the detailed and organized plan she'd create for it.

Really, Owen was a good reminder to her and everyone on her team that there was no fraternizing with the clients. Not with the wedding party, the family or the guests.

It was a hard-line policy, but one Grace felt was necessary. Weddings were ripe for sexcapades. Alcohol flowed, bodies pressed against one another on the dance floor, while everyone was groomed and dressed to look their best. And with the cultural overtones that were wrapped up in the idea of a wedding night, sex was on the brain.

Grace expected her staff to rise above all of that, and to ensure her events stayed classy and professional no matter what. Amorous couples were dispatched to conduct their business in private. Grace had personally caught guests going at it in the garden, in the bathroom and in the limo booked to whisk the newlyweds off at the end of the night. In all cases, she'd politely interrupted and suggested the couple in question might prefer to take their activities to a more private location. Like the bank of hotel rooms she always booked for her events.

She had a feeling she'd need a suite of rooms for Owen Ford.

The moment that thought entered her mind, Grace pushed it away. Owen's personal amusements were none of her business. She was here to plan a wedding, not worry about what kind of problems the brother of the groom might cause. There would be plenty of time to worry about that once the location was selected, the cake ordered and the flowers chosen.

"Let's discuss basics, Ms. Laurent."

"Oh, please, call me Julia."

"Call me Owen."

Grace forced a polite smile she didn't feel. "Of course, Julia. Please call me Grace." She purposely didn't look at Owen, keeping her attention focused where it should be—on the person getting married. "You said during our initial phone call that you're thinking about a winter wedding. Did you have a specific date in mind?"

Julia talked about the quiet time in the restaurant industry and how she and her fiancé hoped to take advantage of that. Grace listened with both ears, but kept an eye on Owen. He looked too casual, too comfortable. And who came to a business meeting, even if it wasn't his business, in shorts and flip-flops? Would it have killed him to put on a pair of pants and some closed-toe shoes?

"So January?" She returned her gaze to Julia. She was going to be an easy bride. Grace could already tell. None of the barely suppressed nerves or the tightly wound personality that some of her brides had.

They discussed a few options. Day or evening. Hotel or private venue. Indoor, outdoor or a mix of both. The number of guests. Their proposed budget made it clear that money wasn't going to be an issue. No, any difficulties were going to come from availability and desire. Grace flicked another glance at Owen, who hadn't added much to the discussion. He'd just sat there.

She felt the burn rise back up her cheeks when she saw he was looking at her and closed her leather notebook with a delicate flip. "I think we've got a good start." She started a new book for each wedding she planned, filling the pages with notes and pictures on anything and everything. The wedding party, engagement parties, photographers, the dress, the food, every detail that might arise and plenty that didn't.

Grace's business offered full-service wedding-planning services and that meant she handled everything no matter how big or small. Though she'd started her own business just four years ago, she'd been in the industry for nine, honing her skills at larger, more established event-planning companies before branching out on her own. She'd already carved out a niche. The wedding planner for those who wanted style and class, traditional elegance.

She was expensive, but then so were her results. But her clients got what they paid for. Every detail was exquisite, every movement planned and prepared so that the whole day was a magical experience.

"I'll come up with some prospective plans and send them to you and your fiancé. Perhaps we can schedule another meeting next week to discuss them?" Grace liked to move quickly. Although winter weddings weren't nearly as popular as summer or spring, the best locations always booked up quickly and often months or years ahead of time. She didn't want to get caught flat-footed on what was sure to be one of the biggest weddings of the season.

She'd manage the media attention, too. She had contacts at the papers, reporters who would be all too happy to feature a pair of local celebrities and their splashy event. Or she could bar them, keeping photos and attention directed elsewhere to allow the bride and groom privacy.

"And please let me know if there's anything else I can do for you," Grace said. She'd learned over the years that keeping in regular contact with her clients was the best way to manage any surprises. This way there were no last-minute bombs dropped that she couldn't negotiate.

"Absolutely." Julia stood, pushing her dark hair off her shoulder. "Thank you so much, Grace. I'm really looking forward to this."

Grace was, too. Not just the wedding day, but the deeper meaning behind it. Grace could always tell which brides were about playing princess and had been planning their wedding since they were six and which were motivated not by the ceremony, but the future it represented.

She smiled, feeling Julia's happiness wash over her. This was why she did it. To know that she had a hand in creating a happy day that would hopefully lead to a long and happy future. A future she wanted for herself. And one she planned to start working toward now that her business was more secure and didn't require her to work quite so many extra hours.

"I'll see you out." Grace was conscientious about not excluding Owen from the conversation, much as she might like to. She led them down her "hall of fame," where she displayed the photos from her favorite events, walking slowly, allowing them to pause and study the black-and-white prints. The reaction often gave her a solid base from which to start.

Did the bride halt in front of garden photos or rocky cliffs? Did her eyes widen at the clean lines of a regimented wedding party or the scattered cluster of bodies? The photos often gave the couple ideas, as well. Most times, they specifically referred to a photo or two during their second meeting.

Grace noted Julia's pauses, the hesitation by the cityscapes. Rooftop patios with the buildings laid out below them. Night shots where the streetlights twinkled in the distance. Good. Very good.

But she didn't feel quite so good when she glanced at Owen. His eyes were on her rather than the pictures. Grace swallowed and kept her gait steady.

She didn't expect him to study them. Not exactly. He likely would have no say in the choices made, but she didn't expect him to gawk at her, either. She longed to fiddle with the cuff of her suit jacket or straighten her skirt, but that would betray the uncertainty writhing within her and she wouldn't do that.

Instead, she took long, slow breaths, the way she'd learned in her Pilates class. The deep and full inhalation and the complete exhalation. It was meant to cleanse and invigorate and Grace generally found this to be true when she was in class. The long, lean bodies stretched around her, each of them working to reach the same goal. But now, she just felt light-headed.

She was glad when they reached the lobby and the safety it provided with both her new hire, Hayley, and the front door.

"Grace, thank you again." Julia turned with a warm smile and took Grace's hands in hers. It didn't surprise Grace, the extra touching. She made connections with her clients—they were entrusting her with one of the most important days of their lives and a connection was natural. But Julia's sincerity did.

"It's a pleasure." Which was pretty much what she said to all her clients, but this time she meant it. "I'll be in touch by the end of the week."

But while Julia moved toward the frosted-glass front door that led out to the sidewalk, Owen didn't follow. Grace felt her molars clamp together, but she made certain there was no other physical indication of her unsettledness. "Mr. Ford? Is there something I can assist you with?"

"I think I forgot something in the boardroom."

Grace held her tongue. Waspishly asking what that could possibly be wouldn't win her any points. Not with him, not with Julia, not with Hayley and not with herself. "Of course. I'll show you back."

"You go on ahead, Jules," Owen said to his sister-in-law with a friendly wave. "And tell Donovan he owes me."

Julia laughed as she pushed the door open and stepped out into the summer afternoon, but Grace didn't feel like laughing. Or smiling. Exactly what was he on about now? She knew he hadn't forgotten anything. He hadn't been carrying anything when he'd arrived and he'd placed nothing on the table or the chair.

It embarrassed Grace that she knew this with such certainty as it meant she'd been watching him, paying close attention even when she hadn't wanted to. "Exactly what are we looking for?" she asked as they walked back down the hallway to the boardroom.

He didn't answer until she pushed open the door and he followed her inside. Grace had always loved her boardroom. The round, shiny table, the padded chairs that had been selected for comfort as well as style, the dove-gray walls and crystal chandelier. It wasn't large because it didn't need to be. Grace didn't have a board of directors and she saw no need for more than eight people to ever be in the room at one time. Any more than that and it meant there were too many voices, too many opinions—usually from everyone other than the couple getting married, which was something she tried to avoid.

But right now, the room felt too compact. Too small. Too full of Owen Ford.

"I didn't forget anything."

Grace's toes curled in the points of her high-heeled shoes. She'd known that, but she hadn't expected him to come right out with it. No, she'd expected a staged search that would end when he suddenly "remembered" that he hadn't brought along whatever item he'd pretended to leave behind with him in the first place. She moved across the room to straighten the line of water glasses that were slightly off. "Was there something else, then?"

"Yes." He moved toward her, all warm intent and male conceit.

Grace felt the unwelcome response of her own body. The tug of heat, the whip of interest and the curiosity that flooded her system. She forced herself to hold her ground, not to back up until she bumped into the wall. There was no need to give him the high ground, moral or otherwise. They were in her space. She was in control. She left the glasses—those could be straightened later—and crossed her arms over her chest, stopping him in his tracks. "What is it you want, Mr. Ford?"

"Well, first, I'd like you to call me Owen." He grinned, a charming, rakish grin that Grace had little doubt got him what he wanted most of the time. "And second, I'd like you to go out with me."

She didn't need time to consider her answer. "No."

"Is that a *no* to question one or question two?"

"To both." She didn't smile or waver. It would only egg him on and she had a feeling Owen would be a handful without any encouragement.

"Now, why is that?" He took another step forward.

He was crowding her, even though he was too far away to touch. "As I've already explained, I don't fraternize with my clients."

"I'm not a client."

Grace didn't bother to correct him, didn't want to engage him any more than was absolutely necessary. "Is there anything else, Mr. Ford?"

Owen didn't say anything, but tilted his head and studied her. Grace felt like a bug under a magnifying glass, which had been a favorite pastime of her brother's growing up until her mother caught him at it and gave him a lecture on respecting the life of all Earth's creatures.

But if Owen thought she'd flounder, scrabble away or otherwise panic, he was wrong. She did what those little bugs never had—remained completely still and let him look. She knew she looked presentable and put together. She prided herself on it. Not a hair out of place, with understated and expensive jewelry, and artfully applied makeup. He'd find nothing there.

"I can't quite figure you out," he finally said.

"I'm not a puzzle."

Owen shrugged. "And yet I find you puzzling."

Grace had no doubt he'd used this line before. But she was made of stronger stuff. He was handsome and clearly comfortable in his own skin, but that was hardly enough. "Then I suppose I'll just have to remain one of life's little mysteries. I'll show you out."

She moved to step around him. He moved with her, their arms brushing. Grace felt his heat through the thin material of her suit jacket and was glad she'd left it on. "Maybe we could go for coffee," Owen suggested as she led him out of the boardroom and back into the hallway.

"I'm afraid that won't be possible."

"And why's that?"

"Mr. Ford." She leveled a cool look at him as they walked. "As I've explained twice, I keep my personal and professional lives separate."

"I'm not part of your business."

"You're in my office as part of a wedding I've been hired to plan." Grace walked a little faster.

"That my brother and sister-in-law hired you for." He kept up easily, his flip-flops slapping against the soles of his feet. Grace hated the sound, the loud smack disturbing the quiet hush of the space. "I don't have anything to do with it."

"You're family. That makes you a client by association."

"What about if I file for emancipation? My parents will be devastated, but they'll understand when they meet you."

Grace tried not to laugh. She really did, but Owen's playful nature and silly banter finally got to her. She felt the corners of her mouth curl up. "Fine, Mr. Ford. If you file for emancipation, we'll go for that coffee." She pushed open the door that led to the lobby. "Otherwise? I'll look forward to seeing you at the wedding."

He followed her into the quiet space, where the only sound was the click of Hayley's keyboard as she entered files into the system. "I'll look forward to it, too."

Grace turned to look at him and felt a pulse of attraction. His dark eyes, dark hair that flopped over his forehead and mischievous grin. Her throat felt dry and she wished she'd taken a glass of water from the boardroom. Oh well. As soon as she got rid of him, she could chug a bottle in the privacy of her office. She was determined to do so immediately. "It was a pleasure meeting you, Mr. Ford."

His fingers, warm and thick, wrapped around hers. Grace felt another shaft of desire, followed by a stern reminder that Owen Ford wasn't her type even if he hadn't been off-limits.

She preferred slender, elegant men. Men who wore suits to work and most certainly to business meetings. Men who worked in corner offices, many stories off the ground, and had a closet full of shoes in black and brown. Men who didn't hold her hand a little too long and didn't make her feel too warm in her suit.

"The pleasure has been all mine, Ms. Monroe." He brought her hand to his lips and pressed a dry and gentle peck to the back. "Until then."

And she certainly didn't like men who kissed her without asking.

Heart pumping, Grace watched him leave and then spun on her heel and made for the safety of her office and the cooling comfort of a bottle of water or three.

CHAPTER THREE

"I'M AFRAID I must have misheard you." Owen pretended to tap his ear as though clearing it of water. "You want to repeat that?"

It was Saturday night and Elephants was packed. He was pleased that his initiatives continued to bring people in the door, even if it was in the form of his only sister. Mal merely stared back. "I need you to plan an engagement party for Donovan and Julia." She said this with a straight face as though it wasn't the funniest thing in the world.

Since Mal hadn't been in much of a laughing mood these past few months, Owen did it for her. "Right."

"I'm not kidding." Mal pinned him with her patented bratty-kid-sister stare. "Mom and I discussed it."

"Oh, did you? And what other parts of my life did the two of you plan?" He was only half joking.

"Owen, you're the best man. Consider it part of your duties." Owen still wasn't sure how he'd been roped into being the best man. Sure, he and Donovan were getting along better than they had been a year ago, but they were hardly close. He suspected Julia—who he considered a good friend—and his mother and sister were all conspiring to bring them closer together.

"No, my duty is to plan the bachelor party, ensure Donovan doesn't freak out last-minute and get cold feet, and make sure I show up on time and in my tux." And find the sexiest woman at the reception and see if she'd consider going home with him. Though really, that was just being humble. More likely, he'd be the one getting propositioned, which suited him just fine.

Despite her little bomb, Owen was glad to see Mal out on a Saturday night. Since her breakup with her boyfriend a few months ago, she hadn't been herself. Owen wasn't sure exactly what had happened, since she wasn't talking and neither was Travis. Not even when Owen had gone down to Aruba, where Travis now lived, for a visit and asked him point-blank. All either of them would say was that things hadn't worked out, but Owen noted neither of them had exactly moved on.

"Well, consider the engagement party an added bonus."

"Bonus for who?" Owen grumbled.

Mal patted him on the shoulder. "For you. Think of it like planning for your own future."

He snorted again. "I'm not even dating anyone. Kind of a prerequisite."

"Good. Then you'll have plenty of free time to plan the engagement party."

"You know, I think I liked it better when you stayed home on Saturday nights."

Mal's hand dropped, as did her head. Owen saw her hands clench in her lap. "You aren't the only one."

"Hey." He reached out and put his arm around her shoulders. He and Mal had always had an easy relationship. Even before she'd started dating one of his closest friends. "I wasn't serious. You know I love having you here."

But Mal only sighed.

Owen turned to look at his sister. She'd always been thin, but these days she seemed downright emaciated. Not that he could say anything about it to her. The one time he'd joked that she should eat a sandwich, she'd about taken his head off. Still, despite her extreme thinness, Mal was a good-looking woman. Owen noted the interested glances that were coming her way even if she didn't. "You okay?"

She sighed again. "Not really, but I don't want to talk about it."

She never did. But since Owen wasn't sure

how it would help to force her into discussing the problem, he didn't push. "If you change your mind…" He left the sentence hanging.

"I know. You, Donovan, Mom and Dad, even Julia the last time I saw her." Mal sat up, shrugging off his arm. "But I'm fine, really. I'm just adjusting. That's all."

Owen didn't point out that she'd had months to adjust and still hadn't managed it. If Mal wanted to think she was fooling him, he'd let her. Maybe she'd eventually fool herself and get back to the Mal he knew. "So, how exactly did you and Mom come to the conclusion that I needed to organize the engagement party? Isn't that something the parents of the groom should do? Or the sister?"

"No." And some of the tension slid from Mal's face at the change of subject. At least, the lines around her mouth didn't look so prominent. "Plus, Mom already tried to pawn it off on me, which is how your name came up."

"You threw me under the bus."

"That's such a cliché. I prefer to think of it as giving you a gift."

Owen shook his head. "A gift? Please, more like an obligation." One he didn't know how to get out of. If Mal and his mother had already joined forces? Game, set and match.

"Oh, I don't know. Julia mentioned how interested you seemed in the wedding planner." Mal shot him a smirk.

Owen picked up the water bottle he was drinking from and rolled it back and forth between his palms. He wasn't embarrassed to have been caught out. He hadn't exactly been subtle about his appreciation for the cool Grace Monroe. But she'd been pretty clear that even if she found him appealing, nothing would come of it. "I'm not sure what that has to do with anything, but for the record, she wasn't interested."

"You didn't think you'd have to plan the party on your own, did you?" Mal rolled her eyes. "You'd be working with her. Just think—the two of you could join forces. Maybe spend some late nights during the planning stages."

Owen wasn't fooled. "Don't try to distract me. I won't forget that you used me as a shield." But he certainly wouldn't mind the excuse to see Grace—ahem, Ms. Monroe—again. "You don't care about my dating life. You just don't want to have to plan it yourself."

"I see no reason that I can't care about both things." And for a moment, with her little smirk and sassy tone, Owen saw the sister he knew. Then it was gone, replaced with something quiet and a little sad. "I know it's a lot to ask, Owen. But I don't think I can do it."

He looked into her eyes to see if she was try-

ing to trick him. Mal would be fully capable
of letting a fib trip right off her tongue with
no body language to indicate anything but the
deepest sincerity, but her eyes always gave her
away. A combination of fear, shame and a deep
pain stared back at him. Owen felt it in his own
stomach.

"It's just…too close."

Too close because up until earlier this year,
Mal had been the engaged Ford sibling, the one
who'd be wedding-planning and holding the
ceremony on a beach in Aruba in the near future. But when their father had had his heart
attack, everything had changed.

It had changed for all of them. Donovan took
over running the company, while Owen began
to pay more attention to work instead of treating it like a fun place to hang out in the evening
for a few hours and collect a paycheck. But Mal
had uprooted her life in Aruba and moved back
to Vancouver. Sold her stake in the beach restaurant to Travis and come back to work for the
family business.

"Fine. I'll do it." Owen huffed out a breath,
putting on a show of being put out because he
thought Mal needed it. Needed to feel as though
things were normal, that her older brother still
found her an annoying pest and loved her anyway. They'd all been careful with Mal over

the past few months. Doing their best not to upset her, tiptoeing around the question of what had happened between her and Travis because even when it came up indirectly, she got visibly upset. But that clearly wasn't working and Owen wasn't about to dump Travis as a friend without cause. "But this means you owe me."

"I got you alone time with the wedding planner. Consider yourself paid in full."

"Not enough." He crossed his arms over his chest and put on his I'm-older-and-know-better-than-you look. "Tell me what's going on with Travis."

Mal's lips pursed and her glare could have melted plastic. Good thing Owen was immune to it, seeing as she'd been using it on him since they were kids. "Nothing is going on."

Semantics. Owen recognized her answer for the dodge it was, but he wasn't about to let her use a loophole to get out of this. "Maybe nothing's going on now, but something happened earlier. Tell me."

"No."

"Mal."

"Drop it, Owen." And there was sorrow as well as anger in her gaze. "I'm not discussing it."

Owen drummed his fingers on his water bottle and then shrugged. "Fine. But if you won't tell me, then I can't console you with free alcohol and ice cream."

Mal's look was withering. "You think I can't comp myself?"

Owen shrugged again. "I'm the manager here. They do what I say."

"And you'd tell them not to serve me?" When he nodded, his sister's eyes narrowed. Owen was glad to see it. At least she wasn't going to curl up in a ball or slink away the way she would have done a couple of months earlier. Progress. "You'd starve your only sister?"

"I'd do whatever I had to if I thought it would help."

Her face softened and she reached out to lay a hand on his arm. "I appreciate it, Owen. But I'm okay."

He wasn't sure he believed her, but he nodded agreeably. He preferred compromise to conflict. "All right, then. Tell me what I need to know about this party. I'm sure you have some ideas."

This time, Mal's smile reached her eyes. "I'm so glad you asked."

OWEN CALLED GRACE Sunday morning. A woman like her would spend her Monday morning returning phone calls in order and he hoped to be one of the first. Perhaps he could convince her to go out with him yet. A business meeting. Over lunch. Totally aboveboard.

He was surprised when she answered.

"Grace Monroe."

But he recovered quickly. "Grace. It's Owen Ford."

"Mr. Ford." He was pretty sure he heard a sigh in her voice, but it was immediately replaced with cool professionalism. "What can I help you with?"

"A party. I need to plan one."

There was a brief pause. "You're aware that I specialize in weddings? But I'm happy to send you the names of some other planners in the city who can help. What kind of budget do you have?"

"It's not for me. An engagement party for Donovan and Julia." Owen had attended his fair share of parties over the years. More than his fair share and even hosted some. But a couple of blowouts when he'd been in high school, a kegger in his parents' backyard before he'd told them that he'd officially dropped out of university and a housewarming when he'd bought his apartment that had turned into forty-eight hours of drinks and debauchery weren't exactly going to cut it. "I'd like to hire you to help."

Grace exhaled. Owen heard the slow escape of air. "You've already hired me, Mr. Ford. I can certainly add the engagement party to the wedding portfolio."

"No, it's a surprise." Another little gem Mal had informed him of once he'd committed to organizing it. He heard the rustling of paper, imagined Grace flipping through a sheaf of them at her desk. "You aren't at the office, are you?"

"I'm not sure how that concerns you, but yes, I am."

Owen glanced at the clock. It was only nine in the morning. On a Sunday. He'd been up for an hour and a half, getting a run in before the day got too warm to be comfortable, but most people would still be lounging in bed or treating the worst of their hangovers at a local breakfast café. And Grace was in her office. What a waste on a beautiful weekend morning. "Listen, why don't I swing by to pick you up. We'll go for brunch and discuss."

There was a short pause. Marshaling her resources no doubt. "That's not necessary, Mr. Ford. Why don't you tell me what kind of function you have in mind over the phone and I'll start putting some ideas together that I can send to you."

"So that I can feel guilty for making you work the entire Sunday? I won't allow it." He had a few hours before he needed to go into work himself and he thought spending it with Grace sounded like a fine idea. Better than his original plan, which was to lie on the couch until it was time to leave. The old Owen would have still been in bed, presumably with a gorgeous woman beside him, but since taking on a more involved role, his late nights out with the beautiful people of the city had come to an end. In truth, he didn't miss it.

While it had been fun for a while—partying all night, sleeping most of the day and then doing it all over again—eventually it had started to bore him. There were only so many times he could see his picture in the paper under a caption proclaiming him one of the city's most eligible bachelors, only so many times he could get up after only three hours of sleep and pretend that he couldn't wait to hit the club that night. He'd done it longer than he'd wanted. Partially because he felt obligated to keep up the guise of the playboy Ford. Unlike Donovan and Mal, who'd finished university and then worked in the family offices putting their education to use, he'd dropped out in the middle of his second year and accepted a job as assistant manager at Elephants only because his parents had explained that he'd be cut off financially otherwise. But he'd done as little as possible those first dozen years.

It had gone on for so long that once he realized he'd changed, he didn't know how to change his situation. His attempts to convince Donovan to give him more responsibility had been met with a steely stare and refusal. It wasn't until their father's heart attack that Donovan had been forced to accept Owen's help. And though there were times that Owen felt overworked and in dire need of a break, he was happier now. He had a reason to get up in the morning, a sense of pride in his life.

But he still liked to have fun.

"Owen—"

He cut Grace off before she could decline again. "It's just brunch. To discuss work. Or have you eaten already?" She probably had, some dry toast and half a hard-boiled egg with strong tea followed by flossing and the recommended two minutes of teeth-brushing.

She sighed. "Just coffee."

"Great. Then I won't take no for an answer. I'll see you in fifteen." Which would give him just enough time to shower, throw on some clothes and make the five-minute drive from his condo in Coal Harbor, which overlooked the water and Stanley Park, to her office in Yaletown. On a normal day, Owen would have walked, enjoying the city morning, the way the sun glinted off the buildings and the cool, fresh breeze that swept off the ocean.

But he wasn't going to give Grace any extra time, any extra opportunity to decline his suggestion.

SHE SHOULD HAVE turned him down. Grace knew that before she'd even agreed to Owen's suggestion. But it was a glorious morning and she'd already attended her Pilates class and brunch in the city sounded lovely, even if it was just a work meeting. Which was exactly what she wanted. Nothing more, nothing less.

Still, her heart beat a little faster when she heard the knock on the front door and she rose from the main desk to slide the bolt and let him in. He looked good. Too good. Dressed in dark jeans and a white V-neck tee, he looked every inch the city playboy the blogosphere and papers claimed he was.

Yes, she'd looked him up. Had done a thorough and intensive investigation through internet searches and online newspaper archives. She was merely information-gathering for her wedding portfolio, making sure that she was aware of any possible pitfalls before they could appear. It was simply good management. But the heat warming her cheeks hinted at something else. Something Grace wasn't quite as comfortable with.

So she pasted on her professional smile, greeted him with a quick air kiss and prepared to step back and gather her purse from the desk drawer. Except Owen pulled her into a loose hug. "It's good to see you."

And her pulse jumped before she gathered her composure and stepped out of his embrace. "Yes, well..." She let her sentence drop off, unsure what else to say. She wouldn't agree that it was good to see him, too, because she wasn't sure it was. He looked good, that was true enough, but was it actually good to see him? Even if he hadn't been a client, albeit an indirect one, there was the small matter that he was absolutely not her type. Not even close. And certainly not the kind of man she saw herself settling down with in the future.

Grace strode back to the desk and grabbed her purse, hoping the flames in her cheeks weren't visible.

"You look good," Owen noted, leaning against the wall, easily, as though he'd been here a million times and had long since picked out his spot.

She refused to be rattled by the compliment. Since it was a Sunday, a day her office was closed unless she had a meeting scheduled, she'd selected a more casual look than her usual business wear. A racerback sheath dress that reached the tops of her knees in the palest periwinkle and flat gold sandals. Her hair was pulled back into a loose knot and she wore simple gold hoops at her ears and wrist. She did look good, but it was nice that he'd noticed. "Thank you."

As Grace ushered him out of her office, she wondered again why she had agreed to go out for a meal with him when their time would be much more usefully spent in her boardroom or, better yet, discussing this by email so that she could consider his ideas and then get back to him with a list of possibilities. But she didn't say anything as they headed down the sidewalk, the morning still cool despite the sun high overhead. It wouldn't really heat up for a few hours and by then Grace would be back in either her office or her apartment. And it would be good to get some sustenance if she planned to spend the rest of the day working.

She lifted her face to the sun, appreciating the warmth that might disguise any lingering heat in her cheeks. She didn't often spend time outdoors, a fact that her family—organic farmers—couldn't understand or value. But then they sort of felt that way about her, too. The one who left home and the business. The one who studied business and commerce in university. The one who stayed on the mainland after graduation and started a business there. A commercial business that, according to her mother, "benefited off the backs of social conventions that no longer had a place in today's world."

Grace didn't agree. She often rebutted her mother's arguments with some of her own. That marriage created a sort of social stability, provided a cornerstone on which to rest. A minicommunity that spread out to embrace the surrounding areas. But the truth was she liked the romance of it all.

The promise to share a life together, to protect and support each other. Granted her parents had done the same thing without ever getting married. Cedar Matthews and Sparrow Monroe—though they disliked using last names, claiming it supported a patriarchal society—had been together for more than thirty years and fully committed to their family without ever making it official. But it wasn't the same.

Grace shook the unsettling thoughts away. She was different than her parents, than her younger brother, Sky, who'd always been content to toe the family line, to learn the business of farming, and who, along with his girlfriend, lived in the small guesthouse built beside the main farmhouse where Grace had grown up. And she was okay with that.

They didn't have to appreciate what she did or recognize the worth of the services she provided. She appreciated herself.

"So, tell me what kind of party you have in mind," she said as they crossed the street and headed down toward the rows of restaurants and cafés that ringed Yaletown, a popular Vancouver neighborhood. No time like the present to get started.

"Let's get settled first," Owen suggested. As though she wasn't totally unsettled by the mere fact that they were out together.

But Grace kept that insight to herself and nodded as they made their way down the cobblestone sidewalks that were common throughout much of the area. Most restaurants had tables pulled out that were exposed to the sun and already filled with customers eating and drinking.

Owen didn't stop at any of the ones they passed, continuing down the sloped sidewalks toward False Creek and a view of the water. Grace was content to keep the peace and simply enjoy the silence of companionship. This was the kind of thing she hoped to make a regular part of her life with her future husband—being elegantly dressed for a casual brunch, enjoying a meal of eggs Florentine or seafood crepes while they discussed travel plans, art, music or theater.

Next year, she reminded herself. At the end

of the five-year plan when her business was flourishing and she no longer needed to oversee every detail. When she had staff to handle meetings and make certain decisions without coming to her for approval. Then she'd block off some time specifically for finding the right kind of man to marry. She didn't think it would take longer than a year, eighteen months at most.

She was an attractive woman who kept herself in good shape. She had her own money, a thriving business and a condo in the city. She was a good conversationalist, cultured and well-read. She was, in short, a great catch. Even in a city of great catches, she knew she'd stand out. Just as soon as she put herself out there.

Her eyes darted to Owen. He looked the part, but she knew he wasn't. According to what she'd uncovered online, he was a regular at the city's hottest nightclubs and a well-known playboy who rarely showed up to any event with a woman more than once. Not husband material. Not even close.

Owen stopped in front of Gascony, a popular spot for brunch thanks to its location on the water and fabulous food. The place was full even though it was still early for many people, but Owen seemed to know the hostess, who found them a small table for two by a window that looked out at the marina. Grace unfolded the cloth napkin and placed it in her lap.

She left her notebook in her purse, determining that while pulling it out might be useful for remembering everything that was said, it would be considered tacky. Gascony wasn't the kind of place where people took notes or dictated business deals. As soon as she got back to the office, she'd write down everything she could recall and then follow up with an email to Owen to confirm.

A server came by and filled their water glasses. Owen ordered a pot of coffee and tomato juice, while Grace stuck with the more traditional orange juice. She waited until the drinks arrived and their food orders were taken before returning to the reason for the meeting. "So, about the party."

Owen smiled. "I wondered how long you'd hold off. I had twenty that you wouldn't make it to the restaurant."

"Twenty with whom?"

"With myself." He offered the cream and sugar to her, but she shook her head. She liked her coffee strong and black. Owen put the small tray near the edge of the table without adding anything to his cup, either. "It was a brilliant bet. I couldn't lose."

Grace pressed her lips together so she wouldn't smile. It didn't work.

But rather than acknowledge her grin or make another joke, Owen merely smiled back, seemingly content that he'd been able to make it happen. "And for the record, I've never planned an engagement party, so I was kind of hoping you'd take the lead."

She was certainly capable of that. She had more engagement parties under her belt than she could remember. Grace took a sip of her coffee, enjoying the hot sharpness. "Are you sure you should be the one organizing it?" She didn't mean to be rude, but in her experience, a party was more successful when the organizer had some sort of idea of what they'd like to see occur.

"As it happens, I agree with you." Owen didn't lose his relaxed pose. "But the family has decided that it should be my responsibility." He shrugged.

Grace knew about living up to or not living up to family ideals and demands and didn't push. "Fair enough. Then let's talk basics. Time, place, that sort of thing."

Owen nodded. "Soon, I think. I'd like to take advantage of the summer weather."

"When? We'll have to print and send invitations, book the space." Grace began counting off the multitude of preplanning details that went into throwing a truly great party. "Decide on catering, make sure the bride and groom are available."

Owen reached out and placed a hand over hers. His fingers were warm when he gave her a gentle squeeze and sent an unanticipated shudder through her. "It'll work out."

As it happened, Grace knew that wasn't the case. Oh, sure, it might seem that way from the outside. That a fantastic party came together naturally and with ease, but that was usually because there was someone like her behind the scenes, making the phone calls, juggling the vendors and putting out fires before they could morph into infernos. If things just "worked out" then she wouldn't have a career.

She slid her hand out from beneath his and wrapped her fingers around the glass of chilled orange juice instead, allowing the cold and her common sense to seep back into her brain. "It'll work out because we have a plan in place." And a contingency plan, as well. But that was her job, not Owen's. He was simply there to assist in the big picture. She'd be handling the minutiae. "The earliest we can schedule is probably the end of August." At the surprised lift of Owen's brow, she clarified. "First we need to select and order invitations. That'll take a couple of weeks.

Then they need to be mailed about a month before the party."

He blinked.

"And that's assuming we can book a location. Summer is a popular time. It's possible nothing will be available." Or nothing that would fit the type of party Grace expected the engaged couple would appreciate. Though she'd once organized a do that took place on the side of a mountain in a snowstorm, so she suspected she could make something work.

"The location won't be a problem. We own three wine bars and a restaurant. We'll use one of them." He looked at her and Grace felt another shudder. Tinier but still unexpected. "I'll take you on a tour."

"Great." Grace lowered her hands to her lap and curled her fingers into her napkin until the tingle under her skin eased. It really was too bad Owen didn't tick any of the boxes on her husband list. No office job to let him be home with the future kids when she had a demanding wedding. No long-term relationships in his past, which she took to mean he wouldn't or couldn't settle down. And when he wasn't wearing flip-flops, he was wearing sneakers. She focused on the reason for their meeting. The engagement party. "An evening reception, I assume?"

Owen nodded. "And probably on a Sunday,

since Fridays and Saturdays are our peak times. Not that we mind shutting down for something special, but the guests are in the same industry. It's hard for people to get away on busy nights."

"Of course." Grace was impressed he'd thought to mention it. Owen might not seem to be a particularly serious person, but he wasn't dumb. She mentally upped the percentage of people who were likely to attend from 70 to 80 percent. Although there would still be some who would decline, holding the party on a Sunday meant a prior engagement was unlikely.

"So, what had you in the office bright and early on a Sunday morning?"

"Work." She had a lot of it and she was grateful. There were many wedding and event planners who barely managed to make enough to pay the rent on their offices, so she wasn't going to complain about being busy. Of course, she knew it wasn't a long-term plan. Not only was it an impossible pace to keep up, but she also did have plans for her personal life. Although the money was excellent and it provided her not just the ability to hire more staff, but also the opportunity to have her name and her work on display for other potential clients to enjoy. Grace figured that come the end of summer and her busy season, she could revisit her business plan and make adjustments to get her life in better balance.

Perhaps she could hire another assistant. She could definitely raise her prices. She was good enough at what she did to justify that.

"What else did you do this weekend?"

"Actually, I had a lot of work to catch up on from the week, which is why I was in the office." She didn't explain that this had been her life for the past six months. It was both boring and none of his business.

"Well, then it's a good thing I could convince you to come out for brunch." Owen's expression was cheerful, no sign of the admonishment that she'd see from her mother. Her parents understood the value of hard work but not at the expense of her personal life.

Grace nodded slowly. "Yes, it is." And she wasn't lying. "What about you?"

"I had to work last night, but I spent yesterday morning hitting some golf balls at the range. Today I went for a run before I called you. I like running in the morning before it gets too hot. And I'll work tonight."

So he worked, too, but made some time for himself. Of course, he wasn't a sole proprietor, nor was he building something from the ground up. He'd taken over a business that was already stable and successful, so really not the same at all. Still, Grace felt a niggle of envy that he seemed to manage both so fluidly. She hoped she'd be able to do the same.

"What do you do when you're not working?"

It had been so long since she hadn't worked that Grace wasn't sure how to answer. She liked gardening, but living in a downtown condo, she was restricted to doing so out of a container. She kept meaning to take advantage of one of the community gardens around the city, joining one close to home where she could avail herself of a larger plot of land to grow something more than herbs and sprawling annuals, but there never seemed to be time. When she was married and had a proper house with a proper backyard, Grace planned to have a full vegetable garden, one where she and the kids could pick ingredients fresh off the vine for that night's meal. She liked reading, though most nights she fell asleep before she got through a single chapter. She worked out six days a week. Pilates three days and an hour on the elliptical machine the other three. But that was as much for health as for fun.

When she thought about it, it was kind of sad. "I have a patio garden," she said. "I grew up on a farm, so it's a way to keep in touch with that." She wondered why she'd added the last bit. She'd never really thought about it, but she realized after she said it that it was true. She hadn't followed in the family footsteps, but many of their lessons and beliefs had stuck. Communing with nature, the feel of digging her fingers deep into the dirt below the warm topsoil and into the coolness beneath.

"My mom's a longtime gardener. And my dad has recently taken it up, too, though I'm not sure my mom always appreciates that." Owen leaned forward as though to share a secret or private thought. "He took over some of her space and planted vegetables. And now they regularly battle over who actually owns the spot. I think he dug up some peonies to make room for some tomato plants."

Grace smiled. "I wish him good luck with that."

"So you've met my mother?"

This time she laughed. "I've not yet had that pleasure, but peonies are hardy plants and they're perennials." When he looked at her blankly, she explained. "They bloom every year and are difficult to get rid of once they've rooted. I wouldn't be surprised if they continue to spring up around the tomato plants."

Owen laughed. "Dad will love that."

Grace smiled again. His story reminded her of her own family. Not that her parents ever battled over gardening space, not with twenty acres of land at their disposal, but the idea of working together, of being a team. She felt a small clutch in her stomach. It was a team she didn't really have a place on.

"I like to run," Owen offered and Grace was grateful for the distraction. "And golf, though I don't get out as often as I'd like these days. And I love seeing live music, preferably at one of the smaller, less well-known clubs in the city."

"I've heard," Grace said, thinking of the photos she'd found of Owen at any number of clubs both well-known and not.

"Oh?" He raised an eyebrow. "Have you been checking up on me? I'm flattered, but you could have just asked. I'll tell you whatever you like."

Now she felt embarrassed and a little foolish. Not that she'd done the checking up—that was just good business—but that she'd let down her guard enough to admit it. She changed the subject. "What kind of food were you thinking for the party? Will it be a cocktail reception or a full dinner?"

Again, Owen eyed her closely, seeming to understand that he'd landed on something she'd prefer not to talk about. This time, he didn't let her off the hook. "Have you been internet-stalking me?"

"No, of course not," Grace lied without a blink. She didn't like to lie, but she was good at it. A skill learned when she'd still been a teenager. A thirteen-year-old who only wanted to go to her friend's house to watch *Dawson's Creek*, since there was no TV at her house, so that she could be part of the conversation about who was cuter, Pacey or Dawson, that invariably sprung up at school. She hadn't had a computer or internet access, either, and the only way she got to listen to music that wasn't performed by a family member was on an old Walkman one of her friends had given her when that friend had gotten a fancy new Discman for her birthday.

Grace had loved that Walkman. She didn't care that it wasn't the latest in technology and that the only tapes she had were those donated by the same friend and her parents, and mainly consisted of '80s hair bands. It provided an audio oasis. A way for her to shut out the rest of her world and indulge in something normal, in a life closer to the ones she saw on TV at her friends' houses.

"Oh, re-e-ally?" Owen drew the second word out, clearly finding her lying skills lacking.

She met his gaze head-on. "Do you really think I have nothing better to do than plunk your name into a search engine and see how many hits there are?" Answer: about one million in 0.31 seconds.

"I don't want to sound like I'm bragging."

His dark eyes twinkled with laughter. "But yes, that's exactly what I think. Did you like what you found?"

Grace exhaled and sipped her coffee, choosing not to answer. The man certainly didn't need the ego boost. "I thought this was supposed to be a business meeting."

"It is, and it's my business to find out if you've been researching me."

"Why?" Grace put the china cup down on the saucer with a click. "Why would it matter?" Who cared if she'd looked him up or not? It had nothing to do with her ability to plan an engagement party, nor did it answer the questions of what kinds of things should be included.

"Because then I'll know if you're likely to agree to go out with me or not."

Grace shook her head. "We've been over this. My answer hasn't changed."

Owen tilted his head to the side. His hair was a little long and fell across his forehead. "And yet here you are with me now. On a pseudo date."

"This is a business meeting."

"With coffee and food and conversations about our families. I don't know. Seems kind of date-like to me, don't you think?"

"No." Grace adjusted her napkin on her lap, though it hadn't shifted since she'd first put it there. But she was lying again. Here at a beautiful restaurant with the hushed conversation of other couples around them and the gorgeous view of the water, it did feel like a date.

"I like you," Owen said.

"You don't know me." And she wasn't going out of her way to change that. Owen Ford was dangerous. Dangerous to her life both professionally and personally.

"I'd like to get to know you."

Grace ignored the flash of heat under her skin. She wasn't here to be cajoled and flattered. Not even by a man who made her teeth sweat. "I'd like to talk about the party."

"We can do both." Owen leaned forward, resting his forearms on the table. Grace hated that she noticed the muscles in them. Probably from swinging a golf club. "You answer a question about yourself and then I'll answer a question about the party."

"No, that's not how this is going to go." She was sure this had worked for him before. Probably many times in the past, but she was no starry-eyed twenty-year-old awed by his charm and banter. She was almost thirty and she had a job to do. "We'll discuss your ideas for the party while we enjoy a nice meal and then I'll return to my office and draw up some plans, which I'll send to you for review."

"That doesn't sound nearly as much fun."

He was right, but to Grace, it sounded infinitely safer.

CHAPTER FOUR

GRACE EXHALED SLOWLY, pushing thoughts of her date—no, it wasn't a date—her *meeting* with Owen out of her mind, and focused on her line budget. Because the breakdown of costs for the engagement party Owen wanted to throw was far more important and interesting than how he'd rocked those dark jeans. Okay, more important, at least. And if she just hurried up and finished the stupid budget, she could work on something else. Something unrelated to Owen Ford and his family.

She fanned her face and checked the numbers on the page again, but her mind wandered back to those jeans and the way his butt looked in them. Dangerous ground. Would have been dangerous even if he was her type, which luckily, he was not.

Grace wasn't looking for a playboy or a casual relationship. In fact, she wasn't looking for anything right now. Not with the summer upon her and an absolute flurry of weddings over the next eight weeks. Each one would be given the same amount of attention and care because each couple had trusted her with their special day.

And that's what she should be thinking about. Not Owen's butt.

She actually managed to lose herself in the numbers for a couple of hours, making notations and edits. Using what she'd learned from previous weddings to make the next one better.

But when her phone rang, the ringtone an elegant measure of Beethoven that she used for work, her brain snapped to customer-service mode and seated there. Even when she saw the caller was Owen.

"Mr. Ford. How can I help you?"

"I thought we agreed to be on a first-name basis, Grace."

The way he said her name sent a brief curl of pleasure into her bones. In his mouth, her name wasn't cool or patrician. It wasn't formal or chaste. It was soft and sexy. The kind of name a woman slipped on when she wanted to seduce someone.

Grace pushed the pleasure away and focused on business. "Well, then, Owen, what can I do for you?"

"I wanted to set up a time for you to come to the wine bar. See the space and layout, so you can get an idea for it."

"Great." She was already pulling up her calendar, which was synced to all her devices. "When were you thinking?"

"How about tonight?"

Grace's fingers stilled on the keyboard. There was no reason she couldn't go tonight. She had nothing planned and it would be better to see the space now, so she could start drawing up options immediately. And yet, she didn't confirm. Because she'd just spent the morning having brunch with him.

"Unless you've got a hot date?"

"No." Now, why had she answered that query immediately? Almost as if she was worried he'd think she was unavailable to go on a hot date with him. Which she was. She cleared her throat. "Tonight would be fine."

But even as she took down directions on location and time, her mind continued to wander. And every time, it flashed on that hot butt in those hot jeans.

Not. Good.

OWEN SWIPED A CLOTH along the already clean bar, earning a glare from Stef, the bartender he'd poached from La Petite Bouchée, the restaurant owned and cheffed by his soon-to-be sister-in-law. It hadn't been an intentional poaching.

He'd needed some extra help for the summer and Stef had wanted the extra hours to help pay for her next semester of schooling. It wasn't his fault that Stef loved Elephants and working for him so much that she'd asked if she could make the position permanent. And it wasn't as if he'd left Julia or her restaurant short-staffed. He'd interviewed and found a qualified candidate to replace Stef at the restaurant before getting Julia's agreement. Not that this stopped her from claiming that he owed her.

But hell. He'd not only attended a wedding-planning session with her, he was going to make sure she had an amazing engagement party, too. And he was going to keep it a surprise. So, really, she owed him.

He swiped the cloth across the bar again, this time earning not only a glare from Stef, but also a comment. "You sure you got everything now?"

"No." And he wiped again, grinning as he did.

Stef rolled her eyes and plucked the cloth out of his hand, replacing it with a glass of water. "Go," she told him. "Mingle. I'll make sure the bar top stays clean." She would, as well as juggling multiple drink orders, keeping an eye on the customers and prepping the bar for tomorrow.

Owen nodded and began to move around the room, but he kept one eye on the door and when it finally opened and Grace walked in, he smiled.

She looked good. But then, in Owen's opinion, she always did. Her pale gray jeans were tight and paired with a black T-shirt and a dark blue jacket with white polka dots. Her hair was down, the blond strands spilling over her shoulders, loose and free.

"Miss Monroe. Twice in one weekend. Are you stalking me?"

The pinched look around her mouth softened just as he'd hoped. "If you'll recall, you issued me a personal invitation. And the preferred honorific is Ms."

Owen offered his arm, pleased when she barely hesitated before taking it. "Well, *Ms*. Monroe, let's start the tour."

She loosened up a little more as he took her around, pleased to show off the bar and his hard work to improve it. But when he asked her to stay for a drink, she declined.

"I really can't."

"Big day of wedding planning tomorrow?" By the way she looked up at him and then looked away, Owen knew that wasn't it.

"Something like that."

His natural inclination was to let it go. He'd found the subtle-nudge approach to be usually far more successful than a direct request. But he had a feeling that with Grace, subtlety would get him a whole lot of nothing. "Just one drink. It's early."

She checked her watch. "I still have work to do tonight."

"All work and no play..."

"You sound like my mother."

"Then she must be a wise woman." And Grace was wavering. "Have you eaten?"

"Not since brunch."

And there was his answer. She wanted to stay; he merely had to provide the opportunity. "Then consider this a working dinner. You can try some of the foods. Research for your party."

She tilted her head to look at him. Her blond hair, free of its sleek knot, fell around her shoulders. Owen would bet money that it would feel as cool and silky as it looked.

"I won't bite," he joked and was rewarded with a rosy flush coloring her cheeks.

"Owen—"

He cut her off. "It doesn't have to be long. I have some pull in the kitchen. You'll be back working before the sun sets." Seeing as that was a couple of hours away, he figured it was a safe promise.

"Owen," she said again. But when he broke out his patented sad face, she capitulated. "No more than an hour."

"Sixty minutes or less." Unless he could talk

her into changing her mind. It wasn't exactly a date, but it wasn't exactly not a date, either.

Or it wasn't, until they were halfway through their meal and she said, "You realize this is only a business relationship." Which it clearly wasn't or she wouldn't feel the need to clarify.

Owen simply smiled and popped another bite of food in his mouth.

Grace put down her fork, carefully and quietly so that he doubted there would have been a sound even if the bar was dead. "I shouldn't have stayed."

He quickly swallowed his mouthful. "Of course you should have. You were hungry and we have food here."

"You're my client."

"This again? I'm not a client. I'm not the one getting married." And never would be. There was nothing wrong with marriage. For other people. Maybe he'd change his mind someday. But not today.

"Close enough." She pushed her plate toward the center of the table. "I should go."

"Stay." He placed a hand over hers. "Just until you've finished eating."

Grace slid her hand out from under his. "I'm done." She slid out of the booth. "If there's anything wedding- or engagement-related, please call me."

"But, otherwise, lose your number?"

Her smile wasn't cheerful. "I wouldn't be that harsh."

But it was basically what she meant. Owen ignored the disappointment pooling in his veins and slid out of the booth, too. "I'll walk you out." Just because she'd told him he didn't have a chance with her was no excuse not to be a gentleman.

"That's not necessary."

"Grace." And this time there was no underlying teasing in his tone. "I'd like to."

She nodded and anchored her purse over her shoulder. No chance of her leaving it behind, so he'd have an excuse to call her.

They walked toward the large wooden door. Neither of them spoke until they were outside.

"So." Grace's fingers curled around the strap of her shoulder bag. "I guess this is it."

Owen kept his tone light. He was good at keeping things light. "I'm sure I'll see you at the party and the wedding."

She nodded, but didn't expand on his comment and Owen nodded, too. He was interested in her, attracted to her, but if she didn't feel the same way, he wasn't going to throw himself at her.

"And I'll call you if I have any engagement-party questions."

"Please do."

He waited until she was a block away and out of sight before he headed back inside.

The table they'd been at was untouched—no doubt his staff expected them to return and finish the mostly full plates. Owen bussed it himself, letting his hands work while his mind whirred.

Not that he had a whole lot to think about. Grace had made it clear that she preferred to act as though the attraction between them didn't exist.

"Shot down by the blonde?" Stef asked when he brought the half-filled water glasses to dump at the bar.

Owen noticed Mal sitting at the bar grinning. "I wasn't shot down." He thought about that for a moment. "No, you're right. She totally shot me down." He was man enough to admit it.

Mal gave him a healthy pat on the shoulder. "Do you need a moment to cry into your water?"

"I might."

She and Stef shared a snicker.

"I'm glad you can find my humiliation amusing. I may have to swear off women forever." When neither of them said anything, Owen helped out. "See, this is the part where you both assure me that it's her issue that has nothing to do with me and that I'm an excellent catch who any woman would be lucky to date."

Silence.

"Nothing?" he asked. "Seriously? Not even a consolation hug?"

"There, there." Mal patted him on the back. "Now you know how all those women you loved and left felt."

"I didn't love and leave. It was always a mutual decision."

"Is that what they thought?"

The conversation had taken on a serious tone and Owen was glad when Stef moved to the other end of the bar to check on her customers.

"Of course they did." Just because there hadn't been long, drawn-out discussions on the topic didn't mean they hadn't been in agreement.

"You sure?" Mal tapped a finger against the side of her glass. Her gaze drifted. "Sometimes you might think you know the other person's feelings only to realize at the worst possible moment that you were wrong."

And they were veering again. Owen absorbed her words fully, then asked, "Are we talking about you now?"

Mal sat up, her attention snapping back into place, that raw emotion he'd briefly glimpsed ducking back under a neutral look. "No, I'm simply pointing out that getting shot down might be good for your personal growth."

"Not that I'm admitting to anything, but I think I've done enough growing." And if Grace wanted to pretend that this sizzle between them wasn't there, she was certainly within her rights to do so. Didn't mean he wouldn't be available should she change her mind, but then he was good like that. Always looking out for the happiness of others.

Owen smiled at his sister. "So what brings you out here tonight? Boredom? Ennui?"

Mal smirked. "You know those words mean the same thing."

He slid onto a bar stool, keeping one eye out for a patron who might use it instead. "Yes. But one is all fancy and French."

Mal glanced around. "Someone you're trying to show off for?"

"Just practicing."

GRACE KNEW THE engagement party would go perfectly. At least, on the surface, which was all that mattered.

No one cared if the DJ's car broke down or if the fish they'd selected for the entrée was unavailable due to a typhoon last week. They didn't care if there weren't enough seats for everyone or if there was one lone bathroom for three hundred guests and someone had just thrown up all over it. All they cared was that Grace took care of it.

Her job was as much about minimizing damage on the day of the event as the actual planning. And she took great care to control as many variables as possible. Like her attraction to one Owen Ford.

She'd managed to plan the engagement party, including another visit to Elephants, without running into him. Some people might think her cowardly or even unprofessional by choosing to schedule her visit when she knew he wouldn't be there. But Grace saw it as taking advantage of opportunities.

She'd been meeting with Julia and Donovan about their wedding and Julia had mentioned that Owen was working at the restaurant all week. Was she supposed to ignore the snippet of information? Purposely delay her visit by a week so that she wouldn't appear to be avoiding him?

And she wouldn't avoid him tonight, either. She'd be too busy to chat with all the various jobs and duties she and her team would be attending to, but she wouldn't avoid him.

She was already at the wine bar, preparing the initial setup even though the party didn't start for another four hours. Her team of three would arrive in forty-five minutes, but for now it was just Grace and a pair of Elephants staff members prepping for tonight.

Grace was glad for the solitude. Glad Owen wasn't here to grab her attention and refuse to let go. She hadn't gotten to bed until almost four in the morning after a wedding the night before. The bride and groom had wanted to party, as had everyone else in attendance, and Grace had been required to negotiate a time extension on the fly while her team checked to make sure the caterers wouldn't run out of food and drink.

When she'd finally crawled between her clean sheets, she'd been so exhausted that she almost forgot to set her alarm. And when it had gone off at six this morning, she wished she had forgotten. But she had her Pilates class at seven and she never missed that unless she was out of town.

Being tired and having a headache were not good excuses. So she'd slipped into her workout gear, grabbed a bottle of water from her tidy fridge and was warming up in the gym ten minutes before class.

But keeping to her routine didn't fill her with any sense of clarity or moral satisfaction. She just felt more tired.

She would be glad when tonight's event was over, though no one would ever know. On the surface, she'd be poised and friendly, her exhaustion hidden beneath a polite veneer.

By the time her team arrived, Grace had moved the tables and chairs into her preferred groupings and downed two bottles of water to keep hydrated.

It had been a warm day and was promising to be an equally warm night. Her thin silk T-shirt was beginning to stick to her back. "Hayley, will you check on the AC, please?"

Nothing would put a damper on a party faster than having guests uncomfortable.

"Right away." Hayley scampered off to do as she was bid while Grace went over the event plan with the other two members of her team. They all knew the plan, but Grace made a point of holding a quick overview on-site at every event she threw.

While it was usually unnecessary, those rare occasions where they caught something that had been overlooked made it a worthy practice. Hayley returned and Grace doled out jobs so they'd be ready come showtime.

The staff Owen had handpicked for this evening were beginning to trickle in. Grace took a moment to speak to each of them personally, making sure they knew that, while technically this party was for Julia and Donovan, in fact it was for all the Fords, so any problems or issues should come directly to her. All part of the full-service experience she provided.

The staff were cheerful and quick to lend a hand to transform the room into an elegant space. It helped that Elephants had good bones, with its long white bar, dark flooring and sleek furniture.

Grace had chosen to forgo a traditional tabletop flower arrangement, those blooms that sprang up and demanded to be seen. Instead, she'd gone for something a little smaller, a little less typical and a little more Julia and Donovan. She'd found beautiful white birdcages with a white stone bird perched atop and stuffed them with small blue flowers that poked out from between the bars. The effect was cheerful containment on the tables covered in pristine white cloths. She trucked in some fake trees, leafless and dark, and strung them with small fairy lights. She'd created some temporary chandeliers out of wire, wrapped in a feathery material and strung with the same fairy lights. With the lights in the wine bar turned from their usual pinky hue to soft white, the space turned from a hip see-and-be-seen establishment to one of classic elegance with a modern twist.

Grace stepped back from fixing a light string that was drooping instead of artfully swooping and surveyed the room. A swell of pride filled her chest. It was beautiful, yes, but more than that it had a sense of the couple the party was being held for.

While anyone could appreciate that the room was worthy of a photo shoot in a magazine, those who looked closer would spot the attention to detail. The two typical flower arrangements, a bustle of lavender, blue and white by the front door, were set up in trifle bowls. The guestbook on the edge of the gift table was set with a silver Montblanc pen identical to the one Donovan always used. There were other little touches of tradition and style that fit the couple.

"This looks amazing."

Grace recognized Owen's voice and blinked before turning, a polite smile already in place. But she felt it waver when she looked into his face. His easy grin and the way he seemed to be checking out her instead of the room. Hadn't she been clear that nothing could happen between them? "Thank you."

"How long did this take?" He reached around her to finger the tiny cages on the table, the movement making the small flowers inside rustle.

Grace felt the heat from his arm sink into hers. She took a small step sideways, away from Owen. "I got here around two."

"Amazing," he said again, but this time he was definitely looking at her.

Grace felt the heat creep into her cheeks. She knew she didn't look awful. Even during setup, she was careful to maintain her image. Hair pulled into a tidy ponytail, clean jeans with no rips or loose threads, a simple, black silk T-shirt and ballet flats so she could do any necessary hard labor. But *amazing* was a bit of a stretch.

"Can I do anything to help?"

"It's all under control." She was happy to give the party line. "Your only responsibility is to enjoy yourself."

"You sure? I am the host. I've got the suit and everything."

And a fine suit it was, cut slim to show off his physique and made out of poplin. The light gray shade set off his dark coloring and he wore it with a plain white dress shirt, the top two buttons left undone.

Grace yanked her gaze away from that small patch of exposed tanned skin. She had no business thinking about that skin, wondering if it would feel warmed by the sun or if it would taste like sugar, rum and mint.

Her eyes fell to his feet and the bright green kicks he wore. The tightness banding her lungs loosened.

This was who Owen Ford was. The kind of man who not only wore bright green kicks, but also wore them with a designer suit. The kind of man who didn't get serious. Not the kind of man she was looking for at all.

"It's all handled," she told Owen, drawing in a calming breath. "If you'll excuse me, I need to get ready."

OWEN WATCHED GRACE glide off, noting the way her jeans clung to her long legs. What he wouldn't give to feel them wrapped around his waist.

"Here." He blinked when a bar napkin was shoved in his face, then saw his sister grinning. "To wipe the drool from your chin."

Owen accepted the napkin and dabbed at his chin. "Thanks."

Mal's smile widened. It was good to see her laughing. She hadn't done enough of that lately. "Of course, it'd be better if Grace would quit giving you the brush-off."

"True." Owen tucked the napkin in his pocket. "She does like me, though."

"She has a funny way of showing it."

"Grace has some funny ideas. Says she can't get involved with me because I'm a client."

"Does Donovan know you're planning to steal his bride and marry her in his place? Tacky, Owen, and just when the two of you were starting to get along."

Owen snorted because the idea of him marrying anyone was a joke. "Maybe you should tell Grace that and put in a good word for me while you're at it."

"No." Mal seemed to relish turning him down. "I won't be your wingman."

"So you just came over here to harass me?"

She nodded. "That and to help you with your drooling issue. You are the host tonight, Owen. Show a little couth."

"A little—" He started to laugh, long and hard. He'd missed this snarky side of his sister. Even when it was directed at him. For the past few months, she'd been muted, all her color washed away. He threw an arm around her now, wrestled her into a headlock the way he had when they were kids.

"Owen, if you mess up my hair, I'm going to kill you." But she was laughing, too.

He grabbed a handful of strands and gave a light tug. "How's that for couth?"

"A poor showing." Mal extracted herself—but only because he let her—and smoothed her hair. "Very poor. See, Owen, it's behavior like that that keeps me from acting as your wingman."

He laughed again. "If I promise not to touch your hair anymore, will you do it?"

"No." She took a quick step back, hands raised to deflect any further hair-touching.

"What about if I act as your wingman, too?"

Her face fell. Damn. He'd thought she was

doing better, was moving past whatever had happened between her and Travis.

"My offer to beat him up still stands," Owen said. Yes, Travis was one of his best friends, but Mal was his sister.

Mal's eyes were sad, her voice soft. "No. I appreciate the support, but it's not necessary. No fighting required."

Which was good because Travis was a good two inches taller than Owen's own six foot one and his friend outweighed him by fifty pounds, all of it muscle. So really it would have been less of a physical beating and more of an "I don't know what happened between you and Mal, but fix it because I promised her I'd beat you up and I'd prefer not to lose a tooth."

"You sure?" This time when he put his arm around her it was to give her a hug.

"Positive." But she held on to him a second longer. "Thanks, Owen."

He watched his sister go, wondering if there was something else he could do to help. But Mal was proud and refused to tell anyone what had happened.

Owen grabbed a bottle of water from behind the bar and cracked it open. Which was why he thought it was better not to get too serious when it came to relationships.

Sure, he could end up like Julia and Donovan

or his own parents, but they seemed to be the exceptions to the rule. Most people didn't last, and wasn't it better to go into the relationship with that already in mind?

Owen sipped his water and glanced at his sister, who was talking to Stef and smiling. But the cheerful expression didn't reach her eyes.

Yes, it was definitely better to keep things light and casual. And a hell of a lot less painful.

GRACE TWITCHED THE HEM of her silvery-gray dress into place, ran a smoothing hand over her hair and slicked on a coat of pale almost-nude lip gloss as she eyed her reflection in the mirror of her compact. It was her standard event-planner uniform. Finished off with sapphire-blue kitten heels and a discreet pair of silver hoops at her ears, she looked cool and elegantly classic.

She knew some planners preferred suits. An exhibition of power and control, a statement that they were in charge and could handle any issue, but she found the same aura could be projected without looking as though she'd come straight from the boardroom. And, in her mind, she really shouldn't be standing out at all. She and her team should move seamlessly among the crowd, looking like every other guest, just with earpieces.

She fussed with her dress again. Something

looked off or maybe it was the twin flags of color on her usually porcelain skin. Grace pressed the back of her hands to the offending warmth on her cheeks, breathing slowly until the rosiness began to fade.

Better. Now she just looked as though she'd gotten a little sun. Which she might have if she didn't have weddings every weekend.

Not that she was complaining. It was all part of her five-year plan, of which she had one year left to complete. She'd successfully started her own business, had three employees reporting to her, planned at least twenty weddings a year and last year had bought her own condo, a gorgeous one-bedroom with soaring loftlike ceilings on the downtown side of False Creek.

Surrounded by other affluent, educated types, Grace Monroe had come a long way from her roots and was proud of what she'd accomplished, even if her family didn't understand. They didn't have to. She was satisfied, which was more important.

She was actually a little ahead of schedule, since she hadn't planned to buy the condo until next year. But she'd booked a wedding of one of the local hockey players, which had gotten her front-page coverage in not just the newspapers—both in print and online—but local magazines, too. All of that would have seen an increase in her business on its own, but when coupled with the inclusion of the wedding in a national lifestyle magazine that had dedicated an issue to the country's most popular athletes, well, she'd hired that third assistant and receptionist pretty quickly.

"Grace?" Hayley spoke through her earpiece.

"Coming out." She'd snagged access to the assistant manager's office for the night for storage and anything else. Like changing clothes.

Grace locked the door behind her as she left. All her employees had stored their bags and purses inside, plus whatever financial items might be put in the assistant manager's filing cabinet.

She adjusted her earpiece, eyes scanning the room. "What's going on, Hayley?"

"The photographer just texted that he's not coming."

Small problem when Grace considered what else could go wrong. "Thank you, Hayley. I'll handle it."

The photographer was a new one whom she'd used once before and been pleased with his work, but she wouldn't be using him again if he wasn't reliable. And he clearly wasn't. She'd be removing him from her list of contacts immediately.

Luckily, Grace had a solid list of vendors. She

called Sherry Sanders, one of her most dependable photographers, and begged her to come for a last-minute gig tonight.

She'd figured the mention of Julia and Donovan's names would be enough to pique Sherry's interest, and she was right. Sherry had promised to grab her equipment and get there as soon as possible. Because there was a good chance a picture from the party would end up in one of the provincial papers, a photo credit line that would create an uptick in business. Not to mention, if Julia and Donovan were happy, they'd probably book Sherry for the actual wedding. And no serious photographer would be foolish enough to turn down the opportunity to work what looked to be one of the most talked-about weddings of the year.

By the time Sherry arrived and Grace had issued instructions about the number of family members and other important people in the couple's lives, their style and general preferences, and made sure her team knew that Sherry was going to be handling all the photography, the wine bar had filled up. Grace recognized many of the guests. The who's who in the city's social scene, familiar faces in the papers' society pages and industry professionals who were often as well-known as their restaurants. They glittered in expensive summer dresses and well-tailored suits. Jewelry and wineglasses shimmered under the lights.

Grace spotted Donovan's parents and sister across the room. Gus Ford looked a lot like his sons, a blend of Donovan's stoic seriousness and Owen's easy smile. He wore a suit as well as they did, too. So clearly, there was no reason for her to get all jittery over the way Owen filled out his suit. It was simply good genetics. Like pheromones. Which Grace chalked up to animal instinct. Something she had overcome, much like her nontraditional childhood.

Evelyn was petite and energetic. Her eyes were bright as she chattered to her husband. Her elegant lilac dress set off her dark hair and complemented the deep indigo tie Gus wore. Grace smiled. She'd never had the opportunity to dress as a couple, except for Halloween, and she'd stopped participating in the costume and candy-consuming ritual when she was ten.

Grace headed over to greet them in person and assure them that they could come to her if they had any questions or concerns.

"I don't think we've met. I'm Grace Monroe." She held out a hand to the brunette standing with Gus and Evelyn. Even if Mallory hadn't looked like a taller, sleeker version of her mother, Grace would have known they were related by the way her parents looked at her. A mix of pride and love showered over their lone daughter.

"Mallory Ford." Her grip was firm, the sign of a woman who lived and succeeded in a man's world. "This is outstanding. Really. I can't believe it's Elephants."

Grace decided she liked Mallory, or at least liked her taste. She seemed to look beyond the surface to note the effort and time that had gone into making each choice. Her strapless dress was aqua and gathered at one side with a slit that provided a peek of leg. With the wrong accessories or on a shorter, curvier woman, it might have looked trashy. But Mallory, with her hair left down to cascade down her back, simple gold drop earrings and bangle bracelet and matching shoes, looked upscale and luxe. Which Grace imagined she was. "Thank you."

"I agree." Evelyn looked around, appreciation clear on her face. "I know it's our place, and I can recognize so much of it, yet it looks different. Like a version created just for Julia and Donovan." Which was exactly what Grace had been going for. Evelyn clasped a hand around her husband's arm. "Isn't it wonderful, Gus?"

"Better than wonderful." Gus's voice was as warm as his eyes. "You've done a fantastic job, Ms. Monroe."

Grace felt the warmth from the pair of them

seep into her, like a flower absorbing the heat of the sun. She clasped each of their hands in turn, wrapping them with both of hers. "Please, call me Grace."

She jumped when she sensed someone move up beside her and the scent of clover with a hint of smoke, like honey by the campfire, surrounded her. She knew that scent. She loved that scent, but wished she didn't.

"How come you never say that to me?" Grace tried not to stiffen as she turned to look at Owen.

"Owen." Evelyn seemed delighted to see her son. Grace wished she felt the same. Instead, she was left with a discomfiting heat swirling beneath her skin. Mallory hugged her brother and whispered something in his ear that made him throw back his head and laugh.

Grace felt a bubble of envy and shifted a step away, out of reach. She wasn't jealous of Mallory, just of the easy relationship she seemed to have with her brother. Grace hadn't spoken to her own brother in six months. Not since the last time she'd been over to visit the family farm. But then despite the only sixteen-month age gap, she and Sky had never been close. Different priorities, different lives. Sky had decided to stay on the family farm and take over the business with his pregnant girlfriend. While she had done the opposite.

Gus moved to stand beside her by one of the tables. "I like these." He was admiring the bird-cage of flowers, running a thick finger along the cage much as his son had earlier. Grace shoved away the thought of Owen's hands caressing anything, even a stone bird, but her ears were attuned to the conversation he was having with his mother and sister. And she had to lecture herself not to inhale deeply before his scent drifted away, replaced by lemon cleaning products, the spicy shrimp appetizers being passed around and her own grapefruit-and-mint perfume.

"You've done a fine job, Owen. Julia and Donovan are going to love this." Evelyn laid a hand on her son's arm. "Really love it."

"I hope so." Owen's tone was cheerful, as though Grace hadn't just brushed him off. Again. "Grace certainly worked hard enough."

A curl of pride wound through her. Not that she didn't believe she deserved the accolades, but it was always nice to be recognized. And then she felt guilty for brushing him off, since he hadn't been trying anything. Not this time.

She flicked a glance at him. He was looking back. She felt her breath catch, took that deep breath she'd been avoiding and caught a full breath of that smoky sweetness that was all Owen. Her knees wobbled. Or they might have wobbled on a less tightly controlled person. Grace simply locked her knees and turned her full attention to Gus, who was now scarfing down both the spicy shrimp and the slices of warm baguette being served with it, wearing the beatific look of a man on a diet.

"Not too many, love," Evelyn called.

"I know, I know. I'll eat some green stuff, too." But Gus winked at Grace as he grumbled and then leaned forward as though to impart some wisdom. "She's always pushing me to eat green stuff. But I really only like it when I grow it myself. You didn't by any chance create a green-free menu?"

Grace laughed at his hopeful look. "I'm afraid not. But since Julia is a French-inspired chef, it's all been cooked in lots of butter."

Gus's eyes lit up as he called over his shoulder to his wife. "I'll eat some green veggies when they come out, dear."

Evelyn smiled. "It's a celebration. Try everything, just don't overdo it."

Gus went back to stand with her, the two of them drawing Mallory into a conversation about a guest they wanted her to meet. Owen moved closer to Grace, hovering by her side, not touching, but close enough.

She got another whiff of him and tried to take only shallow breaths. "My dad had a heart attack at the end of last year." His voice was low in her ear, his breath warm on her neck. "She's still worried."

"Of course she is," Grace murmured. Mallory had excused herself and left Gus and Evelyn standing together, their heads almost touching as they whispered and smiled. Grace had known them for only a couple of minutes and already she could see how in love they were. It would be hard to recover from losing a love like that. Her heart skipped a beat. Of course, she had to find a man she liked enough to go on a second date with—okay, fine, a first date—before she jumped ahead to love and marriage and a lifetime of togetherness. "That must have been hard."

"It was. For all of us."

Grace tilted her head to look at him. His mouth was close to hers and she knew she should step back, but she was afraid she'd bump the table. Yeah, right. The table. That was what was holding her in place. "He looks good." But she didn't turn her head toward Gus. She was caught in Owen's gaze.

"He does." Owen reached out to brush a strand of hair off her neck. Grace felt the sharp buzz of attraction race through her. "He's doing well."

"I'm glad to hear it." And although she hadn't known Gus Ford even an hour ago as anything more than the founder of the family company and father to Owen and Donovan, she was glad. Grace didn't always understand her own parents and she knew they didn't understand her, but despite their sometimes contentious relationship, she loved them and would be devastated if they fell ill.

"Thanks." Owen brushed the side of her neck again, though Grace was pretty sure that the strand of hair wasn't there anymore. She knew she should mind, should take that step back, table or not, and remind both Owen and herself that their relationship was strictly business. She didn't move.

"And how are you handling it?" Her voice was soft.

"Fine. Most of the time." He shrugged and moved closer. She could feel his body heat radiating through her thick silk dress, could imagine the hard bunch of his muscles beneath that stylish summer suit. "Maybe you want to hug me? Make it all better?"

And just like that the moment dissolved and washed away on the realization that Owen wasn't serious. Not about anything. Grace took that step away and didn't bump the table. "Nice try."

Owen grinned. If he weren't so charming, he'd be obnoxious. Actually, she bet he could be obnoxious despite that overabundance of charm. "Can't blame a guy for trying."

She could, but she didn't. Instead, she pretended that one of her employees was calling her through her earpiece and excused herself from the little family grouping, but she risked a glance over her shoulder as she strode away and saw Owen watching her go, a sleepy appreciation in his eyes.

Grace didn't want to find him appealing. Not with his insouciant manner, his casual attitude toward most things and his bright green sneakers. But she did. She made herself keep walking as a quiet ache unfurled in her chest.

CHAPTER FIVE

INTERESTING. OWEN WATCHED Grace walk away, that silver dress catching each curve as she moved.

She wasn't as convinced that their relationship should be strictly platonic as she wanted him to think. And he didn't need Mal as his wingman.

Owen smiled. No, he was doing just fine on his own. Just fine, indeed.

So fine that he was still grinning like a fool when his lookout texted him that Donovan and Julia had finally arrived. Owen gathered the family by the front door, wanting to give the happy couple a proper greeting.

Julia entered just slightly ahead of Donovan. Her eyes brightened when she saw him. "Owen."

Owen grinned wider. He'd lied and told them that he wanted them to come try a few new items he was considering adding to the menu. Because the taste-testing of food was always guaranteed to get chef Julia out.

She noticed the rest of the family around him and then stopped, causing Donovan to bump into the back of her.

"Not that I'm complaining—" Donovan slipped an arm around his fiancée's waist "—but what's the holdup?"

"Happy engagement." Owen hugged his almost sister-in-law, whom he liked better than his brother most days.

"Why are you smiling like that?" Donovan asked, offering exhibit A as to why—though they'd admittedly come a long way in the past nine or so months since their father's heart attack.

"Donovan, look." Julia pointed to the glittering room in front of them.

Donovan's eyebrows lifted.

"Happy engagement," Owen said again as the family collapsed into a round of cheerful welcomes and surprised hugs.

And Julia deserved nothing less. She was already part of the family as far as Owen and the rest of the family were concerned. She'd been a good friend to Owen and softened his brother's occasionally harsh attitude, though Owen had come to appreciate all that Donovan did as the company CEO and now realized that what he'd sometimes seen as harsh was simply part of running a profitable business. Something he never would have considered a year ago.

"I can't believe you did all this," Julia said as she linked her arm through Owen's. "And kept it a secret from me." She gave him a good-natured swat with her free hand.

"If I'd told you, it wouldn't be a surprise." Which earned him a warm laugh.

"You did good," Donovan told him, which from him was high praise.

"I had help."

Julia squeezed his arm. "A certain attractive blonde wedding planner who I see on the other side of the room?"

"She's the one." And when he looked over, spotting Grace in her pretty dress, he felt his breath catch. Very interesting. Apparently, his body thought he'd gone too long without a date. Owen couldn't disagree.

"Don't tell me you hit on our wedding planner." Donovan popped one of the spicy shrimp into his mouth and chewed. "We need her."

"Fine. I didn't hit on her." Which was technically the truth. He'd politely asked her on a date, which was a far cry from sidling up to her in a dim bar and asking if it hurt when she fell from heaven. Not that he'd ever done that. No, not him.

Now, asking if she believed in love at first sight or if he should walk by again, yes. But come on. That line was a classic.

"And why would it be so bad if he flirted with her?" Julia asked. "He's a good catch."

Owen appreciated her support even though he was perfectly capable of holding his own with Donovan. "Julia? Remind me again why you're marrying this guy instead of running off for a weekend in Paris with me."

"Because she's already run off to Paris. With me." Donovan plucked his soon-to-be bride from Owen's side and gave her a heated kiss.

Owen waited until they came up for air. "Aren't you supposed to wait for us to clink spoons against the sides of our glasses before you do that?"

"Jealous?" Donovan put his arm around Julia.

"Yes." And he was, though not of Julia in particular. It was more that he missed having someone by his side at functions, a date for dinner, someone to go on vacation with. Not that he had time for vacations these days.

Julia disentangled herself from Donovan to give Owen another hug. "Thank you for this."

Owen peeked over her head at his brother, who was watching them with a lazy smile. "See? This is why she's listed first on the invite and you're the plus one."

Donovan's smile turned into a laugh. "As long as I'm her plus one."

Owen felt another catch in his chest. Not that he was looking for anything as serious as marriage, but there were times—not many, but they were there—that he felt a little envious of his brother. It wasn't that long ago that Donovan had seemed as uninterested in marriage as Owen. More so, seeing as he had fewer girlfriends. And look at him now.

Julia gave Owen one last squeeze and returned to Donovan's side, grabbing his hand. "You coming?" she asked over her shoulder.

"In a minute," Owen said. He watched them go, greeting guests and accepting congratulations as they moved deeper into the room. But his eyes didn't stay on them for long.

Instead, he watched Grace. Even her movements were elegant—a flick of her wrist as she straightened a tablecloth, the stride that made it look as if she was gliding across the floor, the turn of her head as she angled for a peek at something in the corner. This time the catch was in more than his chest. He headed toward her, then stopped.

She was working and he shouldn't interrupt that. He made a hard right and integrated himself into a group of family friends in the restaurant industry who wanted to chat about some of the changes he'd made at Elephants, but his eyes tracked Grace as she wound her way through the room. A polite smile was on her face, her eyes alert for anything that needed her attention.

He wondered how he could get her to focus that attention on him.

BY THE TIME the party started to wind down, Grace's feet were screaming, but she kept her smile in place. All part of the service.

Even so, as Donovan and Julia left and the rest of the guests followed suit, Grace let her smile slip just slightly. Not enough that anyone would notice, but just so that her cheeks didn't hurt as much as her feet. Thank God she'd resisted the urge to wear higher heels as she often did at these shorter functions, which generally didn't require quite as much running around.

Her team unfastened the lights from the trees, used the ladder to unhook the faux chandeliers from the ceiling and packed up the centerpieces and tablecloths. Grace helped, checking everything off her list as she did. They'd put everything that was owned by the company in storage tomorrow. They had a large room in the office building lined with shelves, each one labeled and cross-referenced on a master list that they used to check things in and out, so if something went missing they could figure out where and when it had last been seen.

Grace had ordered the trees and chandeliers from a local design company and had arranged for them to be picked up tonight, since she had nowhere to store them. The driver was quick, placing everything inside and grunting when Grace thanked him. She felt like grunting herself. And she might have except it felt as if it would take too much effort.

She saw her team off, told them to come in late tomorrow as they'd earned the time. She, of course, would be at the office bright and early but that was part of being the boss. She didn't have the luxury of taking time off, not when she was so close to completing her five-year plan.

She returned to the bar, eyes scanning the room for anything they might have missed, and relished the deep quiet that followed a loud party. Some of the knots in her shoulders loosened. The place was empty. Just one final walk-through of the room and she'd be off, too. Home to the cool comfort of her Egyptian cotton sheets and the restful sleep that always followed a busy weekend.

"Can I offer you a drink?"

She turned. She'd known it was Owen even before that warm voice had curled around her as gently as those Egyptian sheets, but her pulse gave a hearty thump when she saw him standing behind her. She'd known he was still around, waiting to lock up. But the physical reaction, the pull from her core, caught her off guard.

"Thank you, but I should go." The room looked much as it had when she'd arrived this afternoon to set up. No reason for her to stay.

"Not even one drink? To toast to a job well done? Celebrate your success?"

Grace hesitated. Going home was what she always did, what she expected of herself. But it had been a good night. A great night. Everything had gone smoothly, the bride and groom were happy and she'd worked really hard. Didn't she deserve a moment to revel in it? Wasn't that what her mom was always telling her? That she not follow all of society's rules but create some of her own? Not that having a quick drink was exactly rule-breaking, but it wasn't part of Grace's usual routine.

She looked around the room again. It was just the two of them. They'd both worked hard tonight and there was no reason to deny him the acknowledgment of that. "Okay, but only one." She said it quickly before she changed her mind. It was a drink. That was all. Hardly life-changing. She sat down at one of the empty booths and sank into the soft leather cushion, her body exhaling in relief as she took the weight off her beleaguered feet.

"What's your pleasure?" Owen called as he moved behind the bar. "Wine? Beer? Something a little stronger?"

Grace exhaled again, sinking a little farther into the booth's back. Normally, she would have requested water. To go. "Wine would be nice."

If she was going to break routine, she might as well go all out.

Owen nodded. "Red or white?"

"White. If it's open." She watched as he bent down, then straightened with a bottle in one hand and a corkscrew in the other. Before she could even open her mouth to say it wasn't that important, he had the cork out with a few quick turns and a flick of the wrist. And it would be rude to say anything after he'd opened it and poured her a glass.

He stowed the bottle and carried over a pair of glasses. "Cheers." They clinked.

As Grace lifted the glass to her lips, she noticed Owen staring at her, unmoving. She lowered the glass. "Yes?"

"You can't break eye contact before sipping. Clink again."

"Owen." She'd heard the old tale before, too. Looking away brought bad luck. In bed.

"Do you really want to risk it?"

"I'm not superstitious," she told him, not moving her glass. Besides, it wasn't as if she was getting any, and she seriously doubted it had anything to do with clinking and maintaining eye contact.

"Neither am I." He brought his glass to hers, gently tapped and then opened his eyes wider as he sipped.

Grace sipped, too. "Ridiculous."

"And yet, you didn't break eye contact."

The wine tasted amazing after her work-heavy weekend. A small treat, since she hadn't had time to do anything except make sure everyone else was enjoying the party. That and Pilates.

"Thank you." She focused on Owen, who was still far too handsome for her own comfort. And yet, she found herself checking him out more closely. Like a trainer observing a thoroughbred. Good teeth. Nice hair. Excellent bloodlines.

"See anything you like?" And there was the rub. She did. She saw so much.

"Just the wine." She lifted her glass, pretended that there was nothing else making her temperature rise.

"You sure about that?" He slid across the seat toward her. "I'm willing to play a little show-and-tell if it'll help."

"It won't." But the back of her neck grew hot and she was glad her hair was still up.

He edged closer. "Maybe we should kiss and find out."

"No." Even as her mind lingered on what kind of kisser Owen might be. Experienced. Confident. With flashes of humor that poked through unexpectedly. Her stomach did a long, slow flip.

"Kiss and make up? Kiss and get it over with?

Grace…" He pasted on a concerned expression. "You're going to have to work with me here."

She bit back her smile. He wasn't the type you could encourage unless it was all part of your game. Grace Monroe didn't play games. "I'm afraid you're going to have to sell your charms elsewhere."

"Well, now I'm offended." He didn't look offended with that devilish glint in his eyes. "Implying that I'm a common streetwalker when, clearly, I would be a high-dollar escort."

Her smile threatened to break through again.

"There's really only one thing to be done."

"Oh?" She shouldn't be enjoying this—his overt flirting, the way he seemed to shift a little closer to her with each breath.

"I'm deeply hurt. We'll have to kiss and make it better."

"Owen." Her easy enjoyment slipped away, replaced by the practical side that knew better.

He inched closer. His thigh pressed against hers. "Come on, Grace. Just one kiss. And then you can slap my face and tell me never to touch you again."

Except she knew she wouldn't do that. She wanted to kiss him, wanted to see what he tasted like, feel his body pressed against hers. It wasn't part of her five-year plan, but she wanted it anyway. When she didn't brush him away, he lifted his hand to her hair and slid out one of the pins in her updo.

One lock tumbled down, brushing the side of her neck. She knew if she pulled away and tucked the hair back into her twist, Owen would follow suit. He'd lean back, too, and they'd talk about the party and sip their wine and pat themselves on the back for a job well done.

Grace turned her head to look at him. And even though she'd known he was right there, she shivered at his nearness. His eyes drilled into hers and his usual light humor was gone, a quiet contemplation in its place. And sex.

Grace might have been focusing on work for the past few years and her dates might have ranged from rare to nonexistent, but she knew the sex look when she saw it.

She felt that slow, slippery melting inside her. The heat that followed.

"Grace?"

Maybe it was because she was tired. Maybe because she'd been dateless, solely focused on work for so long now and Owen had awoken her to that fact. It didn't matter. She was aware of it now. And her defenses were worn down, exhausted from pretending that she was fulfilled working twelve-hour days, that her vibrator was man enough for now.

Owen cupped the side of her face and Grace

felt a long lick of pleasure. So soft, so light. So right. He leaned forward, his dark eyes never leaving hers, always giving her the chance to say no, to turn her face or shake her head. She didn't and was rewarded with the press of his lips to hers, a light touch that left her sensitized and hungry for more.

She slipped her hand up the back of his neck, fingering the edges of his hair as she tugged him closer. But it felt so good, forgetting who she was supposed to be for a moment, enjoying the attentions of this shockingly handsome man, even if he wasn't who she was looking for.

But she'd missed this. The warmth, the companionship, the sharp curl of pleasure of wanting and being wanted. And it was only a kiss. And only tonight. Not even worthy of a footnote in her five-year plan. She pulled his head toward her, showing him without words how much pressure she liked, enjoying the way their bodies and mouths fit together to achieve pleasure for both. And then, she gave herself over to the moment.

Owen knew the second Grace stopped thinking, the very moment she let herself fall into what was happening between them. It was about time.

He reached an arm around her waist, hauled her toward him on the booth seat. Though they were already touching, Owen wanted to be closer, needed to feel more of her cool, luscious body pressed against his. Seriously, a man could go under with a body like this and smile the whole way down.

He was sure as hell smiling now.

She tasted like the wine she'd just sipped. Her lips soft, her mouth wet and warm. Welcoming. As if he should just settle in and stay for a while. He certainly wouldn't complain.

Owen urged her closer, half onto his lap now. Their mouths pressed together, tongues tangling as they fought for more.

He wanted to taste more than just the wine. Her fingers twisted in his hair, tugging hard. It surprised him, her sudden amorousness. He'd expected her to warm up slowly, that she'd need coaxing and coddling before she embraced this sizzle between them.

Instead, she'd shocked him by going all in off the start line. As though she'd just been waiting for the signal. Hell, if he'd known that, he would have kissed her weeks ago. He put his hand on her knee, first to pull her fully onto his lap, second to run his hand beneath her pretty dress and up her silky thigh.

Grace moaned into his mouth and then tilted her head back, exposing her long, creamy throat.

And what was a man supposed to do with a sight like that except taste?

Owen ran his tongue along her skin from her collarbone to her earlobe. He felt the rumbling sounds of her pleasure before he heard them. Rich, earthy sounds that only came from a woman who knew what she wanted in bed and wasn't afraid to demand it.

Oh, how he loved a woman who was comfortable with herself in the bedroom.

His hand crept higher under her skirt. He was torn between taking his time to carefully explore her and letting her set the pace, which appeared to be hard, fast, now. Maybe they could do it her way now and his way later.

Yes, he liked the idea of doing it again later.

He ran his tongue back down Grace's throat, biting when he reached the curve of her shoulder and pushing aside the thin strap of her dress. His hand spanned the width from her shoulder to the center of her chest. He looped his finger under the strap and dragged it down her arm, exposing her lacy cream bra.

Owen's entire body reacted to the sight of her, just barely concealed by that tiny scrap of material. He bent his head, working his way down from her shoulder to the edge of the lace.

Her fingers dug into the back of his skull even as the rest of her softened, opening. For him.

"Owen." It wasn't a command to stop or slow down. It was a demand to keep going, to give more.

A primal surge of ownership rocked through him. His. And no one else better dare touch. For that matter, they'd keep their eyes to themselves, too, if they knew what was good for them. He growled and dipped his tongue into her cleavage, letting go of the strap and cupping her breast.

Her nipple beaded against his palm, rising to attention, and he squeezed. She squirmed against him, sending shocks of pleasure through him.

Did he have a condom? He sure as hell hoped so because stopping due to lack of foresight might be the death of him.

He began turning her so she faced him. All she'd have to do was swing that long leg over his hip and they'd be in business. Nothing between them but a bit of clothing and Owen was an expert at dispensing of that.

He squeezed her breast again. They were larger than he'd realized. She did an impressive job concealing them as he considered himself a connoisseur when it came to that area of a woman's body.

He liked legs and asses. Appreciated the feel of hair brushing across his skin and nails gripping tight. But in his personal opinion, there was nothing quite like a spectacular pair of breasts. And Grace's were gold standard.

Owen had just begun to lower the edge of one lacy cup, eager to see what it was covering, when he heard the scrape of a heel on the floor. His head shot up and saw Grace's cute blonde receptionist trying to sneak past the table, her head down, very obviously determined not to look at them.

He felt Grace shift restlessly, knew the second she opened her eyes to see what had taken his attention and absorbed the jolt of her body when she jerked back. "Hayley."

Owen let go of her breast and smoothed the dress strap up her arm in one complete motion. There. Now she looked perfectly presentable. Except for the fact that his hand was still wedged between her thighs, but Hayley couldn't see that from where she was.

He saw Hayley close her eyes and swallow as she kept walking. "I apologize, Grace." Hayley kept her head averted, her blond hair hanging between her and them like a curtain. As though they could just pretend this was a perfectly normal situation. "I think my keys must have fallen out of my bag. I was hoping I could check the office, see if they might be there."

"Of course."

Of course. But Owen didn't move, not his

body or his hand. Not until Grace put her hand on top of his and moved it herself. And even then, Owen was sure to take full advantage of the trip back down her thigh. Just as delightful as the trip up.

Hayley had already walked to the office door, her back turned to them, the stiff line of her back indicating that whatever was happening behind her, she was just going to pretend she didn't know about it.

"Hey." Owen caught Grace around the waist before she slid off his lap and out of the booth. "Hurry back."

But when she looked at him, her expression was different. Gone was that soft, sensual stare that told him she'd be a warm and inventive lover. Instead, it was all business. "Owen, I'm…" Her throat bobbed. "I think I should go, too."

He'd have liked to pretend to be surprised, but he'd known. The second he'd seen Hayley—the second Grace had seen her—he'd known this was how the night would end. Not with a bang but a whimper. Literally. "I'll walk you out." Let it never be said that Owen Ford wasn't a gentleman.

As he shifted to help her off his lap, he stroked a hand down her hip. He was a gentleman, not a saint.

She shot him a look. "I can find my own way."

Hayley remained a few feet away, head tilted so that her hair formed a curtain again, as though they could all just pretend this was perfectly normal. Owen leaned closer to whisper in Grace's ear. "Then when can I see you again?"

Dinner, drinks, a movie, a walk in the park. All of the above if she'd let him.

She shook her head. "Owen. This can't happen again."

He blinked. Not what he expected. "And why is that?" He kept his tone light. He was good at light.

"Because it never should have happened in the first place. I was tired."

He kissed her, both because he wanted to and to stop her from continuing that thought. He didn't care if Hayley saw or not. He felt the slow tilt of Grace's body toward him and kissed her deeper. When she pulled back, she was breathing hard. But Owen spoke first.

"You might be tired, but that isn't why you kissed me. If you don't want to see me, Grace, you can tell me. I'm a big boy. I can take it. But don't insult me by lying."

Her eyes widened before she looked down, her lashes sweeping against her cheeks. He wanted to brush his thumb across them. "You're right. I'm sorry." But she didn't say what she was sorry for. She stepped back, her heels clacking across the floor as she headed toward the office before he could ask.

She reappeared less than a minute later, her coat on, bag over her shoulder and Hayley in tow. Owen didn't ask if they'd found the keys. She stopped in front of him while Hayley continued to the door.

He noted that Grace couldn't hold his gaze. She kept glancing away, her tongue darting out to wet her lips. "Here's the office key. If we've left anything behind or there are any problems with cleanup, please don't hesitate to call."

Please don't hesitate? She was talking as if he was an acquaintance, a person she'd met in passing whose name she'd know only because she'd put it in her file and reminded herself before the meeting. Not like the man who'd made her burn, who'd had her legs spread and her only inches away from achieving orgasm. Maybe only an inch away. His hand had been pretty high.

But Owen simply nodded. There would be plenty of other opportunities to remind Grace of how she'd melted for him. She didn't seem like the kind to melt for just anyone. "It was a great night. Thank you."

He purposefully didn't indicate just what he was thanking her for. She could think about that. Judging from the sudden blush on her cheeks, she got it. "Of course, Mr. Ford." So he was back to being a Mr. was he? "All part of the service."

She tightened her grip on her purse, gave him a brief smile and went to meet up with Hayley. He watched them walk out, Hayley turning only to give him an apologetic smile and polite goodbye, Grace not turning at all. But his eyes followed the swing of her hips anyway. Now that he knew how they felt under his palm, he couldn't stop thinking about them. And her legs. And her breasts.

The door clicked shut behind them. Owen leaned his head against the leather back of the booth seat, exhaled and wished he'd had the foresight to lock that door earlier.

CHAPTER SIX

GRACE SCOLDED HERSELF as she stepped out of the wine bar with Hayley. Foolish. Insanity. Wasn't this exactly the kind of thing she lectured her staff about all the time? All those instructions, all the rules that promised that anyone who found them too difficult to follow would be terminated. And in all her years in the business—not just working for herself, but even when she'd worked for others—Grace had always been careful to maintain a sterling reputation, to display cool professionalism no matter the situation and her own feelings or emotions.

And with only the most token resistance, she'd allowed Owen to sneak past those careful defenses and slide his tongue into her mouth and his hand up her thigh. Worse, she'd enjoyed it.

"Hayley, I'd like to explain."

Hayley darted a quick look before turning her attention back to the sidewalk in front of them. "You don't have to explain anything, Grace. I didn't see anything."

The sound of their high heels clicked along

the cement. There were still a fair number of people on the street although it was late on a Sunday night. But Vancouver's downtown core had a population density twice that of London, meaning there were always people out walking their dogs or running to the store for a forgotten and necessary item.

"We both know that's not true."

Hayley didn't look up from the sidewalk. "It could be."

Grace stopped walking. A woman wearing leggings and a sneer sniffed as she led her dog around them. Grace ignored her and her fashion atrocity. Leggings were not pants. No matter how many people wore them as such. "Hayley. You don't have to pretend. You walked in on me and…" Her throat grew tight. Grace swallowed and forced the embarrassing words out. "You walked in on me and Mr. Ford in a compromising position. It was an error in judgment that I'd like to apologize for."

Really, she should probably fire herself.

"O-o-kay." Hayley dragged the word out as she stopped and looked back at Grace. "Apology accepted?"

"Thank you." Grace nodded and started walking again. "I'd appreciate it if you didn't mention this at the office."

For the first time since walking in on her,

Hayley met her eyes. "I wouldn't, Grace. I would never do that." She meant it, too, which eased some of the pressure in Grace's lungs.

Hayley was so young, Grace realized. Still finding her way through life. And Grace prided herself on being the kind of person a young woman could look up to. She hadn't been born with wealth or prestige. She'd had to pay her own way through school and for everything she currently held dear. But she'd done it. Shown that with hard work and determination, there were opportunities to be had.

Granted, she hadn't exactly been hard done by, either. But still, she'd made a nice little place in life for herself. She wasn't willing to throw it all away over hormones. Not even raging ones.

"This just proves that I still have life lessons to learn, too," she said to Hayley as they waited for the walk signal. Hayley nodded amiably. Grace would like to think she'd learned plenty in her time, but clearly some things hadn't sunk all the way in. She didn't say more, like how it would be easier if Owen didn't make her head feel all muddled, her emotions confused and her body on fire. Like how she had a plan and Owen was messing with the timing of it. Like how even if the timing had been right, Owen wasn't.

Grace believed in keeping a separation between herself and her staff. A thin wall of authority that just made business easier. She didn't want them to be her friends. She wanted them to be her team. It was a fine line, but an important one. And she'd already nearly destroyed it once tonight. She didn't need to go any further down that path by unloading her myriad confusions on poor Hayley's shoulders.

She pulled out her cell and checked the time. "I'll call you a cab, Hayley."

"Oh. No." Hayley stopped, a look of discomfort crossing her pretty face. Grace knew Hayley lived with two other roommates in a less expensive part of town and that she didn't have a lot of money for luxuries. "I'll just catch the SkyTrain."

"It's late." And while Vancouver was an incredibly safe city given its size, bad things still happened. Grace wasn't about to let Hayley head for home on her own on the transit system that didn't even have a driver to offer protection. "The company will pay for it." Thinking about it now, Grace wondered if she should always offer cab fare on these late nights. A small perk that would encourage loyalty and safety.

She flagged a passing taxi before Hayley could offer any further refusals and handed her some cash. She'd have to set up a system for the staff to turn in credit card receipts for reimbursement. "See you tomorrow, Hayley."

"'Bye, Grace. Have a good night."

The cab pulled away from the curb, leaving Grace with a single block left to cover on her own before she reached her building. She passed three more dog walkers and a pair of tourists who asked where they might go for a nightcap.

She should be grateful that Hayley had interrupted them before things went further. Grace's face grew warm as she thought about how easily she'd allowed herself to respond to Owen. But however embarrassing it might have been getting caught with a man's hand up her skirt, it would have been far worse to have to face the next few months knowing that she'd slept with a client's brother. What had she been thinking? Obviously she hadn't been.

Grace pushed open the door to her apartment, glad she hadn't run into anyone on her way up. She wasn't close with any of her neighbors, but she knew them by name and would stop for a chat if she ran into them while she was out. Once there had even been a quick drink. But that hadn't gone anywhere, either. She wasn't about to date someone in her building. Because what if it didn't work out and then they still had to see each other every day in the lobby? Awkward.

She slipped off her shoes, flexing her toes, and carried the footwear into the bedroom, where she put them away in her closet. She took out her jeans and shirt from earlier and tossed them into her laundry hamper. Her sneakers went on the shelf below her high heels. And her dress went into a garment bag destined for the dry cleaners. It probably didn't need it, but Grace always sent her clothes to the cleaners after a function. She created parties, food-and-drink extravaganzas where spills and stains were part of the pleasure. Not to mention the smoke and other scents that clung to material.

Wearing only her bra and panties, Grace padded into the master bathroom. She'd heard that bathrooms and kitchens were the rooms that sold houses and she could admit it had been true for her. Growing up, she'd had to share a bathroom with the entire family. It hadn't been terrible, except for the fact that they only had a tub and she'd had long, thick hair that was hard to wash. She'd had to get up at six in the morning just to make sure she had enough time to rinse it out properly before Sky started pounding on the door demanding to use the toilet.

But no one pounded on her door here, and she had a stunning glass-tiled six-showerhead walk-in that defied her teenage dreams. She pulled the pins out of her updo, letting her blond hair—still as blond as when she'd been a kid with only a little help from her colorist—

tumble around her shoulders. It made her think of Owen pulling that single pin loose. She shivered and flipped the handle to turn on the water in the shower.

She was just chilled from her walk home. That was all. She slipped her earrings off and stowed them in the jewelry box that sat on her long white marble counter and wiped off her makeup. Her nails could use a trip to the manicurist. She kept them medium length and painted a nude shade that matched everything. There was a small chip on her thumb and one of her pinkies needed filing. It grew unevenly thanks to a door-slamming incident as a child.

She'd call tomorrow and try to squeeze it in before the end of the day. The water pounded against the pretty tiles, all white with a thick green strip that ran around the center. When the temperature rose enough to be comfortable, she peeled off her expensive lace undergarments and stepped under the spray.

It would be a quick shower tonight. She just wanted to wash the festivities off before climbing into bed. She squirted a dollop of grapefruit-scented shampoo into her palm and rubbed her hands together to create lather before stroking the suds through her hair.

The warm water flowed around her body, massaging away the knots from her long weekend and many hours of standing. Oh, she could stand here all night. She let her eyes close, slowly rubbing her scalp, making sure to work the shampoo from root to tip and clean each strand. She could forget about things under the water. This was her version of being at one with nature. A pristine white bathroom with fluffy towels and a variety of scented soaps and lotions. She was totally communing, though she knew her mother wouldn't see it that way.

Grace exhaled and reminded herself that it was okay to be different. It was okay to be her own person even if her parents sometimes seemed to think she was surrendering to the man. But she didn't want to be a counterculturalist or drink nettle chai tea or raise chickens. She wanted the life she had now. And there was nothing wrong with that.

Nor was there anything wrong with being attracted to a handsome man. Even one who wasn't good husband material.

It was just…embarrassing. Grace pumped her favorite grapefruit soap onto a puffy bath lily. Yes, embarrassing. She inhaled the clean, citrusy aroma. To think she was a slave to her hormones and incapable of using logic and reason when faced with a hot guy. Sorry, even for a really hot guy that was not the case. Yes, Owen was extremely handsome and plenty charming, which was a dangerous combination. But he was certainly resistible.

She smoothed the bubbles along her arms from her wrists to her shoulders, being careful to lather each bit of skin. Like most things in her life, there was an order to her bathing. First the shampoo, twice to make sure she got every strand squeaky clean, then her conditioner, which she left to set while she washed her body. Her body went in sequence: arms, underarms, front of her torso, legs, feet, bottom, back and shoulders. Her front on the way down, her back on the return trip. Some people would probably think her neurotic, but Grace knew that patterns became habits and routines. A way to control the vagaries of life.

For the most part, she liked her life just as it was. Her career path was on a soaring trajectory. She had good staff. A beautiful home. Maybe her personal life had suffered some, but she had a plan for that, too. By this time next year, she'd be dating and maybe some of those casual friendships that she hadn't explored—people in her Pilates class or some of the neighbors—might become real friends.

But she had to complete the rest of year four of her five-year plan before then. She didn't believe in moving ahead or tossing the plan aside. She'd spent a lot of time coming up with the steps and building in appropriate measures so that she could create a situation ripe for success. Just because things were going better than planned, didn't mean she should jump ahead to her next task. No, she should concentrate on her current one, using the extra time to get ahead. It was what she had done the previous three years, which was why she was seeing a better than expected return now.

Grace saw no reason to change what was working. Of course, that would be much easier when she didn't have to deal with a hot man's tongue in her mouth. Even if it had been delightful.

She finished soaping. She knew what she needed to do. Even as she thought it, a disappointed quiver ran through her body. No more tongue in her mouth, no more hand on her upper thigh. At least, not until next year. But it was for the best. She knew that.

And starting tomorrow, she was going to stick to it. There would not be a repeat performance of tonight. No foolish encounter that ended with her staff finding her in a compromising position.

Starting tomorrow. Tonight, though? Grace ran her hands along her body as she rinsed, being careful to remove all traces of soap. Her fingers played over her nipples. A delicious tingle followed as it always did. Grace ran her hands over her breasts again.

Owen's hands had easily covered her breasts, palming her nipples and making them rise and demand to be touched. Demand to be rolled between a thumb and finger. Demand to be licked and sucked by a warm, wet mouth.

Grace closed her eyes, the water raining down on her head and body as she attended to the ache thrumming through her body. She didn't often give herself over to the pleasure outside her scheduled times.

Yes, she scheduled her orgasms. Knowing in advance that she had the time and no obligations made her come faster, which meant she could come again. Because if one was good, two was better.

Sunday night was not orgasm night. She generally chose Tuesdays as they were the days least likely to have evening meetings and she'd be fully recovered from any wedding weekend exhaustion.

But tonight, even though she was off schedule and in desperate need of rest, her body would not be denied. She moaned, the sound a quiet hum under the beat of the shower.

It was Owen's fault, those soft, thoughtful kisses and clever fingers awakening the desire she carefully held at bay. Her hands slipped down her body, now rinsed clean and slick with water.

Grace kept herself trimmed and tidy even though no one else would see. Good grooming was a ritual that didn't require a man in her life. She threaded her fingers through the blond hair between her thighs, a small gasp escaping her lips.

This orgasm might not be scheduled but it was definitely wanted.

She imagined Owen's hands climbing up her thighs, his fingers nearing but never touching her sweet spot. And she'd have let him. In a bar, with a man she had no future with, Grace knew she would have spread her legs and pulled her lacy underwear aside herself had Hayley been a few minutes later.

Heat suffused her skin, but it wasn't from embarrassment or the water. It was from picturing Owen's fingers sliding along her wetness, circling slowly and thoroughly until her legs began to shake. He wouldn't stop there, either. No, she was certain he was the kind of man who enjoyed giving pleasure as much as receiving. She moaned again. Louder. And her temperature spiked. He'd have lifted her onto that table, disposed of her underwear and slid her dress up around her hips. Then he would've lowered his head and shown her what other wonderful things that tongue of his could do.

She came just thinking about it, his name a desperate cry on her lips, her fingers busy where his should have been and the warm water washing everything away. Everything. Her desire, the ache still pulsing between her legs, the thought that she should do it again.

Because she shouldn't. This was an exception in her well-ordered life and one she didn't intend to make a rule. And all those thoughts of getting naked with Owen Ford could go exactly where they belonged. Through the stainless steel drain of her pretty, white shower.

But she let loose one final hum, a purr of pure contentment, before she turned off the water.

GRACE WENT TO PILATES the next morning. Not just because it was on her schedule, but to clear her head. Because it had been awfully fuzzy last night. What had she been thinking? Not only making out with Owen, but also in a public location where anyone could walk in? She got cold just thinking about the fact that Hayley had stumbled upon them, though she supposed she should be grateful. That had stopped things before they'd gone too far and, based on their conversation last night, she thought Hayley would be discreet.

She pushed open the glass doors to her gym, swiping her membership card at the desk and heading to the locker room. She hung the heavy garment bag containing her suit, shoes and makeup in one of the lockers and headed out to the main area.

Grace had selected a women-only gym. It was a little smaller than the larger coed gyms, but the bigger gyms offered features that she'd never take advantage of while her focus was on Pilates and yoga. And there were multiple classes every day that were easy to fit around her work schedule.

She laid her mat down on the wood floor in the glassed-in classroom and settled herself on top of it. They always started by finding a neutral spine position before moving into any of the exercises. Grace felt her entire body relax as she allowed her muscles to soften and shift to the natural position.

"Grace?"

She blinked and turned her head and saw Mallory with a rubber mat in a tight roll slung over her shoulder. "Mallory. I didn't know you were a member here." Grace pushed herself to a sitting position and reminded herself that Mallory didn't know about her aborted make-out session with Owen last night so there was no reason to feel embarrassed. But that didn't stop her from straightening the cuffs of her work-out pants.

"I don't usually take the early class." It wasn't quite seven in the morning. Mallory unrolled her mat on the floor beside Grace. "I take the eight and then head into work, but I have a meeting first thing, so here I am." She lowered herself to the mat, looking graceful and effortless, but her gym clothes looked loose, as though she'd bought them when she was ten pounds heavier. "Great party last night."

Grace willed herself not to flush, not to give anything away. Nobody knew except her and Owen and Hayley. *And two can keep a secret if one of them is dead.* She swallowed and shoved the worrisome thought away. "I'm glad you enjoyed it."

"I don't think I was the only one."

Grace felt her eyes cut toward Mallory, just a little too fast, a little too sharp. "Oh?" She went for fluffy and light in tone, but that whole darting-eye thing had probably given her away. Definitely if the smile curling the edges of Mallory's lips held any hint of truth.

"I think Owen enjoyed it, too." She didn't say any more. But she didn't need to.

Grace sucked in a breath. It felt as though a weight had been lowered onto her chest. "About that—"

Mallory cut her off with a wave of her hand. "I know Owen didn't want to be the point person for the party at first, but it's clear you won him over. He didn't give you a hard time, did he?"

"No." Grace breathed again and this time it came a bit easier. The attraction between them still wasn't something she was planning on pursuing. She couldn't. Except in the privacy of her fantasies. But it seemed clear that Mallory had no knowledge of anything that had gone on behind closed, if not locked, doors.

"He's single, you know." Mallory twirled the end of her long ponytail around her fingers.

Grace murmured that she did indeed know and busied herself with the cuffs of her pants again. They were still perfectly straight.

"And I see I've made you uncomfortable." Mallory cleared her throat. "Not my intention. I thought…I don't know. Maybe it was the situation. The engagement party, love on the brain, but you seemed to like each other. You look good together." Grace's head shot up in time to see Mallory shrug. "But if you're not interested."

No, no, Grace was interested, which was the heart of the problem. If she was going to meet her future husband, she couldn't be distracted by men who didn't have potential. "He's a client," she said, which didn't address her interest level at all.

Mallory stared at her. "He likes you. I can tell."

Grace told herself that didn't matter, that she wasn't going to ask. "What makes you say that?" *Oops.*

"The way he looks at you. The way he smiles when someone says your name." Mallory stretched her legs out and leaned back.

Grace mirrored her, warming up the muscles before the class actually started. "What are you saying, Mallory?"

"Mal." Her grin flashed. "My friends call me Mal."

Grace felt a little rush of pleasure at the implicit invitation to be friends. Since she spent so much time at the office, she didn't really have friends. A few acquaintances, generally those in the business that she met once in a while for an after-work drink or a lunch to discuss a client referral, but for the most part it was just her and the office and the gym.

"And I'm not saying anything." But Mal was smirking up a storm. "Just making an observance."

"Because?" Grace couldn't imagine that Mal was so interested in her brother's love life that she felt the need to meddle in it.

"Because you seem like a nice person and Owen is a nice guy."

"Does he know you're playing matchmaker?" Another thought occurred to her. "Did he send you here to do this?"

"No." Mal laughed. "He'd be highly offended if he knew I said anything. Claim that I'm cramping his style or making it seem like he can't meet a woman on his own."

"Well…" Grace let the thought trail off.

Mal laughed again. "I guess it does seem that way. Let me assure you, Owen has no trouble meeting women." She frowned. "That sounds wrong, too." But she didn't get a chance to finish the thought because the instructor walked in, greeted them and started them on their warm-ups while she set up her own mat and went around the room repositioning them as necessary.

Grace sweated through the movements, her muscles spasming and clutching as she pushed through each exercise, but she barely noticed. Her mind was stuck on Owen. Again.

She and Mal walked to the locker room together after class, but the topic of Owen didn't come up again. Grace wasn't sure how she felt about that. Part of her was glad. She should just put the whole thing behind her, which was the smart thing to do. But another rebellious part of her refused, kept wanting to relive the feel of his lips on hers, his hands on her body, hers on his.

She felt more like herself after a cool shower. She put on a sleek gray pencil skirt and pale pink blouse and pulled her hair into a low knot. Her suede heels had a hidden platform that not only made her appear taller than her doctor-listed five foot eight, but also made walking surprisingly comfortable as she stepped out of the gym into a bright, warm day.

Mal had headed off a few minutes earlier, on her way to the meeting, but with a promise that next time they'd go for coffee after class, and Grace found herself looking forward to it. The fact that her life consisted of work and working out was just sad. Perhaps it was time she did something about that.

Oh, she wasn't going to go buck wild and change her entire life over a comment, but taking a night or even an entire day to do something for herself—a spa date, going to the theater, meeting people for brunch—was something she could start doing now and still complete her five-year plan on time.

She reached her office, only two blocks from the gym, in just a few minutes and stowed her leather gym bag in the small office cupboard that had been purchased for just this use.

The cupboard door closed with a quiet click. Just the way she liked her life. Discreet and tidy. She made an appointment to get her nails done tomorrow after work and settled into her morning routine at the office. A small black coffee then water for the rest of the day. A banana and a bran muffin at nine-thirty. She called and pre-ordered lunch for pickup so as not to waste time standing in a line. Lunch, a garden salad with some legumes thrown in for protein from the café down the street, would be ready at quarter to one.

Satisfied that she was, if not completely back on track, at least in the train station, Grace settled into the daily activities of answering any emails, booking appointments with clients and contacting vendors.

She heard the low murmur of her team as they stowed the items from last night's party and she left her office to say hello. No one looked at her strangely or hid a smile, so she trusted that Hayley had kept her word. Her already good opinion of the young woman rose. It would have been easy to spill what she'd seen, to share the inside scoop, but she hadn't.

Grace was almost feeling as though she might actually get through the entire incident wholly unscathed when her direct line rang. "Good morning, Grace Monroe speaking."

"Grace. It's Julia Laurent."

Grace felt her heart stutter. First Mal and now Julia? "Good morning." She prayed her voice sounded calmer than her stomach felt. That muffin was feeling none too fluffy at the moment. More like a lead ball.

"I just wanted to call and thank you again for last night. It was exactly the kind of look I'd have chosen myself." The soon-to-be bride's enthusiasm buzzed through the line. When there was no follow-up mention of Owen, Grace felt some of her tension begin to roll away.

"Wonderful." A post-party phone call wasn't unusual, after all. She enjoyed hearing from her clients whether their comments were good or bad, as it helped her continue or correct as appropriate.

"I was hoping to schedule a meeting with you this week while it's all still fresh in my mind. You gave me so many great ideas."

"Of course." Grace was already pulling up her weekly calendar, the days neatly sectioned and color-highlighted. Her nail appointment was shaded a pale lilac, as were all her grooming appointments. Hair, waxing, meeting with a personal shopper at Nordstrom. Clients were always a warm, grassy green that reminded her of the first buds of spring coming to life. Just as marriage was the start of a new life together. "Which day were you thinking?"

Grace always built in extra pockets of time for these types of calls. A bride who panicked that she'd chosen the wrong color of tablecloths and that her big day would be ruined. A groom who decided at the last minute that he actually *did* want a say in the flowers—it had happened. Once. Or a parent who felt that they should be more involved in the choices, since they were paying for the event.

She ran her eye down the segments shaded a soft, buttery yellow. Flex time. "I have time tomorrow morning, Wednesday at three or anytime Thursday."

"Could we come and see you today?" Julia's enthusiasm was evident in the breathlessness of her voice. "The restaurant tends to be quieter on Monday, so it's easier for me to get away during prep."

It would be tight but manageable. "Absolutely." Grace double-clicked to enter today's schedule, already mentally rearranging her appointments to make space. There was nothing that couldn't be shifted or postponed if necessary. "You can come in at two or three."

"Fantastic. We'll see you at two. And, Grace, thank you again for last night. It was wonderful."

Grace wondered if Julia would feel the same way if she knew how Grace had spent her time after the party had shut down. She shook off the thought. Hadn't she already decided she wasn't going to linger over it, but was going to move on?

She placed the meeting in her calendar, let her team know that the boardroom was booked at two and returned to her office. If only she could schedule her emotions as easily as her workday.

THE MEETING WAS much as Grace had expected. Easy and productive. She'd provided Julia and Donovan with some preferred locations, those she worked with regularly that she knew could be relied on, as well as some suggestions for decor and food. They'd meet again in a few weeks and start making some final choices.

She was elbow-deep in the wedding of another client, one who had the unfortunate habit of changing her mind frequently, but a father with the kind of money to pay for any cost the last-minute cancellations incurred, when her phone rang. "Good afternoon. Grace Monroe."

"Do you want to know what I've been thinking about all day?" Owen's voice flowed across her skin like the water from her shower last night. "I thought about those sexy little moans you made last night when my fingers slipped up your—"

"Owen." Her temperature spiked and her office, which had been perfectly comfortable before, suddenly felt too warm. She turned on the small desk fan and grabbed the bottle of water beside it. The bottle was still cool and she rubbed it along the back of her neck and over her temples until her racing pulse slowed. Then she cracked open the water bottle and drank. There. Much better. It was fine. She was fine.

"What are you wearing?"

She told herself this was not a turn-on, even though it was. "Owen, enough."

"Actually, I don't think either of us got enough. Which is why I'm taking you out tomorrow." She had to say no. Even as images from last night poked through her resolve. "Good food, good wine, good company." It would be, too. She already knew Owen would deliver. "Julia's promised to make a special meal. Off the menu."

Grace closed her eyes as a sense of dread flooded her system. "You told her what happened?" She was humiliated. Julia had known? While Grace had been talking about colors and flowers and selecting food to go with the spirit of the ambience, Julia had known?

"Of course not. I don't kiss and tell." Which eased the dread if not her discomfort. "So, tomorrow—"

"I have plans." Which was true. After her nail appointment, she planned to pick up groceries for the week and go over the agenda for the wedding scheduled this weekend.

"Like what?"

Of course Owen wouldn't be satisfied without a detailed explanation. Of course not. "Plans." Because he didn't need to know.

"A date?"

Grace might have felt a tiny bubble of pride at his jealous tone. If he'd actually sounded jealous and if she were the type to get googly-eyed over a man getting possessive. Since neither of those things were the case she merely clarified. "No, I don't have time to date."

"Ah. So you're looking for something with no strings attached. You know, Grace, I'm not a piece of meat. I have feelings."

She smiled, then pressed her lips together to hide it, even though no one was around to see. "You're being ridiculous."

"I think you could use a little ridiculous in your life. So, what time works best for you? Seven? Eight? I could convince Julia to make a midnight supper, but she'd probably make me regret it."

It was on the tip of Grace's tongue to ask how, but she swallowed her curiosity. It didn't matter. She wasn't having a midnight supper with Owen, or any meal. "I'm afraid dinner isn't a possibility. Tomorrow or any other night."

"All right. What about lunch? Breakfast?"

"I work through lunch and breakfast." Totally, completely true.

"What about if we call it a working lunch?"

Grace gave him points for perseverance. Though she didn't much enjoy it being focused on her. "And what would we be working on? You're not the client—Julia and Donovan are."

"Exactly. Which means you are not professionally obligated to turn me down. So about that dinner?"

He'd set a nice trap there and she'd walked right into it. "I think you missed your calling. You should have been a lawyer." Kind of too bad he wasn't. He'd probably have ticked most of her future-husband boxes then. "But I'm still unavailable."

"I think you're forgetting something." His voice lowered.

A shiver rolled through Grace. She loved the low rumble of a man's voice, which was something best kept to herself, as she doubted Owen would have any qualms in using it against her.

"I saw how you responded last night. Are you really going to make me ask if it was good for you?"

Grace took a sip of water, but it did nothing to address the desertlike dryness in her mouth. She exhaled slowly. "Last night was—"

"A revelation," Owen finished for her.

"That's not what I was going to say." Even if he was sort of right. Grace couldn't remember the last time she'd gone home and brought herself to orgasm off schedule.

"No? Well, you can thank me later for helping you figure it out."

"Owen."

"I like it when you say my name. Liked it better when you moaned it into my ear last night."

Grace's cheeks burned. She didn't have to think back to know it was true. She'd always been a talker during sex.

"Tell me what I have to do to hear you moan in my ear again."

"Nothing." Her tongue felt thick. She shouldn't let him get to her. Shouldn't let his little games work their way into her mind and her body. "Because it's never going to happen again."

"Now, that would be a shame. For both of us."

Grace shut her eyes, tried not to think of how she'd come in the shower last night with his name on her lips.

"I'm not going to pressure you, but I am going to ask you to think about it. Just give it a chance. Give me a chance."

And damn if the man wasn't smart enough to hang up before she could deny his request.

CHAPTER SEVEN

OWEN SMILED AS he hung up the phone and left the manager's office at Elephants. He wasn't on duty tonight, but he was around anyway. A month ago, he might have thought of that as sad. Pathetic, even. But now, he found it preferable to anything else he might be doing.

Except Grace.

The floor was busy, which was normal, but more so tonight, since they'd been closed for Julia and Donovan's engagement party the night before. Which was another reason Owen was on-site. He'd already had a night off and felt guilty about taking another, even if Mal told him it was fine.

He worked the room, stopping to chat to some regulars and explain the reason they'd been closed last night, then spent a few minutes chatting with some tourists who were interested in what kind of nightlife the city had to offer.

He wished he'd been able to convince Grace to come out tonight. The old Owen would have just let it—and her—go with a shrug, but this was the new Owen. He was willing to work for things he wanted. Like Grace.

There was satisfaction in making a true effort, even if it wasn't successful. Like his attempt to introduce some of the menu from La Petite Bouchée to the wine bars. That had gone over about as well as his attempt to fly using a towel as a cape when he'd been six and Donovan eight. But that was okay. It had been a learning process. He'd learned that people liked the more casual fare at the wine bar and he felt as though he was getting a handle on some of the back-end business aspects.

He knew how to handle the front of the house, work the crowd, handle questions and concerns and make sure staff was performing well. But the business was about more than that. Following a budget, identifying customer wants and needs before they did and implementing changes so the place never grew stagnant.

Owen found he liked that part of the business, too. He knew Donovan worried that his interest wouldn't last, that Owen would grow weary of the workload and leave when something else caught his attention, but Donovan was wrong. Owen liked what he was doing, liked seeing the changes he was making in the workplace and himself.

He wouldn't push Grace. That would be creepy

and illegal and he wasn't a stalker. But he liked her and he liked spending time with her. And despite her assertions that she wanted to keep things between them professional, he knew that wasn't the whole truth.

Owen might not be an expert in business, yet, but he was an expert in people. And from the tone of her voice to the way she responded to his touch, he knew she wanted him on a far more personal level.

All she needed was permission to admit it.

He decided on a week. During that time, he wouldn't call or email her. Wouldn't send her a funny text message or photo and he sure as hell wouldn't drop by her office. It wasn't exactly playing hard-to-get—for that to work, she needed to actually be actively pursuing him—but it would get her thinking. About him. And hopefully she would miss him.

He was still hoping when he turned up at her office exactly seven days later. Never let it be said that Owen Ford didn't follow through.

Hayley offered him water and a seat. He declined both, feeling antsy to see Grace. It had been a long seven days. He prowled the room while Hayley called Grace to inform her that she had a visitor.

He hoped to take her to dinner tonight, something casual, no pressure. Maybe a glass of wine on a patio after the meal. Somewhere they could get to know each other a little better.

"Owen?" Hayley smiled. "Ms. Monroe will see you now." She pushed open the door that led from the lobby to the back offices, but didn't follow him. Owen wondered if that was policy for people who knew their way around or that she simply didn't want to get another eyeful of him and Grace making out. He liked the idea of the latter.

Grace's office door was glass. He could see her working, fingers zipping over her keyboard, an intent expression on her face. She was wearing one of those sexy suits again. He'd never really liked the buttoned-up look before, but there was something about Grace in those suits. The way the lines followed the curves of her body, highlighting her femininity and the soft colors that invited a person to look. Today's suit was cool ivory and was paired with a bright pink scarf.

He knocked once and then pushed the door open. She was expecting him. "Good afternoon, Grace." He'd decided on coming near close of day, figuring she was less likely to be in a meeting or have one to rush off to. If things went well, he hoped to convince her to leave with him now. Maybe they could have both a pre- and post-dinner drink on a patio.

"Owen." She rose from her chair to shake his hand, but he noticed she was careful to keep her distance. Fine. All the better to check her out.

"You look great." Which might sound clichéd, but it was true. Even with her trying not to get too close, he could smell the bright fragrance she wore.

"Thank you." Her handshake was quick, but he still managed to appreciate the softness of her skin. Especially as he now knew that she was soft all over.

He didn't say anything else, just placed himself in the guest chair and watched her.

Her hands fluttered, smoothed down her skirt. She sat down and folded them in front of her. "Why are you here, Owen?"

He noted that, unlike the other times she'd tried to back away, she called him by his first name. An improvement. "I was in the neighborhood."

She lifted one pale blond eyebrow. "Were you?"

"No." Because he didn't want to start their relationship off by lying. "I came to see you."

"Why?" Her nails were painted a pink just a few shades lighter than her scarf.

"Because I wanted to ask you out to dinner tonight." This time, he hadn't approached Julia about making a special, off-menu meal. She'd harassed him enough about his sudden lack of skills with the ladies last week.

Grace's fingers tightened. Just barely, but since he happened to be looking at those pretty pink nails again, he noticed. "I have plans."

Owen looked into her dark blue eyes. "Do you?" He supposed she could have a standing event on Mondays—dinner with a friend, tennis lessons, beach volleyball at Kitsilano Beach. His body tightened at the thought of Grace in a bikini.

Her eyes darted away. "Yes."

He was almost sure she was lying. "Then how about tomorrow?"

"Owen."

He was encouraged that she didn't say no. He might even consider it a green light. "Then Wednesday or Thursday. Or how about the weekend? Do you have a wedding?"

Her lips turned up in a quiet smile. "Actually, I don't. My clients rescheduled for a later date."

"Then you're free." All weekend, by his calculations.

"No, I promised my family I'd go and visit." That small smile shrank and then disappeared.

Owen wanted to put it back. "That shouldn't take all weekend." He sat forward, caught another whiff of her perfume. "Tell me what you want to do and we'll do it. Sailing in English Bay, zip-lining in Whistler, a getaway to Aruba."

She pinned him with a look, but he thought he saw a shimmer of that smile. "Really? You can organize a getaway to Aruba without any notice?"

"I have some notice, unless you want to leave right now, which I am completely willing to do."

This time, her lips definitely turned up and rewarded him with a grin. Unfortunately, it didn't last. "I can't."

"Sure you can. Tell your family something came up and come spend the weekend with me in the Caribbean." He'd have to rearrange his work schedule, but it could be done. He'd barely taken any time off this year, so he was due a short vacation anyway. And Travis would definitely set him up with a suite in the hotel his beach bistro was attached to.

Grace exhaled and he heard her answer. Disappointing, but he had other ideas.

"Maybe we should save that for later." He wasn't about to let her close off this topic of conversation. "Give you something to look forward to." He was pleased when she laughed. "Why don't we start with dinner. Friday, Saturday or Sunday?"

"I really did promise to visit my family."

"That won't take all weekend, will it?"

She nodded. "They live on Salt Spring and I said I'd stay over."

"I'll go with you." It had been years since Owen had been to the vibrant community and he thought it might be fun to go back.

She hesitated. "To see my family?"

"Why not? Ashamed to introduce me? I'm not that bad."

She shook her head. "I wouldn't do that to you. Besides, we're not dating."

"Aren't we?" He showed off his surprised face.

Grace shook her head and her smile disappeared, replaced by something else. "No. We're not."

"We could be." Their eyes met and Owen felt that zing that kept him coming back. That and the fact that she challenged him, which he'd been surprised to learn he liked. Maybe it was just because it was different and maybe the novelty would wear off, but Owen didn't think so.

"I don't think so."

But she didn't tell him he couldn't come, so Owen marked it as a victory.

GRACE STARED AT HIM. Why wasn't she taking a hard line and telling him to forget it? To move on and find someone else to charm? Because some part of her—and not some deep, hidden part, but a big part hovering right below the surface—was interested. Which wasn't good.

"Owen…" She tried for a firm voice.

"I'm just asking for a chance." He lifted one shoulder in a small, nonthreatening shrug. "We're attracted to each other. I have a good job. I'm single. We're both young and healthy. So I really don't see the problem."

The problem was, neither did she. "Owen," she began again, "it isn't that simple."

He frowned at her. "Of course it is. What's so complicated about it?"

Her business, her plan. "I have a schedule for these things."

"Well, tell me your schedule and I'll accommodate it."

She shook her head. "It's really not that simple. I have my business to think of. I…" Her voice trailed off. She had her business to think of, yes. But that wasn't the root issue. No, the root issue was that she was scared. Owen rattled her, he didn't check any—well, okay, he didn't check *many*—of the boxes on her future-husband list, but she still wanted him. But to what end? Was he looking to settle down? In a year? In five years? Did he want kids or a dog? But these weren't the kinds of questions to ask when they hadn't even been on a real date. Talk about getting ahead of herself.

Owen leaned forward. "I think we could have some fun together."

They could. "I'm not looking for fun," Grace told him. She planned to treat her love life with the same meticulous care that she ran her business. "Dating someone is serious."

"It's supposed to be fun, too." He reached out and placed his warm hand over hers. "Tell me you'll think about it."

She opened her mouth to tell him that wasn't a good idea, but he squeezed her fingers, just a gentle press, and it shot a sizzle right through her, making the words dry up. She studied him, the easy tilt to his head, the friendly smile he always seemed to wear. He had a point about fun. She wanted a husband who was stable, one who could be counted on to follow through on his promises, who would cherish her and their future children—but she wanted to laugh, too. And she didn't actually know what Owen's plans were. Maybe he aspired to more than running a bar. She swallowed. "I'll think about it."

GRACE CHECKED HER travel bag again. Nothing had changed since the last time she'd looked, but she liked to be thorough. Everything was folded in neat squares, toiletries and shoes were double-bagged and she had extra clothing in case of weather or spill.

She zipped up the case and flipped it onto its end. The wheels clicked as they rolled over the hardwood floor and rumbled as she headed for the front door and her weekend away.

Grace wouldn't normally choose to spend a weekend with her family. She loved them and she knew they loved her, but they didn't always understand each other. Which only became an issue when they started to poke at her about her life choices, about how wasteful the extravagant weddings she designed were, about the lack of locally grown food in her diet, about falling into the trap of wanting more when she already had so much.

There was nothing she could say to convince them that she liked her life the way it was just fine, thank you very much. So she no longer wasted her breath. She'd sit and listen, nodding every once in a while to make it appear that she was engaged, and make mental notes and plans for her upcoming week. It was better for everyone that way.

She didn't own a car—it was one of the few things her mother approved of about her city life—so she booked a cab to take her to the ferry terminal and her island destination.

As they cruised out of the city, leaving behind the concrete buildings and buzz of people, Grace wished she had work to keep her home. Or that she wasn't going until tomorrow morning.

A Saturday-morning trip had been her original plan, but then her mother had wanted her to stay for dinner on Sunday. As farmers, they ate early anyway. The only way Grace had been able to talk her way out of it was to agree to come out on Friday instead. But now, she wondered if that had been her mother's plan all along. She resolved not to think about Owen and whether or not he'd actually show up. This weekend wasn't about that. It was about doing her daughterly duty.

The ferry terminal was busy with cars as the large passenger ferries dropped off and picked up. According to the signage, her ferry was 100-percent full, but she knew that number was for vehicles only. There would be no such reprieve for her, a lowly foot passenger.

She joined the winding line for tickets to Salt Spring Island. Since it was summer and lots of people wanted to visit the charming—according to her mother—island, they had a dedicated crossing route. Unfortunately, ferries only ran every two hours and on a schedule that didn't fit hers. Instead, Grace was going to take one of the larger, more luxurious ferries to Victoria on Vancouver Island and then catch a smaller vessel that would take her to Salt Spring.

It was a bit of a hassle, making the transfer, but the larger ship with its private quiet lounge and Wi-Fi connectivity made up for it. And it meant she could stay at work until closing and not have to wait until 8:25 p.m. to catch a ferry. She checked her watch as the line moved forward. It was quarter to seven, which meant she had fifteen minutes to buy her ticket, cross the terminal and get to her berth.

The first crossing took just over ninety minutes and the second another thirty-five. With the transfer time, she wouldn't actually land on Salt Spring until 9:30 p.m. or so. On the plus side, it meant by the time she arrived everyone would either be in bed or close to, so she could do the same. On the minus, it was a long trip even with her laptop and work.

The line moved quickly and when she got to the berth, they hadn't even started loading yet, so the small waiting area was packed with other walk-on passengers—a young family with a crying toddler, who looked at her with wet eyes and a quivering lip as though she might be the soft touch that bought him a cookie. A college-aged couple with backpacks straining at the zippers, their sandals and shorts grimy. Business people returning home for the weekend. There were a fair number of people who owned homes on the island but worked and rented in the city during

there, but it was nice to come home to sometimes. "You can see the sights."

"There's only one sight I want to see." She couldn't breathe. Couldn't look away from him, either.

"This isn't a date." It came out as a whisper.

"Okay." He swiveled his wrist to cup her face. She could feel the warmth seeping into her skin, wanted to rub her cheek against his palm.

"I mean it." She was grasping at straws. Something she sensed they both realized.

"Okay." He smiled and started to draw her forward. And when he kissed her, she practically melted.

Yes, not a date at all.

THEY DOCKED ON Salt Spring before ten. The sun hadn't even fully set, leaving everything bathed in a golden glow. Owen's fingers tightened around the handle of Grace's bag and the strap of his own.

"Do you have somewhere to stay?" She turned those big, blue eyes on him. He wanted to reach out and rub the wrinkle between them.

"No, but I'll find a place." He hadn't planned that far ahead, but surely there would be vacancies. The summer season was over and Salt Spring was a popular destination during the warmer months. Maybe he could convince her to come for a visit. "Want to join me? I can promise no parents."

"Tempting." She looked as if she meant it, too. "But I made a promise and if I canceled I'd get the mother of all guilt trips."

Owen grinned. "Sounds familiar." His own mother had given him one when he'd told her that he wouldn't be attending Sunday dinner. He put a hand on the small of Grace's back as they followed the crowd toward the exit, both for the excuse to touch her and ensure they didn't get separated. "If you need a break from the family togetherness, you can stay with me." When she raised an eyebrow, he shook his head. "Strictly platonic. Now, I won't say that it's my first choice, but I won't push. Two beds. No touching."

He saw some of her tension slide away and her lips turned up in a smile. "Thank you, Owen. That's really thoughtful." He wasn't sure, but he thought she walked a little closer as they made their way off the boat.

The evening had cooled, thanks to the breeze off the ocean, and Owen wondered if he could slip his arm around her shoulders in the name of conserving heat.

"Gaia! Sweetheart!"

He didn't take note of the shout until he felt Grace stiffen. Then he turned to see where the voice was coming from and saw a tall woman with light brown hair frizzing around her face, waving like crazy from the small pickup area. As if they weren't the only two who weren't heading to their own parked cars and as if she wasn't the only person idling in the pickup space, aside from one lone cab with no driver in sight.

"Gaia." She waved again. Clearly looking at them.

He knew he wasn't Gaia... He glanced at Grace, who appeared to be steeling herself as she angled toward the woman. Since he still had her suitcase, he walked with her. "Is that your mom?" Even as he asked, he knew he needn't have bothered. They weren't twins and didn't look like sisters, but there was a similarity to their bearing. And the height. "Why is she calling you 'Gaia'?"

"Long story."

"Sweetheart." Grace's mother enveloped her in a hug. Her long skirt swung as she moved and showed off heavy leather sandals. "And you brought a friend." She opened her arms to include Owen in the embrace, so they were in a sort of threesome. Though not the kind Owen had ever imagined. "Welcome, I'm Sparrow."

Like the bird? But Owen was too polite to ask or even give any visual cue. "A pleasure to meet you, Sparrow." He slid a shade closer to Grace. She looked as though she could use the support. "I'm Owen Ford."

"Owen." Sparrow made a circle with her lips while she pronounced his name, as if she was tasting it. Then she nodded. "I like it. Owen is a good, solid name."

"I'll tell my parents you approve."

Sparrow nodded as she moved around to open the back of the vehicle. "I can tell you not only have the look of the Black Irish, but the charm, as well." She sent her daughter a smile. "A handsome devil you've brought with you, Gaia."

"I didn't exactly bring him," Grace said, but she didn't say it loudly.

"Don't be shy." Sparrow grinned at him as she opened the SUV's hatch. Owen loaded the bags, though Sparrow tried to help. "Will you be staying in the guest room this weekend?" She smiled at Owen as she closed the door. "It's a queen-size bed."

"He's not staying with us," Grace announced.

"Why not? We have plenty of room." She faced Owen. "We have plenty of room."

"I appreciate the offer." He did and even two weeks ago, he would have happily accepted the invitation, but with his sister and sister-in-law's concerns still ringing in his ears and a look at the pained expression on Grace's face, he swallowed the inclination. "But I'll stay in town."

"Absolutely not." Sparrow opened the back door for Owen and then hopped into the driver's side. Grace slowly climbed into the front passenger seat and sent Owen a beseeching look. He could pick up what she was putting down, but he didn't know what she wanted him to do about it.

"I booked a room," Owen lied when Grace sent him another pleading look. "At Bronze Frog farm." He remembered the name from his quick search.

"No." Sparrow pulled away from the curb. Owen thought he saw where Grace got her attitude as well as her height. "You'll stay with us. I won't hear another word about it."

"Sparrow—" Grace began, but her mother cut her off with a wave of her hand.

"Gaia, don't be unwelcoming. I know you're shy. We'll put Owen in the guest room and pretend not to hear him sneak down the hall to your room in the middle of the night."

Owen might have been embarrassed except Grace looked humiliated enough for both of them. She wouldn't even look at him now, just faced forward, her hands fisted in her lap.

"That's very kind of you, Mrs. Monroe. If you're sure it won't be any trouble?"

"I insist, and please call me Sparrow. I'm not Mrs. Anything."

"Sparrow doesn't believe in marriage or changing her name. Except that her birth certificate says Susan."

Sparrow laughed. "She's right. Marriage is simply a way for the government to govern our personal lives. I think they should keep their noses out of my private business. I pay my taxes and that should be enough."

Her attitude surprised Owen, given that marriage was how her daughter made her living.

"And I'm not the only one who changed my name, Gaia."

Grace clasped her hands more tightly. "No, but I respect your wishes about it."

Owen saw Sparrow wince. "You're right. It's just that Gaia is such a powerful name. The earth. The mother goddess."

"I prefer Grace." The corners of her mouth were tight.

"I know." Sparrow sighed and patted her daughter on the arm. "And I'll try to remember to call you that."

Grace nodded and didn't say anything.

"So, Owen—" Sparrow looked at him in her rearview mirror, a bright gleam in her eyes "—tell me about yourself."

Owen knew that gleam. It was the one all

mothers got around him, which was why he tried not to spend time with their daughters unless he was sure things were going somewhere. Up to this point in his life, he never had been. He smiled. And yet here he was, of his own volition, even enjoying the interrogation, gentle as it might be. "My family is in the food and beverage industry."

Sparrow raised an interested eyebrow. "Organics?"

"We try to source locally as much as possible." That wasn't even a lie. "I'm actually very interested in seeing your farm."

"How wonderful." Sparrow's grin lit up the interior of the vehicle. Owen saw Grace relax just slightly and was glad. He didn't like seeing her look so tense, although he had a few good ideas of how to help her get relief. None of which included her mother. Perhaps he'd have to put that hallway to use after hours.

It was a quick drive to the farm. Sparrow chatted the whole way, telling Owen about their farming techniques, how they tried to use those methods that put the least strain on the land. "And you'll have to try some of my nettle tea."

"Sounds delicious." It didn't. But he'd drink an entire pot of the stuff if it meant he got a free pass down the hallway.

They turned up the driveway, gravel crunching under the tires. There were vines and plants along the sides, their leaves reaching out and rustling as though to say hello. It could have been creepy, overgrown and derelict, but everything was well-maintained and pruned to allow full bloom, offering a cheerful representation of what the land could provide when treated right. A large tomato bobbed as they passed, looking ready to fall off and splat on the ground.

Sparrow parked in front of a large, traditional-looking farmhouse. Traditional in the sense that it was a typical build—peaked roof, cedar siding, windows and a door. But that was where tradition stopped. A massive wood carving in the shape of a tree with a bird on the branch sat by the front door. The curtains in the windows were a variety of colors. Red in one, blue in another, a multicolored stripe upstairs. The siding was striped, too—purple and green, yellow and orange. Only the door remained untouched, a glossy oak that gleamed in the twilight.

The scent of dirt and water hit Owen as he climbed out of the SUV. "You don't have to drink the tea," Grace murmured when he held her door for her.

"I don't mind." He closed the door behind her. He wanted to take her hand, but he didn't want to get shot down. Not when things had been going so well.

Grace looked as though she was about to say more, but Sparrow was already opening up the hatch and pulling out their luggage.

"Let me." Owen hurried around to help.

"I'd tell you I could manage and that a woman is just as capable as a man, but I can tell you're not the type that needs reminding." Sparrow grinned and put a hand on her hip. "With you, it's good manners." She looked past him to her daughter. "He has good manners."

"He does." Grace came around to stand beside him. Owen wasn't sure if it was to support him or get support from him, but he didn't mind either way.

"Good. You should put that on your list. And good teeth. People underestimate good teeth."

Owen tapped his own, the product of three years of braces. "I floss every day." Then he looked at Grace. "You have a list?" He pulled out both bags.

"Gaia...Grace, sorry, sweetheart." Sparrow closed the hatch of the SUV. "Grace has a list for everything."

Owen wondered what else was on that list.

"Tall, in shape, educated." Sparrow counted them off on her fingers, the silver rings flashing in the setting sun. "What else is on there?"

"He doesn't have to be educated." A slight blush colored Grace's cheeks. "He has to be intelligent."

"Does one year of university count?" Owen asked.

Grace merely looked at him, the flush on her face growing brighter. She looked beautiful, slightly out of sorts and very much as she had when she'd been in his arms, head thrown back, thighs spread. Owen felt his already piqued interest increase.

Sparrow either didn't notice or chose not to mention it, declaring that she thought any post-secondary education should count. "And traveling. You can learn a lot by seeing the world."

Owen had that one down as he'd done plenty of traveling over the years. He'd even lived in Australia one winter, working in a vineyard and getting to know all the pretty sheilas. He didn't mention it now. "I want to hear more about this list."

"It's not a list." Grace reached for her bag. "It's just some thoughts, some private thoughts," she added, glaring at her mother, "that I had."

"Shouldn't have written them down and left them sitting on the table." Sparrow led them up to the front door. She pushed it open. "Unfortunately, no one else is up to say hello. Farm hours, but I know they'll look forward to meeting you at breakfast."

"They eat at six," Grace told him.

"On purpose?" Even now that he'd become a responsible, hardworking employee, Owen only saw 6:00 a.m. from the back side. He was pretty sure if his alarm ever went off that early he'd throw it out the window.

"We work farm hours." Sparrow flicked on the lights as they moved through the house. The sun outside was no longer high enough to breach the windows. "We get up and go to bed with the sun. Speaking of which, I need to get some sleep. You help yourselves to anything you want and I'll see you in the morning."

She hugged Grace tightly and then Owen. She smelled like earth and leaves. A hardworking, outdoorsy scent. "I'm glad you're here, Owen. You be good to my Gaia." She whispered the last part.

"Always." Owen met her gaze and gave her what he hoped was a reassuring smile. He had plenty of plans to be good. Or bad. Depending on your definition.

Sparrow patted him on the cheek. "Good." Then she headed up the stairs, leaving him and Grace alone in the quiet house.

"Are you hungry?" Grace asked.

"Not really." At least, not for food.

She nodded. "I'll show you to your room." They moved up the stairs and tread lightly on the steps. It was dark, the only light a thin sliver under one of the doors at the back, but even as he watched, it went out. Sparrow had been serious when she said she was going to sleep.

Grace stopped at the first door on the left and flicked on the light. "The guest room. But you don't have to stay. If I had the option, I wouldn't."

"You don't have to stay, either. My offer stands. We'll go to a hotel." They could get room service, run a hot bath, wear those fluffy hotel robes. Really, he could be content just imagining her naked under the robe. At least, until she was ready to admit she wanted more.

"I can't." She actually looked sad about it. "But just because I'm stuck doesn't mean you have to be."

"I don't feel stuck." He reached out to reassure her, catching her hand and giving it a light squeeze. "Really."

"Then you're a better person than me." She sighed, but didn't pull her hand from his. "You're going to give my family the wrong idea."

"And what idea is that?" He had a few. In fact, he'd be willing to share those right now. He tugged her forward a step and lowered his head toward her.

She didn't back away. "That we're dating."

Her blue eyes seemed darker in the thin pool of light that came from the guest room into the hallway. Less Caribbean Sea and more sky at dusk. "That's one of my ideas," he told her.

"Owen."

He waited for her to tell him that she couldn't, that it was against her office policy, her business practices, her religion. She didn't.

"I'll see you in the morning."

He didn't let go of her hand when she started to shift away, heading down the hall to her room. "You could still see me tonight."

From what he could see of the room, before he'd turned all his attention to Grace, the guest bed was large and had plenty of space for two. She was more than welcome to join him. He leaned closer, inhaling her scent. The jeans she wore made a man think of peeling her out of them and that fitted button-down shirt only highlighted her soft curves. His palms itched to touch.

He reached up to brush her hair away from her neck and traced a finger along her pale skin. He saw the small jolt that rocked her. Her throat bobbed as she swallowed.

"Tomorrow." And there was a breathlessness to her tone that he was pretty sure could only be interpreted as interest and a sad attempt to hide it.

"Tomorrow," he agreed, running his finger back up and along her jawline. Her skin was soft, so soft. He wanted to touch it everywhere, touch her everywhere. He settled for smoothing his thumb across her lips. And then, before she could shy away or break the moment, he kissed her.

Just a gentle press of lips, a brief meeting that was over as soon as it started, leaving behind a promise.

And because Owen had some practice, he knew now was the perfect time to step back. He backed into the guest room, keeping his eyes on Grace. "Good night."

He was rewarded by seeing her hand flutter up to touch her lips. "Good night."

Owen watched her walk down the hall, her hips swinging in those tight jeans, and wondered if he should follow her or wait for tomorrow.

CHAPTER EIGHT

GRACE FLIPPED OVER her pillow and pressed her cheek to the cool fabric. It didn't help. She was still hot, still bothered, still far too aware that Owen was just down the hall. Was he awake, too? Tossing and turning? Or was he fast asleep, disengaged from the day and resting for tomorrow?

She turned onto her opposite side and gave the pillow a karate chop. That didn't help, either. God. She shouldn't even be thinking about this. She should be annoyed that he was here. She should have insisted he leave. If not for her sake, then for his. But no. She'd allowed herself to admit that it was nice to have him around.

Of course, there was no guarantee that he was staying. Owen hadn't faced the full force of Sparrow's personality yet. Like when she got on one of her rants about local eating and how global markets were ravaging the farming industry, how many fruit varietals were already extinct because hardier hybrids with longer growing seasons had overtaken the market. Or when she talked about how it was people in cities, out of touch with where their food came from and only interested in saving a buck, that were the source of the issue.

Maybe before tomorrow evening rolled around, Owen would be long gone. Not even to a local B and B, but all the way back to Vancouver, where crazy ladies with dirt under their nails and sandals made out of hemp didn't yell at him. The thought made her sad, even though that was silly. She had no reason to feel that way or even miss him. Or his kisses.

She did her best to distract herself, checking her phone for emails and making notes about things she needed to handle in the office next week, in the hopes she might tire herself out. But it took a long time before she finally felt sleepy and her eyes felt gritty when she woke up the next morning.

Grace didn't need to check the clock on her phone to know that it was earlier than any normal person would be up. She considered herself an early riser. She took a 7:00 a.m. Pilates class Monday, Wednesday and Sunday and was in the gym by 7:15 a.m. other mornings. But at Cedar Sparrow Farm, that was considered sleeping in and good only for people who were sick or otherwise infirm. Which was why her mother was banging pots around in the kitchen downstairs.

Grace stretched and rubbed her eyes. The banging in the kitchen would eventually end, but her mother wouldn't give up. She'd knock on the door and barge in if Grace didn't answer quickly enough. Even if she did answer immediately, there was no guarantee that Sparrow wouldn't push her way in anyway.

As much as she'd like to lounge in bed, there was really no point. She flipped back the covers and shivered as the cool morning air hit her. Nothing to get her up and moving like a blast of frigid air.

Grace could hear the continued banging as she pulled on yesterday's jeans and a fresh T-shirt. She didn't bother to shower, even though starting her day without one made her feel as if she was forgetting something. She only took enough time to wash and moisturize her face and brush her teeth.

The door to the guest room was open and when she peeked inside as she passed, she saw the curtains were open and the bed made. She found Owen at the round kitchen table, laughing as her mother served him pancakes.

"Well, look who finally decided to join the living. Did you have a nice rest?" Her mother turned back to the stove, already ladling more batter into her skillet despite knowing that Grace never ate pancakes.

"I slept fine." She poured herself a mug of coffee from the pot and stood by the counter. "You're up bright and early," she said to Owen.

He swallowed his mouthful of food. "Pancakes." As though those were the answer to all of life's questions. If only it could be so easy.

Grace noted that he didn't look tired at all. Clearly, she was the only one who'd spent half the night feverishly tossing and analyzing exactly what was happening in her life.

"I thought I'd take Owen out to the garden with me this morning." Sparrow slid her spatula under the pancake and flipped it over.

Grace raised an eyebrow. The garden was her mother's sacred space and one she only shared with people she deemed worthy. Grace had been out there exactly once. And though she knew it was silly, it stung a little that Owen had already been invited into the inner sanctum. She'd expected her mother to treat him with polite indifference, the way she treated all the city visitors who came to the island wanting to participate in the farm-to-table craze. "Great."

"Cedar is in the lower field today." The lower field was on the opposite side of the 25-acre property from the garden and where her father nurtured his tomatoes and cucumbers. "He's waiting for you."

Grace nodded and leaned her hip against the counter. She knew she'd be put to work weeding or pruning. She was going to need more coffee.

"Sit," Sparrow instructed, waving with her spatula before loading up another plate with pancakes.

Grace didn't want to sit. She didn't want pancakes, either. "I'll just have coffee."

"Gaia." Sparrow shook her head at Grace's cool look. "Sorry—Grace. Coffee isn't enough to keep you going in the field all day."

"I'll be fine."

They had a brief stare-down before Grace relented. "Fine." She would eat the pancakes. She felt foolish when she noticed Owen watching her. "How did you sleep?" she asked as she took the chair beside him. Anything to take the focus off the fact that she'd just engaged in what amounted to a teen rebellion. At thirty.

"Great." He reached beneath the table and gave her thigh a supportive squeeze. "Better now."

Grace felt a flood of heat travel from her leg to her face. She should pull away, shift her chair out of touching range. Instead, she reached down and put her hand on top of his. Then very slowly removed it.

And told herself it was the right thing to do.

Her father greeted her with a hard hug when she made it down to the lower field, already feeling slow and thick from the pancakes her mother had practically rammed down her throat.

"Hey, Dad." She hugged him back. Although her mother insisted Grace call her parents by their first names, feeling it was important to their locus of identity, when Grace was alone with her father she called him Dad. Because that was who he was. And since he'd never asked her not to, she figured he liked it, too. "How've you been?"

"Oh, you know." Her dad wasn't much of a talker. In fact, her parents—birth names: Susan and Steven—had chosen their preferred names well. Her mother had a tendency to flit around, chattering and chirping the whole time, while her father was stolid both in build and behavior. Like a tall and stable cedar tree.

"Where's Sky?" Her brother still lived and worked at the family farm, though he'd moved out of the main house and into the guesthouse this spring. When he'd returned from his winter wanderings with a girlfriend in tow. A now pregnant girlfriend, according to her mother.

"The shop." Where the family sold fruits and vegetables, both fresh and home-canned, along with Sparrow's nettle tea and offerings from neighboring farms.

"With Laurel?" The girlfriend had changed her name from Lauren to feel closer to the land and her unborn child's heritage, which was what she'd told Grace the one and only time she'd met her. But Laurel seemed nice enough, whatever her name, and she seemed to be a good match for Sky.

Her dad nodded.

"I'll stop by later." Perhaps that would give her an excuse to get away for a short time. "It's good to see you, Dad."

Her father always made her feel more centered. Or maybe it was being outside and working with her hands. Not that she'd admit that to her mother. Not unless she was looking to hear a pitch on how she was welcome to come back to her roots and work at the farm. Which she wasn't.

They worked steadily until lunch and then returned to the main house to find her mother and Owen laughing away like old friends. Grace couldn't remember the last time she and her mother had laughed like that. Maybe never.

"Hello, love." Sparrow threw her arms around Cedar's neck and gave him an openmouthed kiss.

Grace felt her cheeks heat with embarrassment at their PDA. It wasn't that she thought her parents should be celibate or hide their love. But a little decorum wouldn't go amiss, either. She couldn't look at Owen.

Her parents continued making out.

"Grace?" It was a whisper that didn't disturb the love bunnies.

"Yes?" She sensed when he moved closer, the heat from his skin touching hers.

"Why don't you greet me like that?"

Her eyes shot up as did her eyebrows, head and heart rate. "Why did you kiss me last night?"

Owen grinned at her. "Foreplay."

Grace tried to give him a disapproving look, but she was pretty sure she failed. Owen's smile only grew broader and he reached out to tuck a strand of hair behind her ear. "Don't start," she said.

His fingers traced the curve of her neck. "Too late."

She feared he was right.

Thank God her parents were still too wrapped up in each other to hear. Not because she was concerned that their delicate ears couldn't handle hearing that their baby girl might be sexually active. Hello? They'd been known to skip lunch for a quickie in the bedroom. But her parents—really, her mother—would try to help her.

Her mother would suggest they spend the

afternoon somewhere private, then produce a bottle of wine made from the small vineyard on the property before slipping some condoms to them. As if Grace wasn't old enough or smart enough to carry nonexpired ones on her at all times. The previous box had gone into the garbage without a single one being used. The whole thing would end up being the opposite of sexy.

Unlike the way Owen's fingers were still playing along her neck, across her collarbone and back up to her shoulder. Grace shivered and reminded herself of all the reasons why she should take a step back. He was a client, she didn't know him well, he wasn't husband material, she wasn't putting a focus on her personal life until next year, her parents were in the room. And the one big reason she stayed exactly where she was: she wanted to.

OWEN WATCHED GRACE during dinner. Watched her before and after dinner, too. She wasn't the same here, under her parents' roof. In some ways, she was wound more tightly, quick to do the opposite of what her mother suggested and often with her lips pressed firmly together. But in other ways, she was softer. She wore jeans with dirt on the knees to dinner and when she looked at him, there was desire in her eyes. And she'd asked why he'd kissed her. A question he planned to answer tonight.

Sparrow had decided they should eat dinner outside, serving up chicken from the barbecue and salads made from what grew in her garden. The meal was rustic and filling. Entirely different from how he ate in the city, but it fit. They'd worked hard all day. Sparrow had put him to work hoeing a new row for more tomato plants while she chatted away.

The labor was hard. Harder than walking the floor of Elephants all night and dealing with a legion of drunk frat boys. But satisfying. He could see why his father, who'd recently taken up gardening post–heart attack, found it therapeutic. Though he wasn't sure he'd mention it when he got home. Not unless he wanted to be corralled into hoeing on a regular basis.

Owen was aware he spent too much time at work these days, in an effort to prove his newfound reliability, but he wasn't sure digging and planting were the kind of life balance he was looking for.

Grace's parents had a fire pit at the back of the property and once the dishes were put away, they brought out wine made from their own grapes and sat around the flames. Sparrow tried to start some singing, but Cedar said he preferred listening to the sounds of nature. One of the few things he said.

Owen also enjoyed the quiet. The lick of flames on wood, the whisper of wind through the trees that dotted the open backyard, the hum of insects as they came alive with the night.

It wasn't full dark—was barely dusk—but work started at five tomorrow morning. Though Grace, Owen and a newly pregnant Laurel had been told they could sleep in. Owen chatted with Laurel while Grace caught up with her brother. Laurel had done a fair bit of traveling and the two of them had seen many of the same places.

It was only nine when Sparrow stretched and announced that she was going to bed. Cedar went with her and Sky and Laurel weren't far behind.

Owen pulled out the wine bottle, cooling in a small hole Sparrow dug in the ground, and offered it to Grace.

She looked at her half-empty glass and sighed. "I shouldn't." But she held her glass toward him.

He topped up both glasses, then took a seat beside her. The chairs had been carved from wood by Cedar and were surprisingly comfortable, sanded to be soft to the touch and shaped to provide back support.

"My parents would love a pair of these for their backyard." He ran a hand across the seat, which held the warmth of the day's sun. They'd make a great gift. "Do they sell them?"

Grace shook her head. "That would be working for 'the man.'" She air-quoted the last two words. "Sparrow and Cedar try to keep their distance from authority organizations. They only give the chairs as gifts."

"Could I barter for them?"

"You could try, but..." She shrugged and sipped her wine.

"But they'd turn me down." Too bad. They were gorgeous pieces And Owen knew they'd sell for big money in the city.

"They turn down most people. Although you seem to be a pretty big hit."

Owen felt a prickle of pride. "Because your mother thinks we're dating." He found he liked the idea quite a lot himself. Not a *date*, but dating, ongoing. It wasn't the first time he'd felt this way, but it definitely wasn't his usual MO, either. He leaned toward Grace, watching the way the fire turned her skin a delicate shade of gold. "Do you know she tried to slip me a condom this afternoon?" At first, he'd been embarrassed, wanting to assure Sparrow that she didn't need to worry about something happening in her home, but then he'd realized that if she wasn't embarrassed he shouldn't be, either.

"Oh, God." Grace closed her eyes and took a gulp of wine. "I apologize on her behalf."

"She just wants to keep you safe and healthy."

"No, she just likes sticking her nose in my business, which is why I don't visit very often."

Owen didn't think that was the only reason, but he kept that observation to himself. Grace didn't seem to recognize how much she was actually like her mother. Not on the surface— Grace with her sleek style and city life and Sparrow with her flyaway hair and commitment to farming—but beneath everything, they were the same. They believed in family and the truth of their own opinions. And they were willing to fight for what they wanted, even if it was with each other.

"I like them," Owen said, placing his own wineglass down next to his chair. They were very different from his family and their day-to-day life reflected that, but they shared similar core values. Owen was confident that if Grace or Sky were ever in need, Sparrow and Cedar would drop everything to help, and he thought Grace and Sky would do the same for their parents.

"Well, sure. My mom gave you condoms and basically a free pass to sleep with me." Grace stared at the fire. "But don't get too excited— you're not the first."

Owen blinked. "I'm not?"

"Oh, no. She did the same thing to my high school boyfriend."

"I bet that made you popular."

She looked at him and frowned, her eyebrows slanted together. "I didn't sleep with him. I have no idea what he did or didn't do with the condoms, but they were never put into action with me."

"I didn't mean that." Now he felt like a tool. "I was just thinking that your friends would have liked the fact that she didn't hide from the realities of teen life." He'd lost his virginity at sixteen with Mara Lennox. Sweet, sweet Mara with her dark curls and skin permanently tanned from trips to Anguilla and St. Barts. She'd smelled like coconut.

"They weren't my reality." She folded her arms around her waist, protecting herself. "It was humiliating because, of course, he told everyone. And then my mother tried to start a program at school to have condoms available at the office and in classrooms."

"Did she succeed?"

"Yes."

"Wish she'd been at my school." He saw some of the tension leave Grace's face and continued. "You don't know how good you had it. We had to buy our own condoms. The trick was to buy a bunch of other things with it. Car magazines, chips, a newspaper to put on top, as though that would fool the clerk."

"Okay, but your mom wasn't known as the Condom Lady." Grace shook her head, but a smile peeked through on her lips. "They called Sky and me the Condom Kids."

"Condom Crew would have been better. You could have tossed them out like confetti."

Her smile was more than peeking through now. "I really don't think you understand the seriousness of this. The scarring I still have."

"I do see." He shifted his chair a little closer to hers, but stopped there. Much like last night, he wanted to drive her to the point where she admitted she wanted him. Pushing too far, too fast, would cause a knee-jerk reaction and he already knew that line by heart. "Clearly, you underwent great personal suffering. Really, I'm amazed you're a functional adult at all."

"I know. The trials and indignities of my youth were quite something." Her smile was out-of-this-world and damn, did it look good.

Owen patted her knee and left his hand there, waiting to see what Grace would do. She looked down at it, then back at him, but she didn't move it and although her smile faded, it didn't disappear. Promising. He let the connection linger another moment and then sat back. "So, tell me just how you managed to survive your high school years."

She glanced down at her knee again and then up. Owen wasn't even sure she realized she'd done it, but he did. And he knew what it meant. She'd liked it and was likely open to more. Very promising.

They stayed on the back patio until the wine was gone and the sky was fully dark. Grace shivered in the cool temperature. Owen wanted to put his arm around her or offer her a warm lap to sit on, but she spoke first. "I think I'm going to call it a night."

Disappointment swept through him, but he did his best to hide it with a manful nod. He watched her stand and stretch, the way her shirt clung to her body and then didn't. "I'll walk you in."

"You're staying in the house, too."

"Yes, but I can still be a gentleman." He offered her his arm.

Grace smiled and placed her hand on his elbow. Her scent wafted around him. He wanted to tug her closer until their bodies touched more places than just hand and elbow. Instead, they walked inside and up the stairs.

Owen stopped and turned to face her when they reached her bedroom door. She was breathing faster. Or maybe that was just him. Eager for another kiss.

She swallowed. "Well, I guess this is goodnight."

It didn't have to be. He reached out to cup her face, both felt and heard her short intake of breath. "No, Grace." He leaned forward until their lips were nearly touching. "This is goodnight."

And then he kissed her until there was no question that she was breathing hard.

CHAPTER NINE

How was it possible that although she'd spent the day in the sun doing manual labor, she was even less able to find a comfortable spot to sleep in?

Grace tossed around, but it didn't help. Clearly, this was all Owen's fault. Why had he kissed her again? Why had she let him? But even as she thought it, she knew why. She'd liked it. She'd wanted it. He was all wrong for her on all levels and she wanted him.

She rolled over and grabbed her phone, opening her inbox and scrolling through her messages, but it was a sad attempt to distract herself and worked no longer than a few minutes.

Grace put the phone back on the nightstand. She could lie here staring at the ceiling or the screen on her cell all night. Again. Or she could try something else. She was out of the bed before she'd even finished considering her options.

The air was cool on her bare legs, but Grace didn't feel like putting her jeans on under her nightgown. Who was going to see her? Her parents had gone to bed hours ago and slept heavily.

Sky and Laurel were in the small guesthouse on the other side of the property and Owen would probably be conked out now, too.

She grabbed a kimono-style robe from the closet. One her mother had bought for her more than a decade ago. It still fit, though Grace thought she filled it out a little better now. Why that mattered, since nobody was going to see her, she didn't know. She tied the belt around her waist, slipped on her sandals and quietly made her way down the stairs and out of the house.

The sounds of the night struck her as she shut the door. The hum of insects, croaking of toads and the occasional hoot of an owl. The same species existed in the city, but she didn't hear them over the buzz of city life. Oddly, Grace found she'd missed it. Not that she could mention it to her mother. Sparrow would get excited and think it meant Grace was considering giving up her urban life to return to the farm. That or she'd consider it permission to bombard Grace with even more lectures about the health benefits of living in a rural environment. Lectures that were based on nothing more than Sparrow's own biased observances.

Grace hurried away from the house and across the yard, the dew already collecting on the grass and leaving droplets on her toes. But Grace knew where she was going and there were towels.

It took only a couple of minutes to reach her destination. Sparrow and Cedar referred to it alternatively as Meditation Manse or Abode au Naturel depending on what they were using it for, but the small one-room, one-bathroom building on the farm had always been a place of privacy for Grace. A place of privacy with a king-size bed.

The abode was open. Her parents never locked anything. Partly because they believed in sharing what one had with those who needed it and partly because they believed that locking something was inviting the universe to break in.

Grace paused with her hand on the door. Although it was dark out, with only the light of the moon to see by, she noted that the murals on the front of the house were new. She could even smell the fresh paint. And there were sculptures on the small porch that hadn't been there before.

She squinted, trying to determine exactly what they were, and huffed out a laugh when her eyes finally drew the distinction between shadow and light and she found herself staring at a sculpture of a nude woman bending over while a man stroked her from behind. It seemed Sparrow had been redecorating.

Grace pushed open the door, leaving the sculpture behind, and turned on the light. There was an overhead chandelier, made by Sparrow when she'd been in her crystal phase. Last time Grace had been in the abode, the chandelier had been made up of multicolored glass that spread a rainbow effect through the room, but there was no such effect now. And when she checked, she saw the bright colors had been replaced with clear glass for a calm, cool look.

The bedcovers were different, too. Gone were the bright colors that mimicked the old chandelier. In its place was a pale gold brocade with shimmery threads. Grace stopped and stared. With the new white rug, the simple wood tables built by her father and cream-colored walls, the space was downright elegant.

Or as elegant as a space could be with wall art showing scenes from the *Kama Sutra* and a sex swing in the corner.

But Grace wasn't really interested in how the space looked, just the privacy it offered. Here, all alone with nothing and no one down the hall, she could decompress and figure out what was going on between her and Owen. After popping into the bathroom to dry her feet, she sat in the oversize chair in the corner of the room that had been recovered in a dark pink material with a sunrise-orange pillow.

The chair had once been covered in old denim, rivets and all. Grace had to say she found this new version far improved. She kicked off her sandals and curled her feet beneath her before covering herself with the teal blanket hanging over the back. She could have crawled into the bed. The sheets would be clean and she knew it was comfortable, but Grace didn't want to fall asleep. Not yet.

Not until she figured out her next step with Owen. Trying to keep things professional wasn't working. He seemed to insert himself into her life whether she wanted him to or not. Except that wasn't really fair. She certainly hadn't tried very hard to dissuade him from joining her this weekend, her attempt to say otherwise on the ferry ride notwithstanding. But letting him even deeper into her life? Well, that way lay danger, as evidenced by the kissing and the not sleeping and the thinking in the abode.

Which meant... She let her head fall back against the chair. Which meant she should probably remove him from her life altogether. Of course, she'd still have to see him at the wedding, but that was work.

Grace exhaled. She could create a file in her laptop, take note of all the reasons for and against and finalize a clean plan of action, but she didn't need to. She already knew the answer; she just didn't like it.

A small thunk had her head lifting, followed by a knock on the door that set her heart racing.

This was the abode. It was meant for privacy. People didn't knock. Unless they didn't know what the abode was for.

She pushed herself out of the chair and padded across the floor to open the door. The interior light flooded out, illuminating a smiling Owen. "Hi."

He wasn't supposed to be out here. She should send him back to the house. Instead, she pushed the door open wider. "Did you follow me?"

Owen nodded and stepped inside. He moved to close the door and then stopped as the light landed on the new outdoor sculptures. "Is that a man and a—"

"Yes." Grace reached around him to shut the door. "And I'd prefer not to talk about it."

Ever easygoing, Owen simply shrugged and moved farther into the room. "What about the art?" He gestured to the framed line drawings. Although they were simple strokes of black paint on white paper, sex breathed from them. "Can we talk about those?"

Grace decided her best course of action was to just sidestep the topic entirely. She didn't want to talk about sex. Not with Owen. "What are you doing here?"

"I was bored?" She eyeballed him. "I was sleepwalking?" Another slightly meaner eyeball. "I was curious. Why you were getting up in the middle of the night, where you were going." He stopped by the side of the bed. "So?"

"I couldn't sleep and I like to think here."

Owen glanced around the room, taking in the erotic decor and furnishings. "Yes. I can see how you'd get a lot of thinking done here. Clearly, this is no place for action."

She shouldn't laugh, shouldn't encourage him. A small snicker popped out anyway. He did that to her, knocked her off guard and made her forget about her plans.

Owen took that as an invitation to move closer. Grace could feel the warmth rolling off him and smell his toothpaste. He reached out to put a finger under her chin and draw her eyes to his. "I lied."

"Did you?" She raised an eyebrow, wondering where this was going, telling herself that it didn't matter.

He nodded, but didn't explain, just started to lower his head toward hers. Grace felt her pulse skitter out of her control. "I followed you because I wanted to do this." And then he kissed her and she forgot about controlling anything.

His fingers threaded through her hair, anchoring her head as he deepened the kiss. Grace felt the heat of his body and mouth, how it blanketed her, raising her temperature. Oh, it was good. So good.

For a full minute, Owen did nothing more. Didn't shift his hands to stroke her arms or back, didn't slide his tongue into her mouth to tease and play, didn't shift forward to bring their bodies into full contact. He simply cradled her head while he slowly and softly explored her lips. By the end, Grace felt wobbly and as though the control she held so dear might be gone for good.

"Owen." His name was more of a gasp than a command, which was a good indication of how her insides felt.

"That is my name." He ran a thumb across her lower lip and then kissed her again.

Grace felt her entire body slide into the kiss. Her mouth softened under his, her hands clutched at the back of the thin T-shirt he wore and she stepped forward to feel the hard press of his body. They'd barely done anything and she was already halfway gone. She sucked in a hard breath.

No, she couldn't do this. It wasn't appropriate, wasn't professional. Like the good-night kiss outside her bedroom? Like the make-out session on the night of the engagement party? Like the fact that it was his name on her lips and his face in her thoughts when she put her vibrator to use?

Yes, she'd already done this. In her fantasies, in her mind. But that was different than reality. She pulled back and tried again. "Owen."

He looked at her, his eyes dark with desire. "I'm not your client."

Cutting down her most salient point before she could even bring it up. "That doesn't change the fact that I'm working for your family. What would they say?"

"Julia would probably give me a high five. Donovan would say you can do better. Mal would be supportive. My parents would invite you to dinner." He slid one hand down to massage the back of her neck. She hadn't realized how tight the muscles were until he began smoothing out the knots. Loosening them, loosening her.

"Okay, you should stop that." But she didn't step back and her eyes drifted shut.

"This?" He kissed her jaw and then down the side of her neck. "Or this?" He tugged on the belt of her robe.

"All of it." But her voice was back to that breathless gasp again, so her words didn't carry much weight. Neither did her body, since her hands were still wrapped up in his shirt as if they were never letting go and her body strained to get closer to his.

"Okay. You tell me when and we'll stop." He began tracing his way along her collarbone. First with his fingers, then his mouth, the pair of them finding their way into the neckline of the thin camisole nightgown she wore.

Grace shuddered. Again, he'd barely done anything and she was already aching. "Okay." She could do that. They'd have a little fun, enjoy themselves and then she could put an end to it. She'd been without male contact for too long, judging from the way she was soaking this up. And what was so wrong with that? She and Owen were both single adults. There was no reason they shouldn't have a bit of fun together. He slid her robe off her shoulder and pushed one of the straps of her nightgown down. Okay, a lot of fun together.

He hooked a finger in the front of her nightgown and tugged, the now loosened strap providing limited resistance on one side. The cool silky material slid along her nipple. Grace felt it bead in response, rising hard and proud, announcing to the world—or just Owen—that it was ready for attention.

Owen was a good listener. He tugged again, sliding the material farther down until her breast was free, then lowered his head and sucked. Grace's arms rose without thinking to clasp him closer. She felt the swirl of his tongue and the answering tug in her belly.

Just a little fun, she reminded herself. She

could call this off at any time. And she would. Just as soon as it stopped being fun.

Owen sucked again, a bit harder this time, and everything Grace had been thinking flew out of her head.

Grace heard the tremor in her own breath, the long sighs of pleasure he was already drawing out of her. It was the room. Well, no, it was only partly the room. It was also Owen with his big hands and quick laugh and dark eyes. She felt a quiver of something stronger than lust and pushed it away. There was nothing more here than simple attraction. "Owen?"

He licked at her neck again. Grace felt another full-body tremble coming on. His voice rumbled across her skin. "Tell me you want me."

"I…" She couldn't say the words, couldn't say anything when he was doing that wonderful dance with his tongue. Her entire body was melting.

"I want to hear you say it, Grace." There was a softness to his tone that should have distracted from his body, but it only made it seem more powerful.

"Why?" Her eyes were closed again. How had that happened? She was falling down a deep, dark cavern and she wasn't sure where she was going to land, but she was surely enjoying the ride.

"It turns me on." He lowered her to the bed. She didn't even recall crossing the room. "To hear it from those sweet lips." He ran a finger over them as he said it. "Tell me that you want me."

She swallowed. She did want him, but could she tell him that? She forced her eyes open, found him leaning over her, his fingers playing with the straps of her nightgown while his eyes roamed from her face to her toes and back up. "You know this is—"

He cut off her words with a hot kiss, his tongue tangling with hers, pressing close, darting away and back again. "I'm not your client." Maybe not. But his brother was and that was almost as bad. Owen's voice grew quieter. "This is just about us. Look me in the eyes and tell me you don't want this."

Grace's throat felt dry. She didn't know if she could tell him that, either. "Just for tonight." She couldn't bear to turn him away, but she knew she was crossing a line. "One night and then we go back to the way we were before."

"Casual flirting with the occasional make-out session?" He pressed a trail of kisses down her chest, pulling on her nightgown as he did so that both her breasts were exposed. "I can live with that."

"No, I mean..." It was awfully hard to clarify what she meant when he was toying with her like this. One hand palming a breast while his mouth played with the other, then switching. Back and forth until her entire body felt strung tight.

Grace realized her eyes had slipped shut again and she forced them open, forced her tongue to work through the thick heaviness that was enveloping her whole body. "After tonight, we're professional. No anything." Which wasn't particularly descriptive but was the best she could do under the circumstances.

Owen didn't say no or yes. He didn't say anything. Just kept his head bent to the task of teasing her to the point where she wouldn't be able to speak at all. And she let him. There would be plenty of time tomorrow to ensure he knew she was serious, that this wasn't a joke or some sex game. That she meant it. But right now? Right now she just wanted to be naked with Owen Ford.

A long, delicious shudder swept through her body when he began to work her nightgown over her hips and down her legs. The air was cool but Owen was warm and he never left her alone long enough to get chilled.

He pulled back the covers, placed her gently on the sheets as he kissed her, leaving her with just the wisp of pink satin that acted as her panties.

"Oh," she moaned against his mouth. Any remaining thoughts of career and professionalism flew out of her head as he shoved himself against her. The buttons on his jeans pressed against her hip, branding her, and she gripped the hem of his T-shirt, fully intending to rip it off him if she had to.

"Hurry." The need was surging through her in swells that threatened to drown her.

"Hurrying." He helped her yank the shirt over his head and shucked off his jeans in two practiced moves. Then he stood before her a moment, all Greek god and gym-buffed before he fell on top of her, mouth and hands working together to answer the demanding sighs she couldn't quite control.

"Don't stop."

"Wouldn't dream of it." His fingers drifted up the inside of her leg while he kissed her, dipping beneath the edge of her panties without ever touching. Her body arched and strained toward him, intent on fulfillment and, apparently, with a mind of its own.

Why wouldn't he just touch her? She wanted to be naked with him, for him. She wanted him between her legs.

But Owen appeared to have other plans. He trailed a line of kisses across her neck and up to her ear. "You're so beautiful." The words tickled against her skin, drifted through her hair. "Gorgeous." His hand slid over her thigh, pushed it back a little farther. She heard his breath catch and his next words were a bit strangled. "What are you doing to me?"

She didn't even know what she was doing to herself. "Please, Owen." She saw his lips curl at the use of his name, felt another bolt of desire unfurl. "Touch me."

He glanced down between her open legs. "Where to start?" He bent slightly. "I do like those pink panties. Maybe I should take a closer look?"

Grace couldn't say anything, could hardly breathe as he kneeled in front of her. His hands rested on the inside of her thighs, holding them open when she might have let practicality overwhelm her and try to close them.

They were, after all, about to have sex in a semipublic place. Because although the family knew that no one was to enter if the abode was in use, she hadn't turned the sex frog that guarded the left side of the door to face the wall, which was the signal. Anyone could walk in on them. See them. "Owen." She tried to find the words, but they drifted away.

No one was going to interrupt them. Not here. Not now.

And she could hardly think when his hands

were running down her legs and circling her ankles. Slowly, he drew her legs up, bending them at the knees as he placed her heels closer to her hips, and spread them wider so that she was completely, utterly exposed.

He moved his head closer. "Much better." The words brushed against her skin and she felt the start of a long line of tremors at the knowledge of what was to come.

But his hands continued to play with the lacy edges of her panties. She was convinced that if he didn't touch her soon, she was going to explode. But he just kept teasing around the edges, stoking the flames under her skin higher and higher until she could stand it no longer.

"Owen." She spat the word out before it got lost in a moan of pain and pleasure. "If you don't touch me soon, I am going to die. And then you'll have to live with your guilty conscience."

He laughed and stroked the damp material between her legs with his thumb. "Better?"

Better? Better didn't even begin to cover it.

She arched toward him. More tremors rippled through her body as he stroked and circled. It was amazing. Incredible. The feelings coursed through her faster than she could name them, tumbling against one another in a jumble of sensations. She looked down at him. He was watching her and he smiled when he caught her gaze.

And then very slowly and deliberately, he turned his attention to her panties.

Grace's breathing stopped as he caught his fingers around the sides and tugged. Carefully, gently, he eased them over her hips and down her legs. Her heart was racing. Her mind was a muddle of emotions. She was finally completely naked in front of him and all she wanted was more.

She cried out when Owen bent his head and tasted her, his tongue soft and careful. Her hands clawed the back of his head. She couldn't think, couldn't breathe, couldn't do anything except feel. And she felt wonderful.

He sped up his rhythm, lapping faster until her legs shook and her feet began to slide. But he was relentless in his pursuit to bring her pleasure, his hands closing over her ankles, opening her wider while he sucked and licked.

Grace could feel hot pulses shooting up her body and the sweet release that hovered behind it. She heard herself making short mewling sounds that increased in rapidity with every stroke from his tongue and knew that if anyone happened to be outside on a midnight jaunt and happened to pause outside the door, they would hear them, too. But she didn't care.

Her legs shook harder. She was soaked with her own need. His tongue ran up and down teas-

ingly and then centered, bringing her to the edge
of her climax.

"Please…" Grace couldn't get anything else
out, didn't have any words left. All the blood had
left her head and was pooled between her thighs.
Torn between letting him finish and having him
inside her, she exhaled a low, hungry moan.

She was close, so close. He just had to…one
more…and…

She cried out with relief and pleasure when
the quaking started for real. Owen didn't stop,
though, but kept licking, leisurely, incessantly,
until he had drained every last shiver from her
body.

Then he pushed himself to his feet to stand
before her. She felt her legs slide down the bed,
boneless now and unable to remain lifted without support.

He smiled, and his eyes were dark and hot.
"And you didn't want me to follow you."

Grace let out a shaky laugh. "Guess you showed
me."

He chuckled. "And I've got something else
to show you." Her eyes followed his hands as
he stroked himself, and despite the long and
remarkable orgasm she'd just survived, Grace
realized that she wanted him again.

"Let me." She reached for him, taking over,
her hands strong and sure. She watched him, his

eyes on her hands as she moved. She felt him lengthen against her palm. So hot and soft, like silk and fire.

"The nightstand," she told him.

"The nightstand?" He sounded as if his throat was being crushed.

"In the top drawer." She kept stroking. "Condoms."

"Right." He was breathing hard and didn't move. So she did, keeping one hand on him while she fumbled for the drawer and the foil packets she was sure would be inside. She wasn't disappointed and she drew one out like a prize.

Owen practically ripped it out of her hand, opened the foil with his teeth and tossed the packet away. Seconds later, the condom was on and he was reaching for her.

Grace let him maneuver her body, watched as he put his hands on her thighs and spread them wider. She was so hot and hungry. Her eyes slipped shut when he began rubbing himself up and down her body. The tremors hovering just below the surface of her skin grew stronger.

She'd never been the multiple-orgasm type before. Usually, she was so sensitive after that she didn't want to be touched at all. But this was different.

Flares of pleasure made her forget about any lingering sensitivity. She reached up, used his arms for leverage as she pulled herself closer to him. He stroked up and down once, then twice, then slid his finger inside her.

Grace moaned. His finger was magic, dipping and twirling, gently opening her up to accept another. She shook from the pleasure. It felt fantastic, but she wanted more. She wanted him inside her, all of him, deep and throbbing and entirely mind-blowing.

His motions increased in intensity. She knew he must be barely holding on. She was barely holding on. She couldn't imagine how he'd stood it this long when she was about to come again before he'd even come once.

It was time to take matters into her own hands. Grace reached down and grabbed him, led him to the entrance of her body and nudged him inside. Her body shivered, already opening to take him entirely.

He needed no further encouragement. He grabbed her hip with one hand to hold her in place and entered her completely with one long, hard stroke.

Grace threw her head back and moaned. He was big, so big, and there was no softness in their coupling. Here, at last, it was fast and hot. Almost animalistic, definitely primal.

His fingers bit into her hips, clutching her tight so she couldn't move. She wrapped her hands around the back of his neck while he pumped into her, held fast when her body felt as if it was going to tear apart from sheer pleasure, cried out his name when she came again.

His fingers dug deeper into her skin as he stroked his way to climax. She'd probably have a tattoo of bruises, a reminder of their party for two, but she didn't care. He groaned, pumped one last time and dropped his head on her shoulder.

He was heavy and warm. Grace could feel the sweat beading on his forehead. A lone drop fell onto her shoulder and ran down her back. She didn't even make a move to wipe it away. She didn't even mind that he was sweating on her. If that didn't tell her everything she needed to know about her feelings for Owen Ford, nothing would.

It was really too bad that things would end after tonight.

CHAPTER TEN

GRACE WOKE UP already halfway to orgasm with Owen's head between her thighs. She didn't even have time to assimilate to her surroundings, determine what time it was or get a good grip on the sheets before she came, moaning his name. Not once, but twice.

He rose from his position with a smug smile on his lips. "Good morning."

"Hi." She sucked in a breath, then another, waiting for her heart to return to normal tempo. The breathing didn't seem to have much effect, but that might have been because Owen's hand was sliding down her leg, lifting and placing it around his torso as he lowered himself on top of her, blanketing her with his warmth.

Grace shivered. She shouldn't be here, shouldn't have slept with him, shouldn't have spent the entire night with him and shouldn't have stepped foot in the sex house. And yet she didn't nudge him aside, didn't climb out of the bed and didn't refrain from touching him.

His skin was so smooth. A soft covering for

his hard muscles. She liked the contrast and slid her hands up and down his back. She'd get up in a minute, explain that this was a onetime thing, but for just now, she'd enjoy waking up to a rocking orgasm from the talented tongue of a hot man.

Really, she hadn't had enough of these moments lately. For that matter, she hadn't had enough of these moments in life. His body nestled against hers, his thighs pushing hers farther apart, his hand running up and down her side, his head settled into the curve of her shoulder.

"I like waking up like this." His breath tickled her neck. "With you."

Grace exhaled. She'd taken her second and then a few more. She couldn't stay like this. "Owen?"

"Hmm?" He didn't move.

She circled a finger around his shoulder, then realized what she was doing and stopped. "I should get up."

He shifted, seeming to make himself more comfortable. "You should stay right here. With me."

Grace felt a small hiccup of possibility, then brushed it off. "We talked about this last night." She noticed her finger drawing circles again and pulled her hand away. Clearly, it couldn't be trusted. "This was just a one-night stand." And a fine one-night stand it was. Not that Grace had a lot of experience, but she was pretty sure that this particular experience could stack up against anyone's.

She fought back the shudder of memory. His hands in her hair, cupping her face as he kissed her, holding her ankles as he drove deeper and deeper inside her.

"Owen?"

He pulled back, but only enough to prop himself up on one elbow. He played with the ends of her hair with his other hand. "If we stay in bed, does it still count as the same night?"

"It's the middle of the morning." She was making a guess, seeing as the sex house was windowless to provide privacy. But the sounds of the forest animals and birds at full alert were audible, which meant the sun had risen. Which meant her family had, too. And yet, this didn't create any further urge to move.

"Then I guess we'll just have to stay here until it's night again." Owen's expression was one of utter acceptance. "I think I'm up for it."

"You're up for something." She shifted beneath him.

Owen laughed quietly. "When you keep moving like that, it's hard not to be." She felt his body press against hers, felt an answering soft-

ening in her own. Her mouth might be saying
no, but every other part of her was saying yes.

Still, she was nothing if not in control. Her
body didn't make the decisions, she did. "We
can't stay here all day." They had to leave today,
or at least she did. Owen was welcome to stay.

"Then how about just for an hour." He shifted
again, pressing his body against hers.

A shiver swept through her. She should say
no. She really should say no. Her family would
be up. They'd notice her bedroom door open
and her bed empty. They'd notice Owen's, too.
They'd realize the pair of them were together
and not having an early breakfast in the kitchen
or the patio. Grace's cheeks flamed. Her mother
would probably provide a shower of condoms.
Then again, all that was going to happen even if
she got up now. "An hour," she agreed, already
reaching for him. "No more."

"We'll see." Owen lowered his head to press
a tender kiss to her shoulder. Now, why did he
have to go and do that? He was supposed to take
her hard and fast. Hot, dirty sex that didn't include feelings or emotions, but was all physical
sensations.

But even as she tried to pretend that was what
last night had been about, she recalled the gentle way he'd held her face, the light touch of his
lips and tongue as they'd traveled across her

body. They'd been hot and dirty, too, but never emotionless.

She closed her eyes and swore. She wouldn't do this. Wouldn't let her feelings get caught up in anything that was happening here because she and Owen couldn't be anything. Even if he wasn't a client, he wasn't the kind of future she'd picked out for herself.

Of course, it was hard to remember that when he was rocking her world so completely.

She moaned as his fingers slipped between their bodies to slide into her wetness. He was a thoughtful lover, and she was plenty ready for him, but he seemed content to move slowly. Slowly driving her mad with pleasure. "Right there," she said as he hit her G-spot, his fingers curling just right and stroking.

Her entire body clenched, reaching for release. But he seemed to sense that, too, drawing back just when she might have gone over the edge. Grace gripped his shoulders, breathing hard. "Owen, please."

"I love it when you beg." He rolled her nipple between his finger and thumb. "Tells me I'm doing it right."

"So right." So, so right.

"I like it when you say that, too." He covered her nipple with his mouth, alternately sucking and licking. Grace arched back against the bed.

She wanted to give him pleasure, too. Take him into her mouth, touch him all over, guide him into her body, but she was having trouble keeping her thoughts straight.

"Just don't stop."

"Never." His tongue swirled, sending sparks of pleasure arcing through her. Oh, yes. But when she reached, urging him to move faster, to put on the condom, to fit himself between her legs, to hurry before she was ready to come just from the brush of his breath on her sensitive skin, he slowed.

Purposeful, careful. "Trust me, Grace." He tipped her chin up so she had to look at him. "Just trust me."

She didn't want to. She wanted to have sex. Rollicking, romping, noisy sex. But he was staring at her with those sweet eyes, asking her to let him set the pace. Because that was all he was asking, right? To be in control of whether they went fast or slow, hard or gentle. Nothing more. She didn't answer. But she didn't have to.

She saw the flash of surprise and pleasure in his eyes when he read her answer. When she allowed him to take over, to return to exploring her body in a dedicated and thorough manner. And when he finally rolled the condom on and slid into her heat, she almost came from relief. That and he was a really, really great lover.

Her eyes drifted shut, focusing on the ripples beginning to build to a wave. Knowing it would crash down shortly, drenching her in hormones and completion.

Owen pressed a kiss to one eyelid then the other. "Open up for me, Grace."

Her eyes popped open and he smiled. Her stomach jumped in response. His smile did something to her, something she wasn't sure she liked. Or maybe something that she liked too much. She didn't want to think about her reaction, about the repercussions it might have, how drastically it could damage her five-year plan if she allowed it.

Owen stroked deeper, his body setting a rhythm that had her clutching and moaning. Her eyes shut again. She felt one of his hands cup her face. He rubbed his thumb lightly along her cheek. "I want to see you." His voice was quiet in the silent room. "I want to see you look at me."

She opened her eyes without thinking while he moved inside her. Their bodies rocking against each other, slow and deep. "Why?" She couldn't manage anything above a whisper.

"Because." He moved his hand down to her hip, to anchor her while he sank even deeper inside her, reaching her in places she hadn't expected, in places that weren't physical. "I want to see you again."

She opened her mouth to tell him that wasn't an option. That this would be an experience she'd never forget, but it could only happen once. All that came out was a long sigh.

"And I think you want to see me, too." He leaned down to kiss her, their tongues tangling, hot and wet, like their bodies.

Grace felt the pulse of truth roll through her. She did want to see him again. And again and again. She wrapped her legs around him, holding him close with her body, and tried not to think about it, letting his mouth kiss away her thoughts, his hands hold back her feelings and his body shield her from the facts.

That she feared last night and this morning weren't even going to be close to enough.

OWEN DIDN'T HEAR FROM Grace for a week. Six days and four hours to be exact. Not that he was counting. After leaving messages for her on Monday and Tuesday, he'd busied himself with work, filling his time with inventory control, budgets and staff and making sure Elephants ran smoothly.

He didn't want to think she was going to maintain her declaration that what had happened at her parents' farm was a onetime thing, but as

the days and nights drew on, he began to wonder. It made no sense to him. He liked her; she
liked him. They were both single. Both of legal
age. They lived in the same city. Plus, she'd already slept with him. Refusing to see him now
was kind of like closing the barn door once the
horse was long gone.

But despite his friendly messages, asking her
to go out for drinks or dinner or both, she didn't
call back. He knew she was in town thanks to
a casual questioning of Julia—okay, fine, he'd
asked outright—who'd acknowledged that she'd
met with Grace midweek and Grace had told
her she'd be in town all weekend overseeing a
wedding and was available by phone or email.

She was probably swamped with preparations.
He'd seen her at work and knew she didn't leave
anything to chance, making sure her team was
fully briefed on what was supposed to happen
and then putting everything in place to make
sure it went according to plan. But he was busy,
too, and he still found time to call her, think
about her, fantasize about her.

So when his cell rang late Saturday night,
near closing time for Elephants, and Owen saw
her name on the screen, the burden of worry
he'd been lugging around lifted. He smiled, already moving out of the wine bar's loud main
room toward his office. "Grace."

There was no sound for a moment. Owen actually pulled his phone away from his ear to see if they'd been disconnected, but the screen continued to count the call time and when he put the phone back to his ear he heard her sigh. He closed the office door behind him, shutting out the noise of the bar.

"I'm glad you called." An understatement, but he didn't want to scare her away.

"I shouldn't have." There was only the sound of her breathing.

"Yet you did." He sank down in the desk chair. "And you aren't hanging up."

She laughed softly. "I could still change my mind."

He ignored that comment, not wanting to find himself backed into a corner he couldn't get out of. "So, tell me, why did you call?" Owen unscrewed the cap from the bottle of water he generally had on hand at the club and sipped. It did little to cool the heating of his blood.

"I'm not entirely sure."

"Haven't been able to stop thinking of me?" He went for light and breezy. For now. "I understand. I am fairly irresistible."

"Are you?" He could hear the humor in her tone. Whatever reason for her call, she was enjoying this.

"I like to think so. Don't go shattering the

image, Grace. It's carefully cultivated and you know how sensitive I am." He kicked his feet up onto the desk and leaned back in the chair. "How was the wedding tonight?"

"You've been talking about me to Julia."

True, but his brother's fiancée wasn't his only source of information. "You told me. You said you were booked every weekend into October, except last weekend." Thoughts of the weekend flooded him. Not that they'd been very far from the surface to begin with. He'd been in a state of semi-arousal for almost a week. Six days and four hours to be exact. "How did it go?"

"Do you really think I called you to talk about my job, Owen?"

"I hope not, but since you haven't told me I can't be sure. Of course, if you're into phone sex, I'm up for that, too." He had no doubt that phone sex with Grace would be amazing. Perhaps not as good as live action and in person, but a hell of a lot better than in-person sex with another woman. He lowered his voice. "What are you wearing? No, let me guess. A pair of sexy high heels, your hair up just waiting to be freed from pins, matching silk underwear—I'm hoping for white."

"Why white?"

"It suits you. So proper in your business wear and uptight hairstyles."

"I'm not uptight."

"Your hair is. But that just makes it sexier when you let it down." He flexed his hand, imagining those silky strands running through his fingers, along his shoulder and across his chest. Definitely draped across his chest while she rode him. His body tightened. "So those sexy lace panties in white and your breasts spilling out of your bra. Yeah, I'm definitely hoping for that. Do you have any idea what it does to me when you wear that virginal-looking underwear and smile at me with your sweet red lips?"

"I think I'm getting the idea."

"I think I should show you." He felt the pause as much as heard it. The sudden quiet, not even the sound of her breathing, and he wondered if he'd pushed her too far, too fast. But she'd seemed to like the phone sex, the humor, as well as the tease. Had he read her entirely wrong? "Grace?"

One more deep breath in his ear. In and out. Was it sick that it turned him on? "I think you're right, Owen."

He was right? About what? He couldn't think, the blood in his brain mostly hanging out in his groin, thanks to the talk about the white underwear.

"Come over and show me."

He shot out of the desk chair, almost kicking

over the water bottle in the process. He wouldn't have cared. The office furniture was old and shabby, leftovers from the main office upstairs after his mother had redecorated a couple of years earlier. A little water wouldn't have hurt anything. But something else stopped him cold. The idea that Grace might change her mind. That she might call him, but by the time he arrived she'd be talking about how it had always been a onetime thing and she'd come to her senses. He paused with his hand on the doorknob and his heart in his throat. "Are you sure?"

Part of him, the old Owen, who was only out for a good time and wasn't looking for anything serious, shouted in his ear. Asking what the hell was wrong with him. Reminding him that when a gorgeous woman asked him to come over and show her how attracted he was to her, he said yes.

But another part, a newer, more thoughtful part, said he was doing the right thing. Yes, he wanted Grace. Pretty much anytime and any way. But not for just tonight. He didn't want another six days and four hours of waiting in his future.

It felt as if it took forever for her to answer. Time where Owen cursed his new self and wondered if a cold shower could end the torment now rocking his body. And then she gave him her address and said, "I'm sure."

He was all the way out the door before she finished talking and pressing the buzzer at her building before another five minutes had passed. Luckily, she didn't live far from Elephants and he was motivated not to give her time to change her mind.

Good thing he insisted on wearing sneakers with his suits, too, seeing as he'd run the entire way there.

"Owen?" Her voice sounded tinny through the outside speaker.

"Did you invite someone else?"

His answer was the sound of the front door being unlocked. He pulled it open and, after waiting impatiently for the elevator for ten seconds, decided to take the stairs. Grace's apartment. Grace's bed. Grace's body.

He knocked on the door, barely waiting for the locks to click open before he nudged his way inside and kissed her. She said something, but it was muffled. And then she loosened in his arms and kissed him back.

Just as he'd suspected, her hair was up. Owen pushed the door closed behind him and flipped the lock, all while maintaining full lip-to-lip and body-to-body contact. His years of casual dating had paid off in some ways. He began walking her backward, out of the entry and into the apartment.

He got a brief impression of elegant warmth.

Clean lines and natural colors, very unlike her office and the day-to-day impression she put forward. It surprised and intrigued him, but he didn't delve deep. Plenty of time for that later when he didn't have six days and four hours of pent-up affection to work off.

She pulled on the lapels of his jacket, dragging him closer to her as she took charge, leading them down a hall to what he assumed was her bedroom. He sure as hell hoped it was her bedroom, although he thought the hall would do just as well. Pushing Grace up against the wall, lifting her, helping her lock her legs around his waist and sinking deep into her warmth. Yes, he could get behind hall sex.

But she tugged him through an open doorway into a room with a large bed, then she turned them so he was the one moving backward. He was happy to go along for the ride. So long as Grace was with him.

He sat down, landing on the bed when she nudged. She fell with him. Owen groaned when he felt her lush body mashed up against him. He ran his fingers through her hair, tugging it out of its tight twist, feeling the strands slip and slide across his hands. He felt her smile. "See? Uptight hair."

"I wasn't wearing it up." She spread his jacket

open, running her hands over his shirtfront. "I put it up so you could take it down."

Owen stopped, caught her face in his hands and looked at her. "Really?" There was something that struck him right in the chest. His pulse hammered. "And the white underwear?"

She nodded slowly, her blond hair gleaming. "But I was already wearing those."

He practically tore her pale pink dress, form-fitting with a tight skirt that came to her knees, in his rush to get it off her body and show the promised underwear in full.

Grace laughed and pushed herself off him. Owen sat up, reaching for her. He didn't want to watch—he wanted to touch and taste. Or he did until she reached her arms over her head in a long stretch that outlined every curve of her body and reached back to pull down the zipper. She shrugged one shoulder free of the short sleeve. And then Owen thought his eyes might cross from want. The flash of the lacy white strap taunted him.

And then she was before him in her full pseudo-virginal glory and Owen wasn't thinking of anything.

HE WOKE UP the next morning feeling sated and satisfied and more than a little smug. Grace slept beside him, her butt snuggled into his groin, her body warm, her hand holding his arm tight around her waist. As if he was going anywhere.

He kissed the back of her neck, inhaling her. Summery, citrus and mint. He breathed in again. He loved the way she smelled. Or maybe he just loved being here, bundled up in her bed, being held close. What wasn't to love?

He tugged, pulling her more firmly against him. She stirred and let out the sweetest little moan. He loved that moan, too. He set to making her moan again, nuzzling her neck and sliding his hand up to cup her breast. Her nipple rose to attention. Eventually, Grace did, as well.

And after he'd thoroughly pleasured her with his hands and mouth, he said, "Good morning."

"Very good." She stretched, rubbing against him. So soft and so sweet. He couldn't resist indulging in a taste of those pretty red lips. And another. And another. Really, he could spend the rest of the day just exploring her mouth.

But Grace put a hand on his chest when he bent to kiss her again. "Owen." She cleared her throat and dropped her gaze. "Last night was…" She trailed off.

"Magical? Amazing? Best you've ever had? I know. It was for me, too."

She laughed, the light sound filling him with contentment. "I can see your confidence is holding up nicely." Her hand slipped around his side, drawing circles on his shoulder. "But, Owen, this can't go on."

Different morning, same story. "Oh?" Different tactical approach this time, too. "Don't think you can handle me? It's true, I am a whole lot of man." She laughed again and allowed him to gather her close. Her fingers kept tracing those soft circles. He liked it. He liked it a lot.

"You're still a client."

"I'm not." He pulled back just enough that he could see her face and catch her gaze. Her blue eyes were serious. He imagined his brown ones were, also. "I know you keep saying that, but I am not your client, Grace."

"I'm planning a wedding for your brother. You're the best man." She ducked her head and her hand stopped moving across his shoulder. "I don't do this kind of thing."

"Hey." He lifted her chin with a gentle hand. "I'm glad you did this kind of thing with me." And only with him. "Tell me what the issue is." When she shot him a doubtful look, he pushed a little harder. "If you won't talk about it, we can't solve it."

"But there's nothing to solve." Her fingers started tracing again. "I already know what I have to do." She exhaled heavily, and he liked to think sadly, because she didn't want to stop seeing him.

"I'm not a client. I have no say in the wedding even if I wanted one. I just do what I'm told. So really, there's no conflict." If she was concerned that she'd be fired if he asked, well, she didn't know Donovan very well. Or Julia.

"It's not professional."

"Grace." He lifted her chin, which had fallen again. "Who says?"

She blinked and seemed to think about it. He could see the thoughts spinning in her bright eyes. "Me, I guess."

Owen shrugged a shoulder. "Then change what you say."

"It's not that easy."

It could be. "I want to be clear about my feelings here. I like you. I want to keep seeing you. But you're the one who invited me to go with you to your parents' farm."

"You invited yourself."

"I think that's up for debate. At any rate, you seemed happy enough to have me there." Plenty happy on Sunday morning when she woke up with him planted between her thighs. "You let your family think we were a couple."

Grace tried to look away again.

Owen shifted so he was back in her eye line. "And you called me last night. You asked me to come over." He felt the need to point out that this wasn't as one-sided as she occasionally tried to pretend. He sensed they were at a tipping point, a moment when things would fall one way or the other, and he wasn't going to just let it happen. That was the old Owen, blowing whichever way the wind went, happy to simply go with the flow and find happiness in whatever he was doing.

He still had that same joy for life, but he wanted to be the one captaining his boat. Maybe it wouldn't always work out, but when it did, there was a sense of satisfaction that he'd never experienced before with the way he used to live.

So he pushed. "Tell me, is this really for just one night or are you going to call me back a week from now, and then we'll go through this all over again?"

Grace closed her eyes and chewed on her bottom lip. "When you say it like that, it sounds bad, like I can't make up my mind or I'm playing with you."

"You tell me."

She opened her eyes and looked at him. He saw the swirl of confusion and fear and a shimmer of hope. His heart thumped. "I'm working for your family."

He thought it was a step up that she'd moved on from the claim that he was a client. "Julia used to work for the family. It didn't stop her."

She turned her head to look at him. "I'm not Julia." No, because Julia had never made his head spin, made his body ache for more even when he'd just had her, made him think about things past this week, this month, this year. "I have a reputation. A reputation I need to keep to be successful in my field. What kind of bride would want to hire a wedding planner who sleeps with the best man?"

"One who's glad she isn't sleeping with the groom?"

Grace didn't smile. "This is serious, Owen."

He took the smackdown. He deserved it. "You're right. I didn't mean to make light of it." He ran a hand up and down her arm. "But I want to keep seeing you, Grace, and I think you want to keep seeing me, too."

"We don't want the same things, Owen."

He blinked. "I'm not sure how you can say that when we've never talked about it."

Grace looked at him, her gaze thoughtful, her lips pursed in a pout that made him think of kissing. When she spoke, her words came slowly, as though she was still thinking them through. "You're right. We haven't."

Owen ached to reach for her then, to wrap her in his arms while he tasted that pretty pout, but he stayed where he was. "So let's talk." And then they could get to the kissing.

"Where do you see yourself next year?"

Not quite the question he'd been expecting

and he stuttered, but only a little. "I hope I'm managing all of the family bars." Hoped that he'd be entrusted with the responsibility. "I hope we'd be dating publicly." He saw her shuddery intake of breath. "Where do you see yourself?"

She exhaled and seemed to gather herself. "My company will be successful enough that I'll have hired another person, which will allow me to spend less time at the office."

"I like the sound of that." Owen did reach for her now. "I hope you'll plan to spend some of that time with me."

But rather than lean into his arms as he'd expected or lift her chin for a kiss, Grace shifted backward and her eyes were full of uncertainty instead of pleasure. "I'm not looking for casual, Owen."

He let his arms drop to his sides. "Is that what you think this is?"

She nibbled on her lower lip. "I want to know what you think. Where you see things going."

He blinked. He hadn't thought much past tomorrow, getting Grace to admit she was attracted to him. But now? He thought about it. "I'm not looking for a one-night stand." He knew one-night stands and, while he'd appreciated the lack of commitment in the past, they felt empty now.

"But?" Grace nudged him.

Owen didn't say anything, his mind whirring. A one-night stand no longer held the same appeal, but that didn't mean he was ready to jump into forever, either. He looked at Grace. Was she? "I'd like to see where things go. With us."

Her eyes dropped. So did the corners of her mouth. It made his belly twist uncomfortably.

"Grace." But he wasn't sure what to say to make that sad tilt lift. He reached for her then, pulled her to his chest. Everything felt better when he was touching her. "I don't see the need to rush things. Let's just see where they go."

He felt her swallow, her entire body shifting with the movement. "I want to say no." Her words came out as a whisper.

Hope lifted Owen's heart. "But you won't." He whispered, too.

She pulled her head back to look at him. There was confusion and worry in her blue eyes. "Should I?"

Should she? Owen didn't want to think about that, so he shook his head, choosing the easy answer, the one that would allow them to continue. "No. I think we have something good. So let's go with it."

It was something the old Owen would have said. He wasn't sure how he felt about that, especially when Grace blinked again and a small line appeared between her brows. Owen's heart thumped again, but this time it wasn't based in hope or anticipation. It was panic that she was going to tell him that she could walk away, that this had been nice but he was right, that they couldn't go on the way they had been, which meant they needed to stop seeing each other.

But he didn't pull the words back, didn't lighten the moment with a joke or turn it into a teasing game, one where they could both pretend that the words they'd said hadn't meant anything and could be forgotten as though they'd never been said at all.

"What about your family?"

Owen felt a tingle of optimism. At least she wasn't turning him down cold. "What about them?"

"I don't want them to know." The line of her mouth was firm.

"Fine." Owen didn't love the idea of keeping this a secret, but if it was the difference between being together and not, fine. "Hide me away like an illicit lover. I can handle it."

The edges of her mouth flickered. "I'm serious, Owen."

"So am I. Does this mean we're playing master and servant? Do I have to wear chains? Or an apron with nothing underneath, mistress?"

"I don't think we need to go that far, though the apron idea intrigues me." This time her smile

stand, it might not be more than a one-month stand, either. The thought chilled her and she patted herself dry more vigorously. Her mother often claimed that there was little point in worrying about things out of her control or regretting decisions made. There was as much to be gained from a poor choice as a good one if a person was only willing to change their viewpoint.

While Grace often disagreed with her mother's nontraditional approach to life, she had to concede there was merit in this philosophy. Of course, there was also merit in looking at all the factors in a given situation and then determining both the most likely outcome and the outcome she wanted. If the two weren't the same, she could change the factors to lead to her desired result.

But only if she knew what her desired result was.

Grace finished drying off, leaving one towel wrapped around her head while she put on a pair of simple blue undergarments and a blue sundress. She waited the prescribed fifteen minutes recommended by her hairdresser before blowing her hair dry, careful to treat each strand from root to tip on a low setting kept at least eight inches from her head. Once done, she blasted her hair with a cool stream of air. According to her hairdresser, the careful steps improved smoothness and elasticity. It certainly made her hair shiny and bouncy.

Satisfied, she set about applying a careful layer of makeup. Just enough to cover the circles under her eyes caused by lack of sleep and even out her skin tone followed by a swipe of the basics: mascara, blush and lip gloss. So very different from her mother, who never used beauty products, claiming they were the constructs of a patriarchal society that taught women they were only valued for their looks.

Grace didn't disagree, but the fact was their society valued everyone for their looks, regardless of gender. And she wasn't covering up her natural appearance—she was simply making the most of it. No different from a man giving himself a proper shave and putting gel in his hair. Of course, when she'd tried to tell her mother that—at the tender age of sixteen—her mother had promptly decided that Grace was no longer allowed to wear makeup.

A rule she'd abided by only at home, keeping her makeup in her locker and getting to school early so she could apply it in the bathroom before everyone else arrived. But since Grace was used to hiding her "bourgeois" tendencies from her mother, it wasn't a big deal. She already had a Walkman and the accompanying cassettes that she kept hidden in her bedroom, since she knew her mother would never find them. Sparrow had many beliefs that she espoused to whomever was in her vicinity, but one of them was the right to personal privacy and she adamantly believed that everyone needed their own "sacred space," which for Grace was her bedroom.

So Grace had gotten really good at putting on makeup quickly and competently under the most hideous of light fixtures and listening to music quietly.

She gave her nose one final powder and then placed everything back in its assigned spot in the drawer before heading out to the main part of the apartment. She knew Owen was still here because she could hear music and him singing along, only slightly off-key. She grinned as she followed the sounds to the kitchen and then stopped short at the sight before her.

Owen in an apron and nothing else, stirring something on the stove and occasionally sipping from the coffee cup on the counter beside him. She cleared her throat; he turned with a smile.

"Coffee?"

"You're wearing my apron. Naked."

"I am." He turned his back to her as he pulled down a coffee mug and filled it.

Grace's eyes were glued to the wriggle of his butt, which she was pretty sure he was doing on purpose, since he lifted a brow at her gaze being directed down low when he turned back to hand her the coffee. She really shouldn't enjoy this. It was silly and a little juvenile and…funny.

"What do you like in your omelets?"

She pulled her gaze to his face, knowing that to do otherwise would only encourage him. "You're cooking?" Grace didn't recall her fridge being filled with much more than bottled water, bagged salad, fruit and some chicken breasts. She ate more than half her meals at the office and often didn't have time to do much more than throw together something simple when she was at home. She kept meaning to join one of the city's community gardens and take a small plot of land to plant and grow her own veggies. But time always ran away on her. There was always a more pressing need.

"I found some fancy cheese." Owen displayed the wrapped package, a leftover from a couple of weeks ago when her dinner had been a baguette and cheese. "A couple of tomatoes, green onions and half a pepper."

"That sounds great." She sank down on one of the breakfast bar stools, her back to the living room while she watched Owen work. If asked,

Grace wouldn't have said she found the idea attractive, and yet Owen's cute butt winking away at her as he whipped the eggs, chopped the veggies and put a pat of butter in the pan was hugely appealing. She shifted in her seat. "I thought you understood that the outfit was as unnecessary as calling me mistress."

"I did." Owen poured the whipped eggs into the pan. "But you like it." He cocked his hip. "Even if you pretend otherwise." Since Grace had no answer to that, she said nothing.

He finished the omelets, slid them onto a pair of plates like an expert, topped up the coffee and then sat down beside her. "What do you feel like doing today?"

Grace put her fork down without taking a bite. "I have to work today." She waited for him to try to talk her out of it.

Instead, he forked up a bite of his own omelet, swallowed and looked at her plate. "It's good. I can vouch for it."

Grace picked up her fork and had a small taste. It was good. Better than the dry chicken breast and plain salad she'd probably eat tonight.

"What about tonight? Dinner?"

She put her fork down again. "Owen, we're not going out for dinner because we aren't dating."

"My outfit would say otherwise, or do you

think I show this world-class tush to every-one?" When she continued to stare at him, he exhaled. "Fine. I will argue that two people who are *friends* who are strictly *platonic* can go out for dinner and not raise any red flags. But if you're going to be that way…"

Grace stared some more. "It was my one rule."

"Then we'll have dinner in. You need to eat. I need to eat. We'll eat together. I can cook, but I only know one meal."

"The omelet?" Which was very good. Certainly better than she could do.

"Okay, I know three meals. One breakfast— this delicious omelet." He ate another bite as though proving his point. "Lunch—Salad Niçoise on a baguette. And dinner—roasted chicken breasts, potatoes with lemon and rosemary and a spinach salad. Most of which you have here, if you were so inclined to trust my skills in the kitchen again."

Grace was torn. She'd barely agreed to con-tinue seeing him and already he was pushing her boundaries, wedging his way past them as if they were made of nothing more than air. But chicken and potatoes sounded really good. And she did need to eat. "We aren't going out after for dessert or to walk off the food or for any rea-son unless the building is on fire."

Owen agreed rather quickly. "Of course not. I

have other plans for us after dinner." She didn't need to see the heated look in his eyes to know exactly what he was referring to.

CHAPTER ELEVEN

OWEN FOUND HIMSELF eating dinner at Grace's most nights after that. He'd pick up takeout or she would. Sometimes he'd pop in to see Julia at La Petite Bouchée and order a couple of to-go meals. Julia knew who he was buying for, and she'd even tease him about it, but she didn't say anything to Grace, for which Owen was grateful. He felt as though he and Grace were getting somewhere, but if she thought he was breaking her lone rule, he worried that she might put a stop to things.

For now, it was enough. He wasn't looking for claims of love or promises that lasted a lifetime. He was simply enjoying what they had and he thought she was, too. She certainly wasn't kicking him out of her bed. Not even that one time he ate crackers.

The weather had turned cool with the onset of fall, which meant peeling Grace out of many warm layers. He liked seeing them slide away, each successive removal showing off more and more of her body, so that when she finally stood before him in nothing but her lingerie he was so turned on that he could barely hold back. He'd ripped a couple pairs of her underwear in his haste, but since he'd replaced them with other pretty flimsy bits, she hadn't seemed to mind.

Although she still insisted that they not be seen in public in any way that might indicate a relationship, she had agreed to exchange apartment keys. She said it was only for ease of meeting. Owen wasn't so sure, but since he wasn't sure what he wanted it to mean, he was satisfied to leave it alone.

It was easier. Sometimes he wanted to get to her place early, for instance if he was cooking, so that when she got in they could spend their time before he had to leave for his work together rather than trying to chat over the sizzle of a pan. And now, when he got off work, he didn't have to wake her up to let him in. Because he spent most nights with her.

He used his key now, juggling a cloth bag of food, a bottle of wine and flowers. Grace loved getting fresh flowers, so he bought them regularly. She seemed to prefer the simplicity of white and they did suit the decor of her home, so he usually just bought whatever he thought would look best without actually noting what kind they were. He and the florist were becoming rather close friends and she generally guided him in the right direction.

Owen put the flowers in a silver vase and displayed it on her mantel, then he set about prepping for dinner. Which, since the food he'd brought was premade, meant putting into warming dishes and keeping the wine cool.

Grace appreciated a set table, so he put place mats on the small two-seater in her living room. It was placed under the window, so they could look out at the city and the partial view she had of the North Shore Mountains. Then he dimmed the lights and lit candles.

He liked the routine of it, and knowing how much Grace enjoyed it gave him a physical rush. He liked doing things for her, liked the way she appreciated the simple things, liked how she returned the favor, making sure there was always bottled water and beer in her fridge. How she'd even learned the rules of football so she could watch with him on Sundays. The fact that she often worked on her laptop during the games or that he got called into work half the time didn't matter. The point was they both did things for each other and enjoyed it. Just like a real couple.

Owen settled on the couch and flicked on the TV, watching the news while he waited for Grace. Just like a real couple who couldn't be seen together. He'd be lying if he said it didn't bother him. It did. More than he'd expected. But Grace had her reasons and although he didn't agree, he could understand them. He knew what it was like to have an employer deem him wanting. He faced it every day when he looked at his brother, although Donovan had been better of late.

Owen blew out a breath. His brother was tough, which was fine. Owen didn't mind tough, but he often felt as though he was held to a different standard. Yes, he'd earned some of that. When Donovan and Mal had been busy working through high school, university and after, he'd been fooling around. But he was different now. He was a hard worker and while he might not have their education when it came to the food and beverage industry, he brought his own set of skills to the table. He was the best with people. Not just customers and partners, but staff, too.

He wanted to do more. He was ready for more. But Donovan seemed content to keep him at Elephants, permitting him to make small changes, but nothing more. Owen knew he needed to push harder, to demand more. But he'd wait until the wedding was over.

Donovan and Julia were getting married on New Year's Day. It was one of the few days in the restaurant industry when businesses were closed, which meant all the invitees could attend. And it was coming up fast, less than six weeks away.

Owen could wait six weeks. It wasn't very long and he had plenty to keep him busy. Including Grace. Six weeks until he could take her out in public and show her off. Six weeks until he could introduce her to the family as his girlfriend, though he knew Mal and Julia already suspected something was going on. Six weeks until…what? Well, he had six weeks to figure that out.

He watched the news without really watching until the sound of a key turning in the lock interrupted his thoughts and he stood to greet Grace at the door.

She smiled when she saw him, her entire body seeming to lift toward him. After she changed out of her heels and slipped off her suit jacket, she met him in the living room, where he had a glass of wine already poured.

"Lilies." Grace's entire face lit up when she saw them sitting above her fireplace. "You shouldn't spoil me."

"Who else am I going to spoil?" He accepted her kiss as his due. Pointed to his lips again when he thought it didn't last quite long enough.

"They're gorgeous." She accepted the glass of wine, when Owen finally let go of her, and walked over to admire them.

Owen admired the way her body moved in her suit. Unlike some women, who looked boxy and awkward, Grace looked even more womanly. Her jackets nipped in at the waist, her pants draped and her skirts narrowed to a point just above her knee.

"Very holiday friendly. I should consider this look for the office in December." She glanced back at him. "What do you think?"

"I like it." But he was looking at her butt.

She swiveled. "I'm not the holiday decoration."

"You could be." He strode forward and scooped her against him. "We could cover you in tinsel and lights. I'd supervise to make sure we got the look just right."

"And would I be wearing anything under this look?"

"I think we'd have to try both ways. In your sexy underwear and out of it. For research purposes, you understand."

"Of course. We'd have to be thorough."

"Very thorough." He ran a finger along the neck of her shirt. "We should probably start now. December is almost upon us." He flicked open the buttons on her suit jacket and worked it off her shoulders. "And the holidays are always so busy."

GRACE LOOKED AT the gorgeous pine tree she and Owen had set up last night. It wasn't real, but she faked it by spraying pine scent. Her building didn't allow actual trees, deeming them a fire hazard, but she made do.

She'd brought her ornaments and other holiday decorations up from storage last night, also with Owen's help, but she hadn't started decorating. Usually, she didn't bring up any boxes until the last minute as she disliked the messy clutter in her living room. But Owen had left early for work and somehow it had felt wrong starting without him.

Grace had tried to tell herself that this was both foolish and dangerous. She and Owen hadn't talked about their future, not really. She told herself that she didn't actually know what he thought, but she feared she was only lying to herself. Yes, he'd asked her to have dinner in public with him, but he hadn't even done that lately, seemingly content to live their relationship in the confines of her apartment.

Which meant… Well, she knew what it meant. That he wasn't thinking about a long-term future, not seriously, and she didn't need to ask him, to see him stutter over the words, to know, which was why she hadn't.

She'd made real hot chocolate tonight, melting Callebaut wafers in a pot and adding full-fat milk as a treat, but even that hadn't been enough to get her stringing, trimming and hanging. Instead, she'd sat on the couch, sipping her hot chocolate and watching the fireplace. She wanted more than what she had with Owen. She deserved more.

She should just tell him. Explain that since this wasn't going anywhere, they should just end it. And she would. Once the wedding was over. Maybe it was weak or callow, but she thought the event would go more smoothly if she and Owen maintained their status quo. And there was also her burgeoning friendship with Mal to consider.

Grace didn't think Mal would turn her back because things with Owen didn't work out, but she wouldn't know definitively until they were no longer together. Losing both of them in one fell swoop and still having to see them at the wedding, now only four weeks away, bearing down on them at full speed? Well, Grace didn't know if she had the emotional strength to handle that.

So instead, she sipped her hot chocolate and thought about her tree and the dinner she'd picked up from La Petite Bouchée warming in the oven. She knew the coq au vin blanc was Owen's favorite. Her stomach flipped. Going out of her way to pick up special meals and including him in her holiday traditions probably wasn't the best way to act as their relationship's end date neared, and yet she couldn't bring herself not to. It was insanity and guaranteed to hurt, but there was still a small bloom of hope, one that blossomed with his smile or the look in his eyes when she was talking, that made her wonder if maybe, just maybe, they could have something more.

Grace had finished her hot chocolate, probably ruining her dinner in the process, and was busy arranging the boxes for decorating when she heard Owen's key in the lock.

"Hi, honey, I'm home."

Her pulse leaped even as she told herself not to let it. This wasn't his home and he was only kidding. Even if he wasn't, it couldn't work. She'd written down all the reasons only last week in an attempt to control the yearning of her heart. Just because her heart refused to listen to reason and logic didn't mean she shouldn't.

She went to meet him in the hall, where he was hanging his coat in the closet. A bottle of wine dangled from his fingers and his eyes lit up when he saw her. She felt her pulse jump again. "Mr. Ford."

"You know that makes me think you're talking to my dad." He gathered her in his arms, the cold bottle of wine he held pressing into her back.

"Maybe that's why I do it." He smelled so

good. Smoky clover and cold air. She inhaled, burying her face in his neck.

"Oh, yeah? You have a crush on my dad? Am I going to have to challenge him to a duel for your hand?" His arms tightened around her.

Grace shoved down the pleasure that Owen might want her hand. All she had to do was listen to his tone to know he was joking. He was always joking. "Maybe later. I've got plans for you tonight."

"I do love a woman with a plan." He nipped the side of her neck.

Grace reminded herself that this was all part of the Owen Show. The lighthearted, nonserious, short-term show that she'd allowed herself to become part of. But she didn't have to stay there.

The meal was a hit, as were the wine and conversation. Grace almost forgot about the approaching deadline for their relationship. Owen did the dishes while Grace made more hot chocolate and they both returned to the living room to start on decorating the tree.

"Speaking of Christmas." Owen looped lights over and through the branches. "Are you going home?"

Grace stilled the thump of her heart with a sharp breath. He was only making conversation. "Not this year." She pulled out another string of lights and handed them to him. She'd determined years earlier that the perfect number of lights was about one hundred per foot of tree. Or that's what the internet had told her and she'd liked the way it looked. "Don't drape the strings too far apart—crowd them together to fill the space." Because it was safer to think about lights than the unspoken feelings inside of her.

"Aye, aye, captain." Owen accepted the lights and plugged them into the string he was holding. "If you're not going away," he said, shooting her a cheerful smile over his shoulder, "you're welcome to come to my house."

Grace held her breath. Go with Owen to his family's house for Christmas. She didn't dare to breathe. It was a step. A big one. "You mean like…"

"Strictly as friends and no one will think there's anything odd. We always invite friends and staff who don't have family in the area to join us."

And even though Grace had been the one to push for secrecy, to keep their relationship hidden, she felt disappointed that he was content to invite her as a friend and not even a special one because apparently anyone and everyone was welcome at the Fords' over the holidays. "I have to work," she said, which also happened to be the truth.

She had a Christmas Eve wedding this year as well and Julia and Donovan's on New Year's Day. With so many vendors and suppliers taking time off over the holidays, she had to make sure she was organized. She couldn't afford to lose any time, not even for the holidays.

"But not on Christmas Day." Owen reached for the next set of lights as he worked his way up the tree.

"I probably will." She shrugged and tried not to think about how sad that was. She'd worked over Christmas last year, too, but it hadn't bothered her then.

"So come have dinner with my family."

As friends. As much as Grace tried to tell herself that she was okay with this, with all of this, it was clear from the shaking of her hands that she wasn't. "I appreciate the invite, but I wouldn't want to intrude." She paused, waiting for him to tell her that she wouldn't be intruding, that he wanted her there.

Instead, he continued stringing lights. "Well, if you change your mind…"

But Grace knew she wouldn't.

CHAPTER TWELVE

THE DAY OF the Ford-Laurent wedding arrived
quickly for Grace, or maybe it was just trying to
squeeze as much as she could into every minute
she had left with Owen. It was a mistake, she
knew, to let herself live in the moment instead
of recognizing that this was borrowed time, but
she did it all the same. It would all be over after
tonight anyway, so what was the harm in taking
a small bit of pleasure. Pleasure she could use
to warm herself on what were sure to be some
cold January nights.

Even this morning when her alarm had gone
off and she'd needed to get into the shower immediately, she'd rolled over and curled into
Owen instead. Which had led to some delightful touching and kissing and showering. And
then she'd really been late. But she just couldn't
bring herself to tell him she needed to go. Not
when the end was actually here.

Fortunately, she was able to drown herself in
wedding-day details, organizing flowers and
musicians. Liaising with the kitchen on service

and food, both of which were paramount considering the bride, groom and entire guest list were involved in the food and beverage industry.

The venue was stunning, all winter white and dark wood tones, like a snow-covered forest, the secondary color a rich mossy green. Grace wore a simple lace sheath dress in a similar shade of green that complemented the decor without standing out. Exactly as she and her team were meant to do. Of course, that was easier said than done when Owen was around.

But he had duties to attend to as well, which was what she'd told him this morning when he'd followed her into the shower under the guise of helping her wash her back. She'd seen him once before the ceremony, slapping his brother on the back and putting a bottle of water into Donovan's hand before he'd spotted her and turned to come her way.

She'd given him a sharp head shake and put her hand to her ear as though one of the team had just called her through the synced devices, when it had, in fact, been completely silent. Owen had given her a sad look, but stopped and turned back to his brother and other family members in the area, and Grace told herself she was glad. She couldn't kiss him. Not here. No matter how much her body might want to.

She spent the next few hours making sure

everything ran smoothly, from the ceremony to the toasts at the reception to the dancing. Grace had just finished helping a guest get out the red wine someone had splashed onto her lovely silver dress and was on her way back toward the main room to see that everyone was enjoying themselves without verging on rowdiness. It was a fine line between having a good time and having too good a time, but Grace had learned to manage it over the years. Nothing a quiet hand, a firm whisper and a suggestion that some air might be appropriate couldn't handle.

"Hey."

Grace glanced in the direction of the voice and felt a hiccup in her heart when Owen smiled at her from a small, dark alcove.

"I'm busy," she told him, even though her feet had already changed direction to head toward him.

"You've got a minute."

She didn't, but before she could tell him that, his strong, warm hands wrapped around her waist and pulled her into the alcove with him.

He was warm and he looked hot in his tux. Grace had seen plenty of men in tuxes before—nature of the job—but she could confidently say no one had ever looked as good as Owen Ford. He'd even worn dress shoes and though she approved, given the circumstances, a small part of her missed the kicks.

"When this is all over, how about I take you someplace private?"

"When this is over, I plan to sleep for twelve hours." But she'd probably get by on eight.

"I'll join you." Owen massaged the small of her back with his thumbs. Grace sucked in a sharp breath and he eased up. "Too hard?"

She shook her head. "No, it feels good." Her back was always tense during events. All that standing in heels.

He pressed harder, working out the tender knots. "This would be a lot easier if you were naked."

"And we'd get arrested for public indecency."

"Small price to pay." He pressed a kiss to her temple and her eyes slid shut. "God, you're beautiful."

Grace felt herself melting toward him, melting into him, and she allowed herself to enjoy it for a moment. "I should get back."

"You should stay where you are." He kissed her on each closed eyelid, then her lips. "With me."

She'd like to. She really would. Instead, she pulled herself up and looked at him. "Julia and Donovan didn't hire me to stand around and get a massage."

"An oversight. Stay with me."

Grace's breath was a shudder. She wanted so much to believe that Owen meant what he said, that he wanted her to stay with him, for always. But she knew better. She sighed. She had a job to do and she was on the clock. "I can't." It would be easier this way.

But he curved a hand around her hip when she started to move. "I wish you were here with me."

A tiny shudder swept through her. Grace did her best to hold it at bay. One small shudder could lead to a quaver, which would lead directly to a quake and the collapse of everything she'd worked so hard for. She had a plan, she reminded herself. A truly excellent plan and she wasn't going to throw it all away for one tiny shudder. Even if it did have the potential to turn into a quake. "I'm with you right now," she pointed out, glad that her voice sounded even and not shuddery at all.

"I mean, here as my date. Not working, not running around, not having a mere sixty seconds to let me get my hands on you. Not that I'm complaining about this little interlude."

Grace felt the words catch in her throat. Because she wasn't here as his date. "Owen."

"Grace." She could fall into his eyes. So warm and dark and welcoming. When he looked at her, it was as if she was his whole world. She sucked in a breath. "Stay with me," he said.

It would be so easy to say yes. She didn't even have to say anything. A brief nod or the press of her body against his would get the point across. Yes, she would stay.

"I want you." His hands began to make slow circles on her back, gradually pulling her closer until she was pressed up against him again. She could feel the heat from his body and the curve of his biceps as he locked his arms behind her. It felt good. "Right here, right now."

Which was how it always was. Temporary, fleeting. And just like that the slow melting of her insides stopped. All he meant was that he wanted her naked at his brother's wedding.

Grace felt foolish. She knew that, had known it for a while. Owen might be gorgeous, he might wear a tux like nobody's business and he might be able to make her laugh so hard that she gasped for breath. But he wasn't looking for forever. At least, not with her.

She'd do well to remember that.

"I have to get back." She unhooked his hands from her waist.

Owen twisted his fingers to catch hers, to hold her back for one more second. And even though she knew she should shake him loose, when she looked up and saw him watching her with those deep, dark eyes, she froze. "I'll see you later?" he asked.

Grace knew she should say no. She'd allowed this to go on for far too long already, allowed herself thoughts that she knew were impossible, but she weakened when faced with his smile and the magnetic pull that sucked her in every time. But she knew that this would be the last time.

She nodded and extracted herself from his heat. She didn't look back as she walked away. She couldn't look back because she was afraid if she did, she'd do something even more foolish. Run to him. Say something she'd end up regretting. Share everything that was in her heart. And beg him to say he felt the same.

But she already knew how that would turn out. And it wouldn't be according to plan. So tonight would be the last time. The very last time.

It was time to say goodbye to Owen Ford.

OWEN DIDN'T STAY LATE at the wedding. He'd given his toast, kissed cheeks until his lips were chapped and ensured that the limo hired to take Julia and Donovan off at the end of the night was on schedule. He'd also double-checked the hotel suite they'd rented and made sure it was fully stocked with all the newlywed necessities. Champagne, strawberries and chocolate. Then he'd headed for Grace's, feeling as if he'd earned his own celebration. One he planned to share with her.

He hummed as he let himself into her apartment. She'd be another hour or so, but he had his key, which allowed him to set up their own non-newlywed necessities. He liked having his own key. He'd given her one to his place, too, but she'd never used it. Not even when he'd hinted—okay, flat out told her—that he'd like it if she did.

But he figured that would change now. No longer would she have those concerns about her career or anything to keep her distance. He'd made certain the past month or so not to push, to make her feel safe and that she could trust him, but it had been hard. So many times he'd wanted to ask her to join him for dinner at Elephants or have brunch with his family or even something as banal as going for a walk together.

But he'd waited and now he intended to make up for some of that lost time. A warm rush filled him. It would be nice to stop hiding. He wanted to introduce her to the family as his, take her on a vacation, kiss her in public.

He checked the fridge for the bottle of wine he'd brought over last night, then pulled down a pair of glasses. He gave them a quick polish out of habit, even though they were as spotless as everything else in Grace's apartment.

The space still sparkled with Christmas decorations. Shiny silver pinecones in clear bowls, white stockings hanging from a matched set of snowflake stocking holders and the green tree in the corner with twinkling white lights and silver and blue decorations. Though he'd snuck in a few colorful ones when she hadn't been looking. A set of metallic pink stars, lime-green bells and the Popsicle-stick Rudolph he'd made in Grade One. He'd had to play innocent when his mother noticed Rudolph missing from her own tree. *Hmm...nope, no idea where that could have gone.* But his parents' tree was filled with ornaments both elegant and garish. They still had his Popsicle-stick Santa and Popsicle-stick Frosty, so they didn't need his Rudolph, too. And Grace had laughed really hard when she'd spotted it and then moved it to a place of honor in the front of the tree.

It grinned at him now, the googly eyes applied with a six-year-old's slapdash attitude, askew and cross-eyed. Owen grinned back and stopped in front of the mantel, where Grace had a pair of silver stags on display. As had become his habit, he mounted one on top of the other then stepped back to admire his handiwork.

He was glad Grace hadn't taken the decorations down and stored them away yet. It was nice, seeing the little celebration they'd created together. And remembering, when he looked beneath the tree, which was still stacked with presents—empty boxes Grace wrapped to make the display complete even if she hadn't finished her shopping—how they'd celebrated the coming of the New Year. Literally.

Which he had plans to do again just as soon as she got home. He returned to the kitchen, filled up the ice bucket she stored in one of her cupboards, put the wine inside and carried it along with a stand and the glasses into the bedroom.

Owen loved Grace's bedroom. It was so her. The pristine bedspread in white with some sort of shimmery pattern worked in. The smooth sheets that never had wrinkles and always smelled as if they'd spent the better part of the afternoon drying in the sun. The blue chair that she sat in to pull on stockings or shoes. And beneath all that perfectly organized, glossy white palette, something hidden and sexy.

The piles of colorful lingerie that filled her drawers. She didn't have anything plain or cotton as far as he could tell. The body chocolate and long silk ribbons that hung in her closet and that he'd put to good use, though not at the same time. And the vibrator she stored in her nightstand that he liked to run all over her body, focusing on her nipples and rolling it between her legs, before sliding it deep inside her.

But he didn't pull any of them out. Tonight, he wanted to be the only thing Grace thought of, the only thing she looked at, the only thing she felt.

Owen put the wine bucket into the stand, arranging the bottle so it sat at an angle and looked nicer, then placed the glasses on her nightstand. Her bed was neatly made, which only made it more fun to muss up. He pulled the covers back, tossing all the pillows she piled on it into the trunk she kept at the foot of the bed, as though the room couldn't be messy even when she slept. There were more pillows added for the holiday season, a silver one with a pine tree etched in a slightly darker shade, a shiny white one and a pale blue one with a snowflake pattern. Most times he just tossed them and their brethren on the floor, but she'd purse her lips and pick them up before getting into bed and he didn't want anything to slow her from sliding into his arms.

She'd looked amazing tonight. She always did, but there had been something special, something extra tonight. When she'd looked at him in the alcove, her lips slightly parted, he'd felt something hard knock in his chest. And then he'd made the joke about the quickie and things had returned to normal. Safer, at least.

Grace wouldn't have gone for any of his suggestions anyway and as much as he teased her, he wouldn't have followed through. Not at Julia and Donovan's wedding. Now, if it had been some other random party, all bets would have been off. But there'd be opportunities for that later. Right now he had other plans.

Owen turned down the lamps in the room, leaving a dim path for Grace to follow. He lit candles. There was something sexy about the way they flickered, the shadows and movement that made him feel as if they weren't in a city of over a million people. Then he undressed, hanging his tux on one of the hooks in Grace's closet, because she would notice if he tossed it over the chair, and climbed into bed, arranging himself with his arms behind his head and stretching into a lounging position when he heard her enter the apartment.

Grace stopped in the doorway when she saw him splayed out like a buffet. He saw the lift of her eyebrow and the slow smile that spread across her face. "This is a nice surprise."

His lips weren't the only things that rose to greet her when she walked over and leaned down to give him a kiss.

"A very nice surprise."

"Glad to hear it." He turned her around slowly, sitting up so he could ease her zipper down. Grace peeked at him over her shoulder, a sexy little peek with hungry eyes, and Owen felt his desire grow. He pulled her dress off, urging her out of it, out of everything.

But when he moved to strip off her bra and underwear, she slowed him, turning to face him and cupping his face as she kissed him, long and slow. His heart thumped, pounding against his chest. Then she picked her dress up off the floor and sashayed over to the closet. Owen drank in every movement. The sway of her hips, the swing of her step. When she emerged, the shoes were gone, no doubt lined up in their spot, but the underwear remained.

"You're overdressed." Owen reached for her, fingers eager to touch. "Let me help with that."

But Grace caught his hands, linking her fingers through his as she crawled on top of him, lowering her body to touch his. Owen exhaled and kissed the side of her neck, the strap of her bra, her jaw, her mouth, anywhere he could reach.

"Slow down," Grace whispered even as her breathing sped up. She rocked against him, the deliberate and measured motion only increasing his need to lose himself within her.

"I can't." His voice sounded scratchy, rough with wanting her, wanting nothing between them. He freed one hand and flicked open the clasp on her bra, grateful that gravity helped the garment slide down her arms.

Grace unlinked their hands long enough to take it off and then returned to her original position. Only now her bare chest rubbed against his. Owen could feel the hard glide of her nipples, the silky plumpness that he longed to fill his hands with.

"Grace." The rasp was deeper now. "I need you."

"I'm here. I'm right here." She kissed the side of his neck, sucked on the skin where it curved into his shoulder, and Owen threw his head back. His body bowed toward her, begging. But she merely continued her careful exploration, keeping their hands tightly clasped together.

Then her mouth was around him, warm and wet and welcoming. Owen closed his eyes and clenched every muscle in his body. "Grace, I won't be able to—" The words cut off in a sharp gasp. And it was no use thinking about cold showers or football stats or any other trick to reduce the desire barreling through him.

He pulled his hands free, hauled her up against him so he could kiss her silly. His fingers stroked the length of her body, slid up her inner thigh to find her as ready as he was. He wasted no time in grabbing a condom from the nightstand and rolling it on. He felt feverish in his haste, but he couldn't wait. Not another day or month or second.

She seemed to grasp his rush and didn't say anything when he maneuvered her back atop him, guiding her legs to straddle his, pressing his hips up to meet her and slide home. "Grace." Her name was a long inhale of appreciation as she closed around him, all smooth skin and lush curves. And when she began to move, her body bouncing up and down, he felt nearly cross-eyed with wonder.

She was his, all his.

"Owen." She began to slow her pace, every move taking a touch longer to finish. And there was something in her eyes and on her face, a pained expression.

Owen allowed the rhythm to slow, matching his moves to hers. She blinked and looked down. He lifted a hand to cup her face, nudged up until she looked at him. He was crazy about her, so crazy, and he didn't like seeing this expression. "What is it? What's wrong?"

He saw her throat work as she swallowed, but she only shook her head. "Nothing. This is perfect."

But suddenly Owen wasn't so certain. He stroked a thumb back and forth across her cheek. "You sure?"

She let out a shuddering breath and nodded. "Hold me." She bent to kiss him, shifting the angle of their bodies so they were mouth to mouth, chest to chest.

Owen wrapped his arms around her, keeping her close, holding her tight as they rocked, finding a new, quieter rhythm. One that didn't lead to long moans of pleasure or demands for more, but left an indelible mark. Something deeper and more precious, as though they were connected everywhere.

He felt a knock in his chest as though it was breaking wide-open, insisting she come in and never leave. He blinked the thought away. She was already here, already there.

Grace lifted her face to look at him, her eyes dark with desire and something else. "I just want it to be us tonight. Nothing between us."

"There is nothing between us." Owen slid his hands up her back to tangle in her hair and kissed her. She softened against him, her body opening to him, allowing him deeper. With every stroke, Owen sensed he was reaching a new, more intense spot.

And he never wanted to stop.

WHEN OWEN WOKE UP, Grace was no longer in the bed with him. A sad state of affairs made doubly so because she wasn't in the shower, either.

Owen pulled on his boxers and padded down the hall. "Grace?"

There was no answer. He found Grace sitting at the breakfast bar in the kitchen dressed in her workout gear, hair scraped back into a tight ponytail. A cup of coffee sat on the counter in front of her, but it didn't look as though she was drinking it.

Owen slid his arms around her and leaned into the curve of her neck, inhaling. "Good morning."

But she didn't lean back into him or turn her head to give him a kiss.

Owen moved around the counter. "Everything okay?"

She smiled at him, but it was as tight as her hair. "We need to talk."

"Sure." He pulled a mug out of the cupboard, a wide-mouthed one in navy blue that he thought of as his, and filled it up. "What are we talking about?"

"I can't see you anymore."

He stilled. Everything except his fingers, which gripped the handle of his mug more tightly. "What?"

Grace didn't look away, but met his gaze head-on. "I can't see you anymore."

This again? He carefully put the mug on the counter and reached out to stroke her hand. "Grace. This is exactly when you can see me. Remember the wedding? It's over, so we don't have to worry about being seen together anymore."

But she didn't smile or turn her hand into his. Her blue eyes were serious. "This wasn't a decision I made lightly."

It wasn't until she shifted her stool back, putting distance as well as counter space between them, that Owen realized just how serious Grace was. He swallowed and pushed his cup away, nauseated by the thought of adding liquid to his suddenly roiling belly. "And just what is this decision?"

"It's over."

He blinked as though that might clear things up. What was she talking about? "It didn't seem over last night."

Or had she already forgotten about that? About that slow, sensitive bout of sex that had been hotter and harder than anything he'd ever experienced in his life?

Because he sure as hell hadn't forgotten.

"Please don't make this harder than it already is."

Hell, yes, he was going to make this harder. Owen widened his stance and placed his hands on the counter. "I want to know why. You owe me that." It was hard to keep his voice steady.

"We both knew this had an end date." Grace

did look away then, her hands wrapped around each other in her lap.

"No, *we* didn't. Look at me." He kept his voice soft—or as soft as he could manage when it felt as if he'd sucked down a truckload of gravel. "Talk to me."

He saw the bob of her throat and the way she bit her lip. "We have different life plans, Owen."

"How can you know that when we haven't talked about them?" He leaned forward. "Tell me. Tell me what you want out of life."

"I want to get married." She looked up at him. "Maybe have some kids, get a dog."

Owen regretted his flinch even before he saw her reaction. He schooled his features into a neutral expression. "Okay." Okay. That was fine. That was perfectly normal, something most adults did. But he felt a nervous flutter around his heart.

"Do you?" She met his gaze.

Owen swallowed. His throat felt tight. So did his chest. Was he having a heart attack? Was he about to have a stroke and collapse right here on her floor? He gripped the edges of the counter more tightly. "Grace."

"I know what I want, Owen. I don't want to waste my time."

That stung. It felt very close to the way Donovan still sometimes treated him. "I don't think I'm a waste of time."

Her expression softened and for a moment Owen thought she was going to move toward him, to agree that there was no reason to make a rash decision first thing this morning. Instead, she sat up straighter and raised her chin. "You aren't, but I don't see the point of continuing if we don't have the same goal."

He studied her. There was uncertainty in her eyes and the press of her lips. "And that goal is marriage and kids."

Grace nodded. "And a dog."

"Maybe we should start there."

Her eyebrows slanted together. "With a dog?"

"I'm just thinking that we haven't been together that long. Only a few months. You haven't even been properly introduced to my family. Why don't we see how things go and then we can get a dog." It seemed reasonable to him, but Grace merely stiffened.

"That's just it, Owen. We don't need to see how things go. We've been seeing how they go for a few months."

"What? When you refused to be seen in public with me? When you hid me away like some shameful secret?"

"We agreed."

"No, Grace. You agreed and I went along with it because I liked you."

She nodded slowly and for a moment, Owen felt his panic recede, the blurring around the edges of his vision clear.

"Then tell me, Owen. Do you want to get married?"

He should have expected it, should have known she'd go back to that one. Instead, he flinched again. He tried to cover it with a cough. "Sure, I mean, at some point, one day…"

Grace's entire body seemed to droop. "That's what I thought." Her voice was a whisper.

"Let me explain." But he didn't know how. "I'm still figuring out my career and other things." *Good one. Other things.* Yeah, that was sure to win her over.

"I want to believe you." She looked at him, but there was no softness there now. Just hard, firm resolve. "But how can I when you can't even say the words?"

She paused and Owen knew this was his last chance, the moment where he could step into the void and fill it with the words she wanted to hear, could infuse his voice with the sincerity he needed to show. He stayed silent.

"I think it's best if you go."

He found his voice then. "I'm not even dressed." But she didn't respond to his comment or his naked chest. "And then what, Grace?" Panic and something else, something hotter and harder, rose in his chest. "And then I go? You're just kicking me out the door and out of your life forever?"

"We never had forever, Owen. You've made that clear."

But he didn't agree. He'd never meant that. "This is crazy. Just because I'm not ready to run to the altar this second, I'm out?" He felt his skin growing warm, thought it might sizzle if someone were to throw cold water on it. Marriage was a big step. One he needed to get used to. He couldn't just jump in without looking. "All I'm asking for is a little time. Time for us both to make sure."

Grace stared at him, lines bracketing her mouth. Then slowly she shook her head and for a second, Owen thought everything was going to be okay. That she'd see the insanity of her demands and would agree they could go on seeing each other and then, who knew? "But that's just it, Owen. I don't need any more time and, if you're honest, neither do you. Do you see yourself married to me?"

That damnable flinch rocked his face again. Christ. Owen scrubbed a hand over it, but it was too late.

"That's what I thought." But she looked sad instead of angry. "There's nothing wrong with that, Owen. But I do want to get married and I won't stay with someone who doesn't."

Grace might not have been angry, but suddenly he was plenty mad for both of them. Just where did she get off deciding what he wanted and how he should live his life? Didn't he get enough of that from his brother? "Well, since you've got it all wrapped up in a neat little bow, I guess that's it. It doesn't matter what I might say or think because you've got it all figured out for both of us. Congratulations."

"Owen."

"Why is this suddenly so important?" He shook his head. It didn't matter, since her answer wouldn't change the outcome. She was breaking up with him. "For God's sake, Grace. You won't spend time with my family. You won't even go out in public with me. But I'm expected to just drop onto one knee and claim everlasting love?" His heart pounded with it. "Pardon me if I'm having a little trouble accepting that."

"That isn't what I said. I just want to know that we want the same things."

"Like meeting family? Going out for dinner? Kissing in public?" Because he wanted those things. They were steps on the way to something larger, something longer.

"Of course, I want those things, too."

"But you aren't willing to wait. You've made

up your mind that marriage has to happen now and not later."

"I didn't say that."

But she had. She'd said she wouldn't wait for him. As if he wasn't good enough to wait for. As if he wasn't good enough for her. And an ugly insidious thought hit him. Had she really been concerned about her reputation or had she just wanted to keep him a secret? "Would you even marry me if I asked?"

Her face went blank and his heart sank. "As you aren't asking, I don't see how that's relevant."

"It's relevant to me." But she didn't answer. And a red, rich anger rose up in him. He was good enough to sleep with, good enough to play with, but not good enough to make a life with. "You're right." He lashed out now, wanting to hurt as much as he was hurting. "I don't want to get married. Not yet. But that doesn't mean there's anything wrong with me."

He was breathing hard now, like a freight train barreling ahead, and he wasn't going to stop until he'd blown off all his steam.

"I'll go now." He'd said enough, letting out those little worries that he worked so hard to keep buried. Fear that he wasn't good enough, smart enough, worthy enough. Fears that had kept him from taking anything too seriously for most of his life. Maybe he'd had the right of it then. Less painful. He scowled. "Don't bother to see me out."

He put on his tux from last night, jamming his feet into the shoes so hard they hurt. Stupid dress shoes that pinched his toes. And yet, he hoped she'd follow him into the room, insist they talk this out so that he could help her understand that things didn't have to end this way.

She didn't.

He left the bedroom, his bow tie clutched in one hand and her keys in the other. She was sitting at the counter again, her chin in her hands, her eyes tilted downward. But he didn't care, wouldn't care. She didn't want him in her life? Fine. He was gone.

"Here." He tossed the keys onto the kitchen counter. They made a loud jangle in the quiet of the room. "I won't bother you again."

"Owen."

"Just drop mine in the mail or by the bar sometime." There was no question of her using it, sneaking into his apartment, all soft and warm and wrapping herself around him, telling him that she'd been wrong, all wrong. Not when she'd never used it when they'd actually been together. And he couldn't stand the idea of sticking around while she dug them out of whatever drawer she had them tucked neatly away in.

Because they wouldn't be in her purse, where they should have been if she'd been in the habit of actually visiting him. "Goodbye, Grace."

He wasn't sure if she responded because his ears were ringing too loudly to hear anything, even before he closed the front door behind him.

CHAPTER THIRTEEN

GRACE DIDN'T MOVE when she heard the door close. Or when her phone rang. Not even when her back, still stiff from working last night, began to ache from sitting on the stool with no support. She felt frozen inside and out.

Owen was gone. Just like that. And though she knew it was the right thing to do—his instinctive reaction every time she even mentioned marriage made that painfully clear—she couldn't help feeling sick inside. Guilty, too, as though she'd done something wrong. Which was so unfair. She was sorry that he was hurting, but that didn't mean she had to give up everything she wanted. All her plans, her dreams for the future.

She didn't have to go into work today. Winter was slow for weddings and January was virtually dead. She had a Valentine's weekend wedding—there were always couples that opted for the day associated with roses and romance—but everything had been in place for weeks and the bride and groom were low-key.

She'd already given her staff the next two weeks off. They'd all worked really hard through the holiday season leading up to the wedding yesterday. Grace hadn't personally minded the heavy load. Despite the fact that Owen kept late hours and often woke her up when he got home, she'd felt energized. Even the grim weather and limited daylight hadn't bothered her.

Of course, that was before.

Grace felt her fingers curl into angry knots. She should be relieved. Clearly, she'd read all of Owen's intentions exactly right. Casual, see where things go, no strings. But that didn't make the ache in her chest any less painful.

She pushed herself off the stool and stalked into the kitchen to dump her coffee. She wasn't wrong to want more, to insist on it. And as she respected his decision, he should show her the same courtesy.

If he hadn't wanted more, then he never should have gotten involved with a wedding planner. What did he expect? That she didn't believe in long-term commitment? That she'd be satisfied with the scraps of a relationship? And sure, he'd claimed that he wanted to take next steps, but to what end? Clearly, he had no plan in mind, no ultimate goal, which was as good as not bothering in her world.

Really, this was all for the best. It would allow

her to focus on her goals, to reestablish her plan and complete it on time. And if her heart was a little worse for the wear, it was only a good reminder that doing things off schedule was not for her.

She closed her eyes and saw the next two weeks stretch out in front of her. She hadn't filled them, hadn't planned events and scheduled appointments on a single day. Probably her subconscious still hoping that Owen might come through. And now she had nothing to do. All the air squeezed out of her lungs as she gazed around her apartment, so happy and bright and filled with holiday cheer.

She couldn't look at the decorations, waving at her, so unaware of her inner pain. Annoying little things.

Well, she'd take care of them now. No need to let the lights and ornaments and everything else linger. She'd stow everything away, then vacuum and dust, and get her apartment back to its normal appearance. Then she'd sit down at her computer and look at her five-year plan. It was time to implement the next step. Whatever that might be.

The fact that she didn't already know the next step, didn't have it residing in the back of her mind just waiting to be called into action, was proof of how badly Owen had messed with her schedule. Usually, she did a monthly check-in, to see where she was and determine that she was on her way to achieving her goals or if there were any superstar goals she could aim for if she'd already succeeded in reaching her base-level ones.

Grace nodded to herself. Yes, she'd bury herself in cleanup and then refocus her mind where it should be. Which was not on Owen Ford. But when she walked into the living room and saw the two reindeer going at it on her mantel, her good intentions fell away.

As he always did, Owen had left his mark. In her living room. With the ornaments on her tree. On her life. Grace scrubbed a hand across her face. She'd already missed her morning Pilates class, she'd missed her annual Christmas cleanup and she didn't even know what her January goals were. Suddenly, she didn't care.

The ache she'd been trying to pretend she didn't feel, the pain that hovered inside her chest, rearing its head with every heartbeat, flared to life. She stared at the reindeers and started to cry.

OWEN WENT STRAIGHT TO Elephants from Grace's. He didn't have anywhere else to go, which was a sad state of affairs when he thought about it. Travis, his closest friend, lived in Aruba, he no longer was in contact with the social-page crowd and aside from Grace, who had just officially punted him out of her life, the only other people he saw regularly were his family.

"Owen." Stef greeted him with a warm smile and pulled a bottle of water from the fridge. "Nice tux. I thought you were off today."

"I am." He grabbed the water offered by Stef, but didn't open it. Probably should have gone home to change first, but the idea of being completely isolated, even for one more second, had been too much to handle on top of everything else. So here he was, tux on, bow tie stuffed in his pocket and his dress shoes pinching his feet.

The bar was doing brisk Saturday brunch business. No doubt half the clientele were still hungover from New Year's Eve celebrations two days ago. Two days ago he'd rung in the New Year in Grace's bed. Where they'd laughed and teased. He'd thought they had a future. Not necessarily marriage—he felt himself flinch at the thought and squeezed the bottle of water so hard, he was surprised the cap didn't pop off.

The whole thing was ridiculous. Grace hadn't even spent any time with his family as his girl-friend. Hell, she wouldn't even let him call her that. And while she had allowed him to meet her family, it was minor when balanced out against everything else. And somehow she thought they'd go from that to marriage?

He snorted, earning a surprised glance from Stef. "I'm fine," he said, answering her unasked question. Yes, he was just fine. Perfectly fine. Finally free.

Because who wanted to be tied down? Not him. He wasn't ready for a wife and kids and the two-story house in a tree-lined neighborhood. No way.

"Brunch?" Stef asked, sliding a menu across the bar to him. Their weekend brunch deal was insanely popular. Along with the typical fare of waffles, omelets and toast that could be found at every eatery in the city, Julia had suggested Elephants add a European flare and offer a sandwich section. Open-faced and piled high with things like cold cuts, cheese, tomatoes, pickles and cod roe, which sounded disgusting but tasted delicious and, according to customers, had proven to be an amazing cure for going a little too hard the night before.

"Not hungry." Owen didn't even look at the menu.

Stef moved the menu away. "So you're here for the water?"

"Something like that." It was better than sitting alone in his apartment. Better than going to his parents' place, where everyone would be full

of chatter about how beautiful the wedding had
been and didn't Julia and Donovan look happy
and how long before Owen found a nice young
woman to settle down with. And sure as hell
better than going back to Grace's and banging
on the door until she let him in and gave him a
reasonable explanation for her sudden decision.

"Owen?" He looked up, registered the concern on Stef's face. "Are you okay?"

No, he wasn't okay, but there was no reason to
drag her into his drama. It wasn't even drama.
Just surprise and disappointment. He'd thought
he and Grace were on the same path, had the
same goals. Clearly, he'd thought wrong. Yet
another person in his life who didn't think he
was capable, didn't think he was ready for responsibility.

He wasn't saying he was against marriage
forever. He just wanted to work his way up to
it. What was so wrong with that?

"I'm fine." He pushed away from the bar before Stef could ask anything else and headed to
the back corner booth. It was usually quiet over
here, which suited him just fine. He didn't want
to be alone, but he didn't want to make inane or
non-inane conversation, either. He just wanted
to sit back and watch, let his own problems slip
away for a few minutes.

Owen sat silently, not opening the water, not

thinking, barely even breathing while the crowd milled around in front of him. They looked happy, even the ones who were clearly suffering from bleary eyes and aching heads, swilling down tomato juice and coffee, shoveling their breakfast sandwiches down as soon as they landed on the table. He'd take the sandpapery eyes and a sore head if it meant he'd feel better. Because while he might look okay on the outside, he wasn't.

He just wasn't.

But he had to try. He twisted the cap off the water and managed to take three sips. They didn't feel good going down, but they didn't feel bad, either. He could handle neutral. He could wrap himself up in a nice little neutral bubble for a while. Just until his insides didn't feel clawed open.

He noted the flow of the kitchen, which wasn't as smooth as it should have been. He needed to look into that, find out where the chain was breaking down, but not today. He didn't have the energy today and if that meant Donovan was right and he wasn't ready for the responsibility of overseeing operations for all their locations, then fine. He wasn't ready.

Owen picked at the label on the water bottle, leaving little scraps of paper on the table while he thought. The tabletop needed repairing. There was a long scratch marring the center, as though someone had dragged a key down it. Owen rubbed at it with his finger. It was mostly surface, just required a little buff and a coat of stain and polish to be brought back to its former glory. He hoped he would be the same.

"Any particular reason you look like someone just stole your dog?"

Owen looked up at Mal, who stood on the opposite side of the booth. She looked cool and polished, all clean clothes and washed hair. Owen glanced down at his rumpled tux and then back up. Mal's expression, despite her cheery smile, looked sad and worried, which only made him feel worse, so he returned to staring at the table. "I don't have a dog."

"It was a joke." Mal sat down without being invited. "What's up?"

"Nothing." Nothing was up. Absolutely nothing. Not his attitude. Not his life. Not his heart. In fact, his life was full of nothing. Yay him.

"Then you're just hanging around the bar on your day off, scaring customers away for fun?"

Owen glanced over at Stef, who looked away quickly and buffed the bar, as if she hadn't been watching them at all. Clearly, she was the cause of Mal's sudden appearance. "I'm not scaring anyone away," he told his sister. He wasn't talking to anyone or making eye contact, and why should he have to? This was his day off. He could do whatever he wanted with it, including sitting at Elephants and drowning his sorrows with a bottle of water.

"You are." Mal signaled to one of the servers, who hurried over wearing a bright smile. Owen couldn't even bring himself to fake one as his sister placed an order. She turned back to him and folded her hands on the table. "Your expression is bad for business. What would Donovan say?"

"I don't care." Owen wanted to let his head fall back against the seat and close his eyes, but he knew Mal well enough to know that wouldn't chase her away. In fact, it would probably give her incentive to stay. "I'm fine."

"Sure you are." Mal nodded. And how she got so much sarcasm in one small movement, Owen didn't know.

He didn't say anything. Neither did Mal. They sat in silence, if not exactly companionable than at least not awkward, until the server brought back a pair of tall tumblers filled with tomato juice, a spear of pickled asparagus and no doubt a jigger of vodka.

Owen stared at the frosted glasses and then looked at his sister. He knew she meant well, but he just wasn't up for it. "It's not even noon."

Mal nudged the glass forward again. "It's a

breakfast bevvy and you look like you could use one."

Owen frowned. "I don't drink on the job."

"An admirable trait, but since you're not actually on the job, it's not an issue. Now, why don't you have a sip and tell your sister what's bothering you."

Normally, Owen would have been happy to sit with Mal and chat about life or work. But right now, he wanted to wallow. He nudged the glass back toward her. "I'm not thirsty."

"Drink anyway." She lifted her own glass and held it forward, waiting for him to do the same.

Owen didn't want to. He also knew that Mal could outwait a turtle. "Fine." He raised his glass and clinked it against hers. "Happy?"

"I wouldn't say that." She sipped from the straw. "But it's certainly better than a kick in the teeth."

"That's hardly a difficult bar to reach."

Mal shrugged. "What can I say? I'm easy." She took another sip and reclined against the booth seat. "So what's troubling you?"

"I told you, nothing." But he heard the sharp edge in his voice, saw it in the way Mal's eyebrows drew up on her forehead.

"Oh, yeah. You sound really relaxed."

Owen frowned and sipped the Bloody Mary he didn't want. It tasted good, so he took another sip. It didn't matter if he got plastered. He wasn't working. He didn't need to stay sober. And what was the point of trying to be responsible anyway? Donovan couldn't see past the person Owen used to be. Even if he could, he was on his honeymoon and wouldn't know. Mal was the one encouraging him. And if a man ever had a reason to drink his sorrows away, now was one of them. He drank half the glass in one glug and stared down his sister. "Better?"

"I don't know. You tell me."

No, he wasn't better. Nothing was better and getting drunk wouldn't change that. He knew that and yet he took another small sip before officially pushing the glass away. The liquid sloshed around in his stomach and made him feel slightly ill. "I'll stick with water."

"Suit yourself." Mal lifted one shoulder, but didn't leave. She took a casual sip from her glass and scanned the room, which was bustling as usual, before she turned to face him again. "Just in case you were wondering, I plan to sit here until you tell me what's wrong."

Owen glared. It wasn't his normal expression, so it should have scared her. Instead, she glared back. "I've told you what's wrong." He fought to keep his voice neutral even as his fingers clenched the water bottle. "Nothing."

Mal looked pointedly at the plastic bottle that was crumpling under his grip. "Right."

Owen let go of the bottle. Okay, so he wasn't fine. How was that anyone's business but his? "I don't feel like sharing."

Mal nodded. "But maybe it will help."

"I didn't see you sharing your personal life when you and Travis split."

She blanched and her throat bobbed, but when she spoke her tone was calm. "That's true. And I think it was a mistake. If I'd talked to you, maybe things would have... Well, maybe they'd be better."

For a moment, Owen's own problems fell away. He studied his sister. She was still thinner than she used to be, but the color was back in her cheeks. "Are we about to have a moment? Share our innermost feelings? Do we need ice cream?" A ghost of a smile lifted his heart. "Will there be hair-braiding involved?"

"Owen. Be serious."

"I am." He gestured to his hair. "I'll need to get extensions."

Mal sighed, but didn't break eye contact. "You aren't going to chase me off the subject by joking."

"What subject?" But he felt his stomach roll, the Bloody Mary and water swirling together. "Hair-braiding?"

"No. Why you're here, without Grace and wearing your tux from last night."

Even hearing her name hurt. "Why would she be here?" Maybe he should be grateful that Grace had insisted on keeping their relationship quiet. Fewer questions to deal with now, since no one actually knew they'd been together.

"Oh, please." Mal waved a hand. "We all know you like her, that you're seeing her." She paused. "Or is the problem that it's now past tense?"

Owen looked down at the table again and shrugged. "Don't know what you're talking about."

Mal exhaled again. A very sisterly, loud and entirely dramatic sigh. "Really, Owen?"

"Yes, really. Unless you'd like to go into detail about why you're here and not in Aruba with Travis." He watched her fingers curl around her glass, saw her lips press together in a thin line. "Yeah, that's what I thought."

"It's not the same thing."

"Oh?"

"Things were fine between you last night," she pointed out. Owen sucked in a painful breath. Things had been fine last night, better than fine. Until they weren't. "Did you have a fight?"

"No. That would have been easier. Would have made sense." He looked down at the water bottle. He'd peeled off half the label without thinking, the scraps of paper in a little pile on the table. "She dumped me."

He was grateful that Mal didn't jump in immediately. Didn't place blame, didn't ask why, just sat quietly while he gathered his thoughts.

"I wasn't expecting it." Owen looked up, thinking he'd see pity in his sister's eyes. Instead, she watched him steadily. "But she was pretty clear that it was over."

"Did she give you a reason?"

Owen barked out a laugh. "She wants to get married, have kids." He shredded the rest of the label. "And I'm not ready for that. Is that so wrong?"

"No." Mal's voice was quiet. "Not at all."

"Well, Grace thought otherwise. She wouldn't even give me a chance." Just like his brother wouldn't give him a chance. It sucked—it *really* sucked—to feel as though no one judged him on his actual behaviors and achievements but on their own expectations. And they always expected so little from him. Maybe they were right.

"Owen." Mal shook her head and this time there was pity in her gaze. "It's not too late for you."

Owen tilted his head. "You say that like it's too late for you."

Mal looked away and something sad flashed across her face. "I don't want to talk about me."

Owen felt bad for bringing it up, but she'd

started this. "And I don't want to talk about me."
He took another sip of the Bloody Mary, then
chased it with water. They were quiet for a moment. "So you still haven't talked to him?"

He didn't need to clarify who he was talking
about. They both knew.

"I came here for you." Mal pinned him with a
narrowed gaze, but even her firm tone couldn't
prevent him from recognizing the deep pain in
her eyes. Whatever had happened, no matter
that she was looking better and acting more like
her old self, Mal still wasn't over Travis.

"My offer to beat him up still stands."

Mal laughed, but it was filled with sorrow
rather than humor. "I'm afraid that wouldn't help."

"Then what would?"

"You talking to me, telling me what's wrong."
She ran a hand through her dark hair. "I've managed to make a thorough mess of my own life,
but you can learn from my mistakes."

"Does this mean you're going to tell me what
happened?"

She shook her head. "No. It doesn't matter
what happened with me."

Owen disagreed, but he didn't say anything.
Neither did Mal. "Well, we're a fine pair, aren't
we?"

Mal sighed and finished her drink. "I know
you care about her."

"That doesn't really matter if she doesn't feel the same way."

Mal blinked in surprise, which soothed his ego a little. "That wasn't the impression I got."

"Well, you were wrong."

Mal nodded slowly. "I'm sorry to hear that. Is there anything I can do?"

Owen shook his head. He felt raw, as though he'd been stripped naked and left exposed to the elements, which wasn't so far from the truth. "I have to work." He decided on the spot not to take the day off because managing the bar was better than pouring a drink down his throat and throwing a pity party.

Mal gave him a once-over. "Like that? No, and isn't this your day off? Go home."

But Owen didn't want to go home. His apartment held no appeal and his social life was non-existent. "No."

"Yes." Mal leaned forward as though she could intimidate him. "I'm going to have to insist. It's not healthy to bury yourself in work."

"You're one to talk." Since that was what she'd done last year when things had fallen apart between her and Travis.

"Exactly." Mal nodded knowingly. "I'm exactly the one to talk because I'm the one who can tell you that it doesn't work."

Owen didn't want to hear that. He wanted to

hear that if he took on enough, piled it up past the tips of his ears, he'd be so distracted that he wouldn't have time to think about anything or anyone else. "I'm not going."

"Owen." She glared. He glared back. "Fine, then you leave me no choice." She whipped out her smartphone and started typing. "There's a flight to Aruba at four o'clock this afternoon. I'm buying you a ticket."

"Oh, are you and Travis making up?"

She shot him a look. "No, the two of you are. Think of it as rekindling your bromance."

"It's not a bromance. It's a much deeper connection."

Mal stopped typing and held a hand up. "Listen, I'm willing to book you the flight. I'll even pay for it. But I do not want to hear about my brother and my ex and their deep connection."

Owen looked at her. He knew he should tell her no, that he was fine, he could handle work and the breakup and everything. That if he was going to visit Travis, he could pay for it. Instead, he swallowed. He needed someone. Someone who would pour him a beer and talk about sports and leave all talk about romance at the door. "And you're okay with that?"

Mal's shoulders dipped. "I don't really have a choice, do I?" Her dark hair rippled. "I promised myself that I wouldn't ask you to end your friendship with him because we broke up."

He wanted to tell her how much he appreciated that, but the words got stuck in his throat. Still, somehow his sister knew.

"You need to talk to someone and that's apparently not me—I'm hoping he'll have better luck."

Owen's voice came back with a vengeance. "I don't need to talk to anyone." He didn't need a therapist and he didn't need to go to Aruba, he just needed some appreciation, a little acknowledgment that he wasn't such a bad guy and maybe some hot, no-strings sex that would chase all thoughts of Grace out of his mind.

"Suit yourself, but I think it would help."

Owen thought her concern was misplaced and told her so, but four hours later he found himself on a flight to Aruba.

OWEN CAUGHT A CAB from the airport directly to his hotel, a tingle of anticipation running down his spine. Blue water, white sand, hot sun. Maybe Mal was right. Maybe this was exactly what he needed. He'd tried to tell himself that he should have fought harder, insisted that he didn't need the break, didn't need to take a vacation. But the truth was he did. Without Grace, his personal life consisted of his family.

Pathetic. They had to spend time with him and pretend to like him.

But here, he could forget about all of that. He could sleep in and stay up late, not to work but to party. He could drink beer instead of water. And he could find a pretty girl to sleep with and shove all thoughts of Grace out of his head.

He'd spent last night in New Jersey, since there were no direct flights from Vancouver, but it had given him time to get in touch with Travis, who was thrilled he was coming for a visit. Owen shoved away the niggle of guilt. He wasn't betraying Mal by maintaining his friendship with Travis. She'd encouraged it, even pushed for it. But part of him wondered exactly how okay Mal was with everything and how much was just her putting on a brave face.

He was still wondering when he wandered into the beachfront bistro she had owned with Travis, looking for the man in question. Owen had stopped by his hotel room only long enough to change into a pair of shorts and flip-flops. He was already starting to sweat in the tropical heat.

The bistro was beautiful and he thought he was qualified to make such a declaration, seeing as he seemed to spend the majority of his work life inside a similar establishment. The walls were blue, the furniture white and made of wood. The front looked directly onto a water view, unmarred by anything but toned, tanned bodies in swimsuits.

Owen snagged a seat at the bar, ordered a beer and asked the bartender to tell Travis he was here. He could have texted Travis himself, but had decided to leave his phone in his room. He didn't need the temptation of Grace's number—which he couldn't bring himself to delete—mixed with a couple of beers.

"Owen." Travis grinned as he came out of the back. His hair was lighter than it had been last time Owen had seen him, his skin darker. But, like Mal, he was also thinner. Even so, Owen felt small around him. He wasn't short, but he felt that way around Travis. "Good to see you."

"You, too." Owen stood and they shook hands, following with a few back slaps, each one harder than the one before until Owen laughed. "You win." Even thinner, Travis was still a burly guy. Owen retook his seat and motioned for Travis to join him. "You have some time?"

"I'm the owner. I can make time."

Owen bit back the comment that he hadn't personally found that to be true. He wasn't here to bitch about work or really anything. He was here to unwind and maybe have a little fun.

"So, what's brought you out?" Travis thanked the bartender, who placed a glass of ice water in front of him. "And don't say my charming personality because I'll know you're lying."

Owen laughed again. A real laugh this time and some of the tightness in his lungs eased. "Well, since you stole my real answer, I'll have to lie and say that it was the sun and sand, but we'll both know the truth."

Travis threw back his head as his laughter filled the room. He slapped Owen on the shoulder. "Good to see you."

"Yeah." And it was good to be there. Owen felt his lungs unclench a little more. Mal had been right. He did need this.

They shot the breeze, talking about surface things: work, hobbies, what the Canucks' chances were at a Stanley Cup this year. Owen hadn't realized how much he'd missed Travis until he was here with him. "I'm really glad I came," he blurted out.

Travis blinked. "Do you need a tissue? A shoulder to cry on?"

Owen gave his friend's shoulder a shove, but Travis didn't move an inch. "You're an ass."

"Yes, but I'm your ass. So what's going on?"

Owen didn't know where to start. How he'd met Grace? Their breakup? Everything in between? "It's all good, man." He faked a grin. Maybe if he acted as if it didn't matter, it wouldn't.

"Right."

Owen stared at his beer, though he wasn't thirsty and he knew any oblivion found at the bottom of a glass didn't last. It just made everything worse the next morning.

"What's her name?"

"Who's name?"

"The woman who made you look like someone just stole your dog."

Seriously, what was it with these people and dogs? Was this the universe telling him to get one because a dog would love him when no one else would? Was it the male version of the crazy cat lady? "I don't have a dog," he said.

"I don't hear any denial. Going once, going twice." Travis slapped a hand down on the bar. "I think we have a winner."

"No winner." Just him and his rapidly warming beer. "And no woman." But his voice rose on the last word as though trying to hold back the lie.

Travis didn't say anything, just studied him. Owen felt as though he was under a magnifying glass.

"What?" he finally asked.

"Well, I'm just wondering, since there's no woman, why you haven't noticed the brunette who's been giving you the eye since you walked in."

What? There was a brunette?

"Or the redhead or the blonde. Or anyone."

"Maybe I'm not here for that."

Travis blinked hard. "Since when?"

"Since always." God, was he really so pathetic that even his closest friend thought he was only here to have sex? Was that what Mal had thought, too? Was that why she'd sent him here?

For a moment, Owen saw his previous self through their eyes and he didn't like it.

"So you're here because?"

"Can't a guy just come and hang out with a friend when he has a break?"

"Of course. But you didn't."

"How do you know?"

"I'm psychic." Travis shrugged. "You want to talk about it?"

Owen gave a sullen shrug. "Nothing to talk about." Grace had made it very clear that he wasn't worth her time. Maybe she was right. He swore and took a slug of beer.

"Seems like there might be."

Owen leveled a gaze at him. "I was seeing someone and now I'm not, okay?"

"Okay." Travis sipped his water. "But I've never seen you this upset about a woman before."

"I'm not upset." But he practically bit his tongue in his haste to get the words out.

"Then I've never seen you this concerned. Is

that better?" It wasn't, but Owen let it slide. He hadn't come here to fight with Travis. "How's everything else?"

"Crappy." He still hadn't been promoted from managing Elephants. Donovan had met with him to discuss ideas, but hadn't moved forward to implement any of them and it seemed no matter what Owen did, he stayed in place. In the little box everyone in his life had built for him and refused to let him out of. He was banging his head against the sides, but nobody seemed to hear.

"Really, man. It's great to have you here. Your sunny disposition makes everything better."

Owen narrowed his eyes, but felt the edges of his lips twitch. "You the kind of man to kick another man when he's down?"

"When that man needs a kick in the ass? Yes."

Owen snorted then and some of the tension twisting his gut eased. "I don't need a kick."

"No, just that tissue, then?"

Owen punched him in the shoulder. "It's so not great to be here."

"It's so not great to have you."

They both grinned.

By the end of the night, Owen was feeling better or at least less ready to pound his fist into the bar top. He'd even told Travis a little about what had happened. Not everything—there were some things he thought it was best to keep to himself—but some. "So I left."

Travis pressed his lips together as he took in Owen's story. "Rough."

"It was." He appreciated Travis's simple assessment. It was rough. What more needed to be said?

"You going to do anything about it?"

"Like what? Throw myself at her feet and beg her to take me back?" But the light tone Owen had been going for never showed up. Instead, his voice sounded as rough as his situation and the sympathetic look in Travis's eye told Owen he'd heard it, too.

"If that's what it takes and that's what you want." Travis shrugged his big shoulders. "Why not?"

"Because." Because. Well, he didn't know. "Just because."

"Good one." They were both quiet for a moment. "I would, if I thought it would help."

And suddenly they weren't talking about Owen anymore. "So why don't you?"

"Because I don't think it would matter." Pain flashed over Travis's features and then hid behind a smile. "But I'm trying not to wallow, you know?" He fished a piece of ice from his glass and crunched down on it. "I haven't had sex in nine months."

"Clearly, the women in Aruba have good taste."

This time Travis punched Owen in the shoulder. "Just for that, I'm going to tell you that it was with Mal."

Owen closed his eyes. "Stop. That's my baby sister you're talking about. And I don't want to have to hurt you." He opened his eyes. "I did ask Mal if she wanted me to beat you up."

Travis, whose arms were about the size of Owen's thighs, snorted. "Oh, yeah?"

"But because she loves me and wants me to remain in one piece, she declined my gallant offer." Owen drummed his thumbs against the counter. "What happened between you two? Everything was good and then it wasn't."

"Story of my life. I was an idiot." Travis met his eyes and shrugged. "I screwed up. Big-time. And now she hates me."

Owen wasn't so sure about that. Mal had never said anything negative about Travis, never even hinted about what had happened between them, and as far as Owen knew she hadn't been on a single date since the breakup. "She misses you," he said and even though Mal had never said that explicitly, he was confident it was true.

Travis's head shot up. "Don't mess with me."

"I'm not. I just escaped engaging you in a scrap—you think I want to try again?" But the look on Travis's face told Owen that now was not the time to joke. "I mean it. She misses you. She doesn't date. She's totally turning into an old lady. When she's not at work, she's at home."

"I think I'm about to prove what a sicko I am, by telling you that I have never been so turned on."

"I'm not willing to act as a surrogate for her, okay?" Now Owen punched Travis in the shoulder again. He was no slouch in the muscles department, but his hand practically boomeranged back on him. "Keep it in your pants."

"I'll try." Travis's grin was back and this time it didn't appear to be hiding anything. "Does she really miss me?"

"I think so, but what do I know? I just got dumped."

"True."

CHAPTER FOURTEEN

"I'M SO GLAD you're here, Gaia."

It was a testament to how happy Grace was to be back that even her mother's slip of the tongue didn't bother her. "It's Grace. I had it legally changed and everything." Which had caused quite the hair-pulling and teeth-gnashing at the time despite the fact that she'd retained Gaia as a middle name.

"I know. And I don't mean to keep slipping up. Sorry, baby." Her mother hugged her more tightly as the cold wind whipped off the ocean at the ferry terminal, making Grace's face and toes ache. Somehow, instinctively, her mother seemed to understand that this wasn't just the postholiday visit Grace had promised months ago when she'd explained that she wasn't able to spend Christmas on the farm.

"It's okay." And it was. It was good to draw strength, to let the wind blow away some of the hurt and to just focus on breathing. The two days she'd spent alone in her apartment had not been cathartic. Not cleaning up the decorations, rearranging her furniture or picking up paint chips with the hopes that a new look would give her a new outlook. Instead, the idea of taping and rolling and starting fresh just felt overwhelming.

"Dad's excited to see you." Her mother squeezed her again. "I had to promise him chocolate to get him to stay home while I picked you up."

"Dad? Chocolate?" Grace was surprised, both by the use of "Dad" instead of "Cedar" and the mention of chocolate. Her parents hadn't had chocolate in the house since Grace had been ten, when she'd snuck it home from a neighbor's birthday party and hid it under her mattress. She'd enjoyed the sweet treat all the more knowing she wasn't supposed to have it. But as far as she knew, her dad and Sky had always followed the rules.

"Organic." Her mother pulled back and picked up Grace's suitcase. "And free range."

Grace wasn't sure how chocolate could be free range, but she wasn't up for hearing the details, which she knew her mother would be only too happy to share. "Are we off the Cedar and Sparrow names, then? Can I call you Mom and Dad?"

"You call Cedar that anyway." Her mother winked at her, tossed in her suitcase and slammed the back door shut. "You didn't actually think you hid that from me, did you?"

Grace was surprised. She *had* thought she'd kept it a secret. She didn't even slip when Sky was around. But apparently, her bat-eared mother had discovered their secret nickname anyway.

"And if you want to call me Mom, then Mom it is."

"Are you okay?" Grace froze, suddenly fearful. Where was her overbearing mother who demanded obedience? "Are you sick? Is Dad?"

"We're both fine." Her mother patted her on the hand. "And while I'll allow you to call me Mom in private, in public I'd prefer Sparrow."

It was the first time her mother had ever loosened her hard-and-fast rules. Grace peered at her, still uncertain. "Are you sure you're okay? No one's sick? Weeks left to live, that sort of thing?"

"Of course not." Sparrow puffed out her chest. "We're healthier than most twenty-year-olds. All the fresh air and hard work and clean eating."

Grace wasn't sure if that was true, but she could admit that her parents did look younger than their fifty-something ages listed on their ID and who was she to say that it was genetics and good luck as opposed to their lifestyle choices?

They made small talk on the drive to her parents' home. Well, Grace made small talk while her mother encouraged her to explore her feelings, which she did not want to do.

But when had that ever stopped her mom before?

Sparrow wheeled into the driveway and turned to Grace. "Let's go inside. I'll make you some chai nettle tea and you can tell me all about what's happened."

"Nothing's happened," Grace said, but her mother was already halfway to the house, Grace's suitcase bouncing merrily by her side. She hurried to catch up. "I'm only here for a visit, Sparrow. Because I wasn't able to come over the holidays." She purposely used her mother's name as a conciliatory gesture and one to sway her into letting Grace set the tone for the visit.

But Sparrow hadn't loosened her rules that much. "Of course something's happened." She pushed open the door and called to the house at large that they were back. "The question is if you're going to tell us about it or spend the next seven days moping around, thinking you're fooling us."

"I don't mope." Grace never moped. She considered her feelings, she debated how long an appropriate mourning or celebrating period was and then she followed the rules she set for herself.

"It's okay to mope." Sparrow started up the

stairs, seeming to make as much noise as humanly possible. "It is a totally valid response."

Grace didn't want to talk about valid responses or honoring her feelings or any other New Age psychobabble that her mother liked to spout.

"We love you even when you mope." Sparrow swung the suitcase into the room that had always been Grace's. "And there's no need to pretend around us." She hugged Grace. "We're family."

Grace wanted to defend herself, but there was a lump in her throat and she didn't think she could talk around it. She swallowed and concentrated on breathing, letting herself be hugged hard.

"There's not always a right answer, Grace. Sometimes things just are." Sparrow gave her a little jiggle that Grace suspected was meant to infer "chin up, buttercup." Then she looked at her daughter. "You unpack while I make the tea."

And all Grace could do was nod.

She walked into her room, still the same clean, white palette she'd selected at twelve. Even then, not yet in high school and years away from being known as the Condom Lady's daughter, she'd already been looking to be different from her parents and find her own way through life.

Grace heaved her suitcase onto the bed and

unzipped it. Nothing had moved during the trip, which was exactly how she'd packed it. There was an art to packing that people didn't realize. Her own mother, who had a tendency to hurl in whatever she thought she might need and then kneel on top of the suitcase to close it, was one of them.

Carefully, Grace unloaded her toiletry bag, double wrapped in plastic bags to prevent any spillage, then a series of small, light items. Her folded clothing, a dress shirt—not that she'd have any need for one here—a nice skirt and a pair of dress pants were all loaded into a dry cleaner's bag to prevent wrinkling. She hung the bag in her closet without looking at it, then pulled out her rolled T-shirts and sweaters, jeans and finally her footwear. Everything was stowed in its place and when she was finished, she felt a little better, a little more centered. As if she wouldn't break at the slightest tap.

This was good, all part of the grieving process. For a breakup, the formula was three days of grief per month spent together. That didn't mean Grace was completely over her relationships once she reached the end of her predetermined period, but it did mean she would no longer allow herself to actively grieve. When the end date came, she boxed up the hurt and got on with her life.

It had always worked before and this time would be the same. She'd count off the months, calculate her grieving period and get on with it. Even if her heart felt shattered. Even if just thinking about Owen made her knees weaken and threaten to buckle.

This was why she'd had to leave the city, her apartment and all the memories that lingered there. They were too close, too much. She could gather herself together here, remind herself of who she was. The memories would still be there, she knew that, but Grace hoped that she would be different.

She closed her eyes and exhaled. She had to be different.

GRACE STARED AT the computer screen in front of her. She'd been back at her childhood home for four days and was already beginning to feel antsy. Living under her parents' roof, coupled with no work and nothing to keep her distracted, left her feeling out of sorts and a little cranky.

It didn't help that Laurel's pregnancy was now obvious and their family dinners were filled with conversations about the baby, child-rearing practices and how they planned to raise her as "her own person." Which was ridiculous. Of course the baby would be her own person. Who else would she be?

Although they didn't actually know the baby's sex, Laurel and Sparrow had decided to use the female pronoun, believing it would somehow offset the innate patriarchy that suffused society. "She's a woman, being born into a man's world," they'd spout.

Grace's mention that the baby might "be a man born into a man's world" had been met with sniffles from Laurel, which made Grace feel like a heel, and a sharp retort from her mother on the benefits of putting positive thoughts out into the world. Grace had kept her mouth shut after that and had taken to hiding in her room once dinner was over. She liked Laurel, but if she had to debate the merits of baby clothing made from hemp versus homespun wool or listen to another treatise on the wonders of going diaper-free—which, as far as Grace could tell, meant having specially marked bowls all over the house and holding the baby over one when necessary—she'd go insane.

She was self-aware enough to know it wasn't just a difference of opinion. That was only part of it, but jealousy was just as much a factor. Grace could admit that. While her younger brother and his partner were bringing new life into the world and were totally content with the life they'd chosen for themselves, Grace was not.

No baby, no partner and although she loved her work, it clearly wasn't enough.

Which was why she was now sitting on the bed, her laptop beside her, staring at the screen trying to decide if her potential partner's age was somewhat important, important or very important.

She didn't want someone too old or too young because they might not be on the same page when it came to a future plan. But at the same time, how much did that have to do with age? Owen was completely age-appropriate and yet totally wrong when it came to everything else. Grace ignored the tug of heat between her legs. Okay, maybe not *everything* else, but most things.

And surely there would be other questions to sift out those potential mates who weren't looking for the same things she was. Grace clicked *important* and moved on. There were more than fifty questions to fill out and a short essay to write. She'd typed up the essay last night, so all she had to do was cut and paste when she got to that section.

She'd decided yesterday afternoon that she needed to prepare herself for the next step in her life plan: searching for a husband. Personal-life planning was something she hadn't done enough of over the past few months. Which was why she found herself in her current situation.

So she'd gone online using her cell phone as a hotspot, since her parents still refused to get internet service. When Grace had pointed out that they could put up a website about the farm and the store, which would increase business, her mother had given her a pitying look and patted her on the shoulder as though Grace was the nutty one.

Maybe Grace *was* the nutty one, at least in this family, but in this family that was okay. No one hinted that she needed professional help, though her mother had been known to leave brochures for holistic retreats on her pillow, which Grace simply stuffed into her suitcase and recycled when she got home.

If things went well and she found a good match, maybe they could go to one of those holistic spots together. The spas looked nice and there were massages and hydropaths and other treatments meant to relax. It might even be fun. She could imagine Owen there, making jokes and probably kissing her when he wasn't supposed to.

Grace's smile faded. That was why she wasn't booking a trip with him. Because the kind of man she intended to marry would take his relaxation seriously. She turned back to the questionnaire. She'd signed up with the city's most discreet and well-respected service. They didn't advertise and the only reason Grace knew about them was because she'd planned weddings for more than one couple who'd met through their services.

The company seemed to know what they were doing. At least, according to the polite and educated testimonials on their polite and educated website. They certainly charged enough for their services, which included a personal consultation with a matchmaker, an invitation to a monthly supper group where she'd be seated at a table with good matches for her, as well as at least three one-on-one dates.

Grace ignored the punch in her stomach at the hit her bank account would take, ignored the little voice that said she could spend that money on multiple holistic retreats or start a university fund for her new niece or nephew. She could afford it, and it would be worth it to meet her future husband, to get started on the next phase of her life and leave this one behind.

She exhaled slowly and worked her way down the list. She heard her brother and Laurel leave to make the short walk across the lawn to their own house and heard her dad come upstairs, his tread even and heavy.

She was staring at the last question when someone knocked at her door. "Grace?"

She pushed herself off the bed, still thinking

about the final question, and opened the door. 'Hi, Sparrow."

She was rewarded with a wide, warm smile. "You finished in here? I thought maybe we could sit down and have that tea."

Though they'd had the past four days together, there had always been someone else around, someone else needing her mother. Grace smiled and felt something inside her release. "That sounds great." She glanced over her shoulder at the computer, which was still humming away on the bed, then stepped out of the room and closed the door behind her. She could answer the question later.

Her mother had already boiled the water and had the tea steeping in a ceramic pot. She carried it into the sunroom, which was more of a rain room in the winter season. But the weather was clear tonight and Grace snuggled into one of the thick woolen blankets draped across the chairs and looked out at the stars. It was almost like being outside.

"Let's talk." Sparrow poured the tea. "What's going on with you and Owen?"

Grace sighed and took the cup from her mother, wrapping her hands around the ceramic. "Who said Owen had anything to do with this?"

Sparrow sent her a withering glare. "Do you really think you can fool me? I'm your mother."

"And that means you're psychic?"

"When it comes to my children, yes." Sparrow nodded and sat down, cupping her own mug between both hands. "I like him."

"I like him, too." It would have been so much easier if she didn't. If he was a jerk or thoughtless or cruel. Grace hardened her heart. She couldn't think like this. It was already going to be hard. She couldn't focus on all the wonderful things about Owen. Not yet, not until she had the distance of time so that her heart didn't ache and question whether she was doing the right thing.

"Then what happened? Because I know he likes you."

Grace seriously doubted that was true now. She shrugged. "It just didn't work out. These things happen."

"They don't just happen."

Grace knew her mother wouldn't be so easily brushed off. If she was honest, it was one of the reasons she'd wanted to come home. She'd wanted to talk to someone, wanted to share everything and hear someone else's opinion. "We were too different."

Sparrow nodded and blew on her tea. "How so?"

Grace sipped the earthy-flavored liquid. It wasn't her favorite tea, but when she was sick

CHAPTER FIFTEEN

GRACE TURNED AROUND to eye herself from the back in the mirror. Were the pants too tight? Too revealing? She fiddled with the sides, smoothing them down, even though they lay perfectly flat, then pressed a hand to her stomach. Which did nothing to stop the butterflies trapped there.

She practiced her Pilates breathing. In and out. She was ready for this, ready to date.

She'd met with the professional matchmaker to go over her questionnaire in detail, flesh out certain areas, so they could better match her. She'd signed up for the supper club next month, which would feature twenty men who could be possibilities.

In preparation for that, Grace had agreed to a blind date. The matchmaker had encouraged it as a way to get comfortable in the dating pool, and so she was meeting a man named Garrett for drinks. Casual, no need to linger and make awkward small talk over a meal if they didn't click. Still, she wanted to look her best because what if Garrett was her match?

She'd been surprised to learn that although the setting was less targeted, more matches were made at the supper club. Grace figured it had something to do with feeling less pressure. At the supper club, you were just one of a group. You didn't know who your best match was, which allowed a sense of freedom. Or maybe it was just the idea of choosing your own destiny, eyes meeting across the room and all that.

She turned back around, eyeing herself from the front. She wore fitted black pants with a matching draped top, an unstructured blazer in white and a multichained silver necklace. With her hair back in a loose knot and strappy black heels on her feet, she looked cool and chic. Elegant but fun. Interested but not trying too hard.

The matchmaker had suggested Grace and Garrett meet at a Yaletown restaurant known for its oyster bar. No personal information was exchanged aside from first names and photos taken at the matchmakers in-house studio. Following a meeting, both parties had to separately contact the matchmaker to release any further information. Though they could disclose cell numbers, emails or anything they wanted in person, the matchmaking service cautioned against it, recommending that they use the service instead.

Grace liked that idea. It was tidy and controlled, the way she liked her life to be.

She glanced at the time on her phone. She still had ten minutes before her cab would arrive. The restaurant was close enough to walk, but January nights were dark and cold, and Grace was in heels.

She added lipstick, a small package of tissues, a sewing kit and emergency Band-Aids to her clutch. She put on her winter wool peacoat and leather gloves, locked the door behind her and went to wait in the lobby of her building.

"GRACE?" SHE LOOKED UP as she exited the cab. A man who looked very much like the picture she'd been provided by the matchmaking service smiled at her. He strode forward to help her out of the cab. "I'm Garrett."

Points for politeness. "Grace." She shook his hand, feeling a shiver crest through her. Too bad it was only from the icy weather outside. "It's a pleasure to meet you."

"You, too." He closed the cab door, keeping her hand in his for a moment. Just long enough for her to realize that she might not have felt an immediate zip, but he did.

He was handsome. Thick blond hair, brushed off his face in a clean style. His eyes were pale blue and crinkled at the corners. The sign of someone who smiled a lot. Grace liked that. His coat was a classic style and showed no signs of wear and tear, and his shoes were dark and polished.

Garrett let go of her hand and offered his arm instead. "Shall we?"

Grace put her fingers on the inside of his elbow. It was a little old-fashioned and courtly. She wasn't used to it, but she could get that way.

Garrett smelled nice. Of toothpaste and soap, and his teeth were straight and almost blindingly white. Grace told herself these were good signs. Indications of good hygiene and genetics.

He shielded her with his body as they stepped into the busy lobby. A harried-looking hostess gave them a forced smile and explained that their reservation system had accidentally double-booked everything this evening. The wait for even a seat at the bar would likely be an hour.

Grace hid her wince. She didn't wear these particular shoes often and for good reason. They weren't meant for standing. But she wouldn't whine. It was her fault for wearing them.

"Do you want to go somewhere else?" Garrett had to lean closer to be heard over the roar of conversation in the lobby.

Grace glanced around. There was limited seating in the waiting area, all currently being used. And while leaving meant she'd have to walk in these arch-breakers, it also meant she'd get relief soon after. "Yes."

"I know a place nearby," Garrett said, pushing open the front door and leading her back into the cold January night. "Do you like wine?"

When Grace said that she did, he launched into a treatise on what he felt was the oversight of Malbec. Grace listened with half of her attention, the rest spent navigating the seams in the cobblestone sidewalks that just loved to grab hold of stilettos and send their owners sprawling.

She should have paid closer attention to the destination instead of getting caught up in the journey.

"Here we are." Garrett reached for the handle on the large glass door.

Grace felt her throat close. Elephants. She swallowed and forced a smile. "Great." Only it wasn't great. It wasn't great at all.

Garrett continued his defense of Malbec as they stepped inside, the door swinging shut behind them while Grace furtively scanned the interior of the wine bar.

It was busy, but not so busy that they wouldn't get a table. On the plus side, she didn't see Owen working his way through the crowd. Maybe he wasn't on shift tonight.

But she kept a close eye out as Garrett led her

through a gauntlet of bodies to a table for two in the back corner.

"So you want to try the Malbec?" Garrett pulled out the tall chair at the table and made sure she was comfortably seated before grabbing the chair across from her. Definitely polite. "We can order by the glass, but there's an amazing one they sell only by the bottle."

"Sure," Grace agreed. Malbec was fine. Her mouth was so dry, she wasn't sure she'd taste anything anyway. But she was going to do her best. She smiled again and tried to think warm thoughts and not worry about whether Owen was somewhere in the building.

She needed to focus on Garrett, on her next step, not on Owen and what she'd put behind her. Luckily, Garrett was a good conversationalist, obsession with Malbec aside, and it turned out he was right about the wine. It was delicious and a beautiful dark red color that was almost violet.

Grace was actually starting to unwind and open up a little about herself. Telling him she had a younger brother and her parents owned a farm on Salt Spring Island, where she'd grown up.

She felt Owen's presence before she saw him, just a little whisper of recognition that swept across the back of her neck and put her on high alert. He stood across the room, arms folded across his chest, watching her. And the delightful wine soured on her tongue. Grace nudged the glass away and tried to turn her attention back to Garrett, but her mind was caught in the beam of Owen's gaze.

What was he thinking, seeing her here? She flicked another glance up. He didn't look happy, that was for sure. A trickle of unease joined the flare of recognition. Why had she allowed Garrett to pick the location? She could have declined, made up an excuse for why they needed to go somewhere else.

"Are you okay?" Garrett had obviously picked up on her distraction.

Grace started to nod and tell him that she was fine, everything was fine. She stopped herself. "I'm so sorry, but could you excuse me? I'll only be a minute." She slid off the seat before he could answer.

Garrett, proving once again that his mother had raised him right, rose with her and helped her to her feet. Grace swallowed and thanked him. Her pulse was thundering and not just because Owen was wearing a suit. But her knees got a little weak when she looked at him again. The man knew how to wear a suit. He looked so tall and strong and... Grace shook the feelings off.

She rolled her shoulders back and managed to cross the room without wobbling until she stood in front of him. "Owen."

"Grace." He didn't drop his arms, didn't offer her a hug or a handshake or anything other than a glare.

"How are you?" It was an inane question, but it was the only thing she could think of.

She saw the flick of tension on his face. "I've been better." His gaze tracked across the room to where Garrett was sitting and then back. "Are you on a date?"

It would have been easier if he'd been mad or indifferent. Why couldn't he put on a brave front and pretend that he didn't care? Or that she'd wronged him somehow? Why did he have to look sad? Grace pushed down the guilt. She was sorry he was hurting, that had never been her intention, but she had to do what was right for her and she shouldn't have to feel that she'd done something wrong.

So she was honest. "I am." She didn't dare look over her shoulder to see if Garrett was watching them, couldn't bear to think of what he might be wondering.

"And you came here?"

Grace could and did feel bad about that. "It was unintentional."

A flash of anger surfaced and then disappeared. "I see."

She didn't think he did. "Owen." Whatever she'd been about to say dissolved when he looked at her. His eyes were so dark and soulful. She felt as if she could see his whole heart in them—the heart that she was grinding beneath her gorgeous stiletto heel.

"I miss you." His voice was raspy.

It pained her to hear it. Her throat grew thick, her breathing heavy with unspoken emotion. She reached out to touch him, didn't even realize that was what she was doing until she felt the steel of his forearm under her fingers.

He looked down at her hand and then back up. "Can we talk?"

Grace was afraid what would happen if she said yes, afraid that she'd let him back in when she knew nothing had changed. Nothing at all. Including her feelings. Clearly, she'd been a fool to think she could calculate her grief as if it was a line item in her budget.

He put his hand over hers. "Please."

And she couldn't say no. "We are talking."

But he was already drawing her away from her date, back to the far corner of the bar near the hall that led to the office, and she was letting him. It should have left them exposed, open to viewing from other patrons in the room. But he tucked himself into a small alcove, pulled her in behind him, and she was reminded of another alcove and another night in their not-so-distant past. "Owen," she said again.

He wrapped his arms around her and lowered his face to her hair. "I told myself to stop caring, to let you go."

Grace swallowed. She didn't want to hear this, couldn't hear this, but instead of doing the intelligent thing, she melted toward him. She'd missed him, too. His scent, the feel of his body, the sound of his voice. The way he made her laugh, how well he got along with everyone. But he didn't want her enough. "I can't do this, Owen."

"So you've said." His hold loosened, giving her an easy out. She didn't take it. She would stay right here. Just for a minute. One long minute to get closure, to say goodbye, to lock away in her heart forever. "And yet here you are."

"I told you." Grace opened her eyes to look at him. "It was unintentional."

"Right. Of all the wine bars and restaurants in the city, in this neighborhood, and you walked into mine."

She opened her mouth to disagree, to explain that she hadn't realized where her date was taking her until they were here and she was worried it would be awkward, would start things off on the wrong foot if she told Garrett they had to choose a different location because her ex owned this one. But she didn't. Because Owen was right. Some part of her—not even a deep, hidden part—had wanted to come in, wanted to see him, wanted to be right where he was this second.

"Come home with me tonight." And when he tipped her chin up, holding her close and looking at her as though she was the only thing that mattered in the world, Grace wanted to. It would be so easy to say yes. Easier yet when he lowered his mouth to hers and kissed her. Not hard and demanding. He didn't mark her as his own, though she knew from experience he could. No, this kiss was light, barely a touch, and it left her lips tingling. A connection.

Her heart stuttered and then slammed against her chest. "How will that change anything?"

He stared at her, but he didn't drop down on one knee and claim true love. "We'd be together."

It was so simple for him. They would be together and that would be enough. But it wasn't enough for her and she didn't feel like going over this ground again. Grace didn't need a dictionary to decipher the meaning of his words. She stepped back, chilled by the loss of his body heat. But she had to step back, had to make space before she threw herself into his arms and never let go. "That's not enough, Owen."

"Fine. Then marry me."

For one long moment, she stared at him, her heart and her hope in her mouth. Until she saw his eyes flick away. It was just a small twitch but one that told her he wouldn't follow through. "No."

His hands tightened on her arms. "Why not? I thought that's what you wanted."

She did. With everything inside of her. "But you don't." And she wouldn't do that. Not to either of them. It hurt now, but Grace knew it would hurt far, far more if she allowed it to continue. "I need to get back to my date." She didn't wait for his response, simply pulled away, turned on her heel and headed down the hallway and across the room to Garrett.

She heard his footsteps behind her.

"Grace. A minute."

But she didn't have a minute. She didn't have a second, not if she was going to make sure the internal shaking threatening to tear her apart stayed buried inside. She slowed and flicked what she hoped was a cool glance over her shoulder. "You've had your minute, Owen, and I'm on a date."

The crowd swirled around them, laughing, flirting, completely unaware that something so important, so life-changing, was occurring in their midst. Owen reached out and placed his hand on her arm. "I'm not finished."

Grace jolted and moved her arm behind her. "I have nothing left to say."

"Then listen." He leaned forward, his dark eyes insistent. "Listen to what I have to say."

She let her eyes flutter shut. It was easier to think, to separate her true feelings from the maelstrom of emotions swirling inside her, when she didn't have to look at him, to see the yearning on his face. "What could you possibly have left to say?"

Hadn't he already said enough? Hadn't she?

But when he remained silent, she opened her eyes to look. It was a mistake. He watched her, his gaze naked and longing, and she felt her poor bruised heart warm. Even when she reminded herself that nothing had changed, that there was nothing he could say to change anything, she hoped.

"Give me a chance and find out." He held his hand out but didn't touch her. He just left it there, left the choice up to her.

She looked at it then at him. "Owen."

"One minute." He moved his hand a little closer, so she could feel the heat from his skin reaching out to hers. "I'll even set a timer."

Grace knew it was a terrible idea. She still

loved him, and he still had the ability to send her life into a tailspin. She was on a date with another man. She looked at Owen's hand again. The touch she knew so well, within reach. She clasped her hands behind her back and gave a sharp nod. "Fine. One minute and not a second more."

She followed him out of the wine bar, back down the hallway and into his messy office. It was the first time she'd seen it since the engagement party. The realization surprised her. In some ways, she felt as though she knew Owen so well, but looking around this tiny room, seeing a part of his life that she'd held herself back from, she wondered. Not that it mattered. She crossed her arms over her chest and waited.

"I feel like I might not have explained myself."

Grace raised an eyebrow, but said nothing.

"I don't want to lose you. I…" Owen ran a hand through his hair. "I care about you." His voice lowered. "I need to know if I can make things right. If I still have a chance."

Her lungs tightened and she was stunned into silence for a moment and then her self-preservation kicked in. "Exactly what are you saying, Owen?"

"I want to ask you this properly." Her heart stopped. Just came to a screeching thud of conclusion. "I don't want to live without you, so I'm asking you to marry me. Again."

She started breathing then. "Oh." Same old, same old. No ring. No getting down on one knee. No sweeping her off her feet with declarations of love or offering proof that he was anything other than the man who'd seemed to find marriage so distasteful such a short time ago. "I've already answered this question and I can't imagine anything has changed in the few minutes since then."

Owen stared at her, his eyebrows forming a V. "Exactly. Nothing *has* changed. I always cared about you."

But if he thought that was the way to win her over, then he really didn't understand the problem. Proclaiming that he cared for her was a start, but coupled with his assertion that nothing had changed? Grace wasn't so sure. "I see." But she didn't. And she suspected Owen didn't, either. "Is that all?"

"What do you mean, 'is that all'?" His eyes narrowed. "Isn't that enough?"

No, it wasn't. It wasn't even close. But she saw that he didn't understand. In his mind, she'd wanted marriage and now that he'd offered it, she was just supposed to accept and give no further thought to why he'd done it or whether he'd change his mind again two weeks before the wedding. "Owen." She unfolded her arms. "I don't want you to propose because you're afraid of losing me."

Some of the tension on his face morphed into confusion. "Then why did you give me an ultimatum? Marry me or we're done?"

"Is that how you saw it?" Grace was stunned even as she recognized why he might have seen it that way. Her mistake in not making things clearer, in not explaining her feelings. "I didn't offer you an ultimatum. I wanted you to want the same thing I did."

"And now I'm here, asking you to marry me, which is what you said you wanted." She could see the redness rising in his face, the way his hands clenched into fists. She wanted to cry, but she'd sworn she was finished with that. She wouldn't cry anymore, but would get on with her life.

"But you don't want to get married." Her chest grew tight and she felt her breathing begin to wheeze.

"How can you know that?" And he looked at her with such open questioning that for a moment she halted, hovered on the edge of a decision that had the potential to change everything. Except he hadn't changed and he still didn't understand.

She exhaled slowly. "Because you're only

doing this because you think it's what I want. Owen, you didn't even get a ring." If he'd been sincere, he would have a ring. Even the least romantic soul in the world knew a ring was generally considered a key part of a proposal. A symbol of unity, forever unbroken.

He stuffed a hand in his pocket then and for one small second, Grace wondered if he was about to pull out a small square box and prove her wrong. He didn't. "I want to be with you, Grace, and if you want to get married then..."

"No. That's not how it works." How it worked was that he was supposed to *want* to marry her, supposed to *want* to spend their lives together. "You're not supposed to choose me as an alternative that beats being alone."

"I'm not." His hands once again fisted by his sides. "I need to tell you that I've thought about it and realized that I do want this."

He couldn't even say the word. She tilted her head and looked at him. Really looked. Peering into those deep, dark eyes to find the truth. "Owen, I love you."

"Then say yes." His hands unclenched and reached for her. She shifted, just slightly, just so he couldn't reach her, because if he did, she didn't know if she'd be able to go through with it. And she had to do this for both of them.

"I'm doing this because I love you." Grace

was glad her voice sounded calm and firm and not nearly as shaky as she felt inside. "I'm not going to trap you into something you don't want." Even though it felt as if her heart was breaking all over again.

"But you love me."

She exhaled slowly. She only had to hold on a little longer, keep a brave face and act as though it wasn't taking everything she had not to crumple into a ball as she sent him away. "Sometimes that's not enough."

"Why not?"

"I make a living planning weddings and I've learned what makes for a successful long-term relationship and what doesn't. Despite what the movies and music industry tell you, it requires more than love."

"Sex? Because we've got that part down." He grinned, his innate humor shining through. Grace didn't return the smile.

"No. It's not just about sex." Marriages that lasted, that stayed loving and supportive, were based on a multitude of things, a shared set of values and beliefs, laughter, loyalty and attraction. Marriage wasn't just about choosing a lover; it was about choosing a best friend. A best friend you liked to boink.

"Then tell me what it is. Help me understand."

But she didn't have any explanations left to

give. Either he got it, or he didn't. He didn't. Grace could feel her control beginning to wobble. She needed to get out of here. "We had a nice time and now it's over. Now you get to head off into the sunset and think of me fondly."

"Grace." But he didn't say that he didn't want to go. He just looked down at his empty hands.

"You're a wonderful person, Owen. I wish you the best." She was going to go home and indulge in a long, hard cry, but she would hang on until then. "Goodbye."

"I want my minute." She blinked. She'd been in here at least five. "Starting now."

"For what?" She lifted her hands. "What's left to say? You don't want to get married."

"Stop saying that."

"Then stop acting like it." Grace grabbed for control, calmed her breathing, her rattled nerves. Saying yes when he hadn't fully bought in to marriage would be an epic mistake. One she might never get over. She was doing both of them a favor by refusing. Even if he couldn't see that. "I think I should go." Because she didn't think she could last another minute here without losing her grip on her emotions. She swallowed and tried for levity. "You'll thank me one day."

Owen's answer was immediate. "No, I won't." His hand shot out to catch hers. "And if this is your version of the 'it's not you, it's me' speech, it sucks."

He wasn't wrong, but Grace shrugged it off. She had no other choice. Not one that she could see. Oh, sure. She could be swayed by her own longing, her own wants. She could choose to buy in to the fantasy that Owen really did want to get married. But she knew what would happen. He'd wake up at some point in the future and realize that she'd been right all along. That he hadn't been ready for marriage, and then what?

She couldn't risk it. But as she opened the office door and walked away, it felt as if that deeper hurt she was saving them both from had already burrowed deep into her soul.

CHAPTER SIXTEEN

A WEEK AGO, a month ago, Grace's rejection would have been enough for Owen. He wouldn't have been happy, but he'd have brushed it off and moved on. But not anymore. He was tired of brushing things off, of going with the flow, of not fighting for what he wanted, for what he deserved.

He slammed a fist on his desk so hard that the locked drawers rattled. It didn't make him feel better, but it did distract him slightly from the hurt in his heart. She was right. He wasn't acting like a man who wanted to get married.

Where was the ring? The planned proposal? Hell, he hadn't even gotten down on one knee. Well, if she needed proof that he'd changed, he'd find a way to give it to her. In fact, he'd find a way to give it to everyone in his life. Because Grace wasn't the only one in his life who seemed to think he couldn't be serious, that he was merely a laid-back, easygoing sort who could be counted on for fun but not much more.

It was time to show everyone they were wrong.

Owen yanked his keys out of his pocket, jamming one into the lock on his top drawer. It gave a mighty crash when he yanked it open and everything inside rattled and spilled over. He didn't care. He needed only one thing and the green folder was easy to find.

He plucked out the folder and slammed the drawer. The old Owen wouldn't have bothered to lock it or the door. But he was changed, so he spent the few seconds required to make sure everything was secure, then headed for the back exit of the bar, which opened onto a plain hallway. There, he took the stairwell that led to the company offices on the top floor of the building.

As he climbed the stairs, he planned. He knew Donovan was up there, working away, the perfect hardworking son. But Owen was a hardworking son, too, and he was tired of being treated like the second son, even though he was. He wanted more. He'd proven himself the past year since his father's heart attack. He'd stepped in at Elephants, increased sales, streamlined waste and made Elephants even more popular than it had been—and since Elephants had always been popular, it was something to be proud of.

Now he was going to do it for the rest of their

locations. Owen had pitched the idea to Donovan a few months earlier at the meeting his brother had promised for filling in at that first session with Grace, but nothing had come of it. Owen was going to change that.

He found Donovan in his office, his head bent forward as he studied his computer screen.

Owen paused in the doorway only long enough to snap, "We need a meeting," before he continued on to the big corner office, the one that had been their dad's, the one that would soon be his. Because he'd decided that it was time to make his mark on the company and on his own life. He was as much owner of the Ford Group as Donovan and Mal, and it was time he started acting like it.

Owen took the seat behind the desk, the captain's chair of power, and laid the folder in front of him. He didn't flip it open to look over the reports or refresh himself on the details. He didn't need to because he'd spent the past year studying them.

Donovan appeared in the large office a moment later, a frown on his face. "What's this about, Owen?"

"Have a seat." Owen gestured to the large chair across the desk, pleased when Donovan, still frowning, did as requested. "I'm here to talk shop."

"Talk shop?" Donovan raised one dark eyebrow.

"I'm bringing eighties slang back. Get used to that, too."

Donovan nodded slowly. "All right, then." He folded his hands over his knee. "Tell me what's so important that you walked away from Elephants to stomp up here and demand my attention."

His voice was calm and cool. Controlled. And Owen felt some of his newfound confidence slip. Was this really the best way to go about things? Storming up here on a whim and demanding to be heard? He took a breath and shoved down all the old thoughts. It wasn't a whim. The thick folder on the desk between them proved that.

Maybe Owen had once been the kind of employee satisfied with limited or no role, had tried to do as little work as possible and had grown itchy and anxious at the very idea of responsibility. But no longer. He'd changed and he was here to show his brother just how much. "I'd like to take on a larger role in the company."

Donovan didn't move. "Such as?"

Owen swallowed his nerves, his fears, his worries that Donovan might point out something he'd missed, some obvious flaw that he should have seen, and told him. His vision to bring what worked at Elephants to their other locations, how they could streamline inventory and purchasing at all locations. How he planned to oversee this, spending time at each location while changes were applied and remaining until they were just part of the process of doing business. His end goal was to oversee all locations from head office. He'd still work a lot of evenings, be on call for issues, but he wouldn't be installed at the bar anymore.

Donovan listened, asking a few questions, but mainly just absorbing. When Owen finished, he sat quietly for a moment. "You've given this a lot of thought."

"It's important. To me and to the business."

Donovan nodded slowly. "Your ideas are good."

Owen felt his lungs release the breath they'd been holding. "My ideas are great." He also didn't believe in false modesty.

Their eyes met, brown on brown, the same dark chocolate color. "You know, I think you might be right."

Owen glanced around in search of someone, anyone. "Can I get a witness? The mighty Donovan Ford has acknowledged that I was right and he was wrong."

"I didn't say I was wrong." But his lips twisted when he tried to hide his grin.

"It was implied," Owen told him. He shifted forward in his seat. "I've developed a six-month plan. But depending on other factors, we could shorten or lengthen that." If he could either train the management he had or bring in some experienced people, he believed he could speed up the process. He'd be able to spend less hands-on time at each location, simply giving them the tools and guidance they'd need, which would give him more time with Grace. Because he'd win her over to his side, too. Whatever it took.

Donovan sat back in his seat. "What brought this on?"

Owen sat back, too, lounging in the clear seat. It felt good to be here, bonding with his brother, being taken seriously. "A couple of things. Mostly Grace."

"I knew I liked her."

"I love her." When Donovan lifted an eyebrow, Owen nodded. "Yeah, I didn't expect it, either."

"It sneaks up on you sometimes." Donovan got a swoony look on his face. Owen would have pointed and laughed except he was pretty sure he got the same look when he thought of Grace.

"More like a punch to the chest."

"That, too." They were both quiet for a moment, thinking. Then Donovan cleared his throat. "What are you going to do about it?"

To Owen, the answer was obvious. "I'm going to convince her to marry me."

"Really?"

"Yes." Owen thought he would have come to that conclusion on his own, but seeing Travis had clarified things for him. He loved his sister and he loved his friend, but he didn't want to end up like them. Drawn to each other, but refusing to act on it. It was a sad way to live and he worried for them. Would they move on, past each other, or would those feelings always linger, the what-ifs, the one who got away? "And as my best man, you'll be responsible for my bachelor party. I want strippers."

"Have you met my wife?"

Owen grinned. Julia would kill Donovan and him. "Okay, fine. A trip to Vegas." Which had been his goal all along—he was just practicing some of his new business negotiation tactics. Asking for more than he wanted so that when he pitched his real desire, it sounded reasonable.

"Done. Has she said yes?"

"Not yet. But she will." Owen was sure of that. "Book something for a couple of weeks from now."

"You think things will move that fast?"

Owen didn't see the point in waiting. "I've decided to start going after what I want."

"I'm beginning to see that."

"Don't worry. I'll remind you if you forget." He crossed his legs and leaned a little farther back in the seat. "Any questions?"

"No." Donovan smiled at his brother. "I think you've answered them."

And for the first time in maybe forever, Owen thought he had, too.

BEFORE SHE EVEN got back to the table and lied to Garrett, claiming she had a headache and needed to leave, Grace had already decided that she wouldn't be seeing him again. Instead, she started working longer and longer days, arriving at the office before the sun was up and not leaving until long after dark. Even though it was the slow season and the number of weddings she had booked over the next two months was two.

But even though there wasn't a whole lot of work to keep her busy, working was preferable to dating. All she had to do was look at the fiasco with Garrett to know that success was not on the horizon. Garrett had been perfectly presentable. Handsome, smart, kind. All the things she was looking for. And she didn't want to see him again.

Grace had tried to tell herself that it was just a lack of attraction, that they were missing the zip that woke up the butterflies in her stomach. But that was only part of the answer. Because when she'd gone in to meet with her personally assigned matchmaker to select other dates, ones that might provide that missing zip, she discovered that not only was she not attracted to good-on-paper Garrett or his blindingly white teeth, but she also wasn't interested in meeting Jason of the green eyes who was an investment banker. Or Magnus with the big shoulders who climbed mountains and kayaked. Or Tom with the dimples who enjoyed wine tasting and fine dining.

Since she knew each one of those men had potential, good jobs, good genes and had been screened by the matchmaking service, there was clearly only one reason for her lack of interest. It was all Owen Ford's fault.

Sadly, knowing the root of her problem didn't bring her any closer to solving it. And so she thought it best to put a temporary hold on the process until she was in a better mental space. One that didn't involve comparing every man she met to Owen. It was time to take a break from the next step in her grand life plan and suspend her matchmaking account.

So she filled her time by researching new vendors, visiting potential location sites and taste-testing caterers. Even now, alone at the office after giving her team the afternoon off, she stayed and worked. Categorizing and subdividing her lists of suppliers according to various factors: time of year, number of seats, style of bride and groom.

She no longer thought about her own wedding. That was too painful and too far in the future. Especially since she wasn't even dating. Maybe in another month, though she'd already been dateless for just that long. But April was when the spring buds began to pop. Yellow daffodils reared their heads announcing new life had begun. Maybe at that point, Grace could shut away her old life and start her new one.

She was still playing with her lists, renumbering and adding colors, when the phone rang. She was grateful for the interruption. She'd renumbered and colored her lists so many times that even she was beginning to grow confused. "Grace Monroe Weddings."

"Hello, Grace."

She knew his voice even before her body flared to life at the sound. Owen Ford. She sucked in a cool breath. Oh, God. Why was he calling? What did he want? But her throat was too tight to ask.

"How are you?" She still didn't answer, but that didn't stop him. "I hope you don't mind me calling." She did, but she couldn't find her voice to tell him so. Instead, she clutched at the receiver like a lifeline, as though it could stop her from drowning in the wave of emotions. "I'm managing all the family properties now."

Grace swallowed. Why was he telling her this? How did this matter? But even as her lips buzzed with questions, she pressed a finger to them for silence.

"But that isn't why I called." Why did his voice have to rumble through her like that? Why did she have to feel the pull of desire? Why was he calling her? "I wanted to ask you out."

She grabbed hold of her voice then and used it. Self-protection. Instinct. Something else. "Owen, I've moved on." With her work and eventually her five-year plan. When she could force herself to get around to it.

"I've changed, Grace."

Sure he had. "Congratulations."

"Let me show you."

"No." She sucked in another long breath, wished she'd never picked up the phone.

"You said you loved me." Grace squeezed her eyes shut, yearned to shut out his words as easily as the familiar sight of her office. But Owen would not be denied. "If you meant that, just give me one chance to show you and if you don't believe me, I'll never bother you again."

Was that what she wanted? Her legs felt wobbly and she was grateful she was sitting down. To never be bothered by Owen again? Never see his smile? Hear his voice? It was how she'd lived her past month, which had been far from a resounding success. And yet maybe she hadn't. Maybe she'd wondered, held on to some foolish hope that one day he'd drop in or call or insist that he'd meant it when he said he cared for her, loved her, wanted to marry her.

"Grace?" For the first time, he sounded uncertain and it pierced her heart in a way his confidence couldn't. "Are you still there?"

"I'm here." She swallowed. She could say no. Cut this off before it ever started. Slice open her heart all over again. Not that it had ever healed. She exhaled. She couldn't say no, couldn't deny her own need to see him again, even if it was likely to end in more hurt. Maybe that was what she needed. One final stab to the heart to put this and Owen behind her. "Fine." Her throat was tight. "When?"

"Are you free tonight?"

OWEN PRACTICALLY CHEERED when she said yes. If she'd said no... Well, he wasn't going to think about that because she hadn't and so his plan was still in effect. "When will you be ready? I can pick you up in one minute."

"One minute?" She sounded dubious.

"I'm right outside your office." He grinned,

unable to slow the spill of hope racing through him. "I couldn't stand the thought of waiting."

Grace murmured something potentially unflattering but she didn't hang up or tell him she'd changed her mind, and she only kept him waiting five minutes. "This is completely abnormal," she said when she stepped out of the office and turned her back to lock up.

"I've been called worse." He ached to touch her, to hold her and kiss her, but reminded himself not to rush her. Not yet. He led her down the sidewalk to his silver convertible.

She shot him a questioning look. "Where are we going?"

"I'm surprising you." He helped her into the passenger seat and refrained from pressing a hard kiss to her lips. Barely. "You'll be pleased to hear I have a plan."

She sniffed, but allowed him to shut the door behind her. "Just so long as I end the night the same way I started it."

In fact, he was counting on that not happening. But that wasn't something she needed to hear yet. "I'm going to refrain from acknowledging that statement so I don't incriminate myself."

"Incriminate?" Her fingers edged toward the door handle, gripping the smooth leather as he pulled away from the curb. "Owen, where are we going?"

"I promise it's nothing illegal. Nothing dangerous. And something I hope will make you happy." If not, well, he'd cross that bridge when he came to it. He pushed down on the accelerator and headed toward his future.

"A FLOAT PLANE?" Grace stared as Owen proudly pointed out their next form of transportation. "I don't think so. What does this have to do with showing me you've changed?" In fact, he seemed the same fun-loving, not-serious man who'd stolen her heart. As though it sensed her thoughts, her heart gave a solid thunk.

"Consider it expanding your horizons."

"I don't need my horizons expanded." Nor did she need to get on a plane to who knew where with only the clothes on her back. "Owen?"

He touched her, for the first time all night, the first time in weeks, he touched her. His hand capturing hers and bringing it up to his chest. "This is one of those things where you're just going to have to trust me." His fingers flattened hers. She could feel the beat of his heart. "I know I haven't earned your trust." She felt his pulse quicken. "But I'm going to ask you for it anyway."

"Why?" She wasn't sure he heard her over the roar of the surf, the street noises that were part of city life. But relief showed on his face.

"I promise that everything will become clear. But you need to get on the plane."

She didn't want to think about the sweet look on his face, the hope in his eyes. Just because he thought he'd changed didn't mean he had. But she didn't move her hand from his chest. "And if I say no?"

"Then I'll take you out for dinner in the city or a walk or a movie or whatever you want."

She felt some of the tension knotting her muscles slide away. "But this is important to you."

"Like I said, it's all part of my plan." He brought her hand to his mouth, brushed his lips across the back. She felt the sizzle all the way to her toes. "But I would understand if you'd prefer not to."

Grace exhaled away the last of her reservations. She was already out here, had already said yes to giving him a chance. Who was she to say no to a plan?

She looked at the tiny plane bobbing on the water and nodded.

"Thank you." He kissed her hand again and this time, she was pretty sure the sizzle went through her toes and around again.

She'd been on a float plan before, but this plane was nothing like that one. Rather than the shoulder-to-shoulder setup she'd been expecting, the cabin was pure first-class with wide leather seats that were swiveled to face a sofa and a fold-out table in bird's-eye maple. It would have looked like a businessman's paradise except that the table held a massive vase of red roses and a bottle of champagne.

Grace turned to look at Owen. He'd stopped to chat with the pilot, who was looking over the plane. He seemed to sense her gaze and smiled that smile that nearly knocked her backward. She gripped the side of the door, hovering half in and half out of the plane until he finished his conversation and moved to join her. "Owen?"

"You were expecting someone else?"

"What is all this?"

"Just part of the surprise." He bounded up the stairs in two long strides.

Grace looked back at the setup. It was beautiful. And quality. She stepped into the cabin when Owen nudged her. The petals of the roses were velvety soft and their scent tickled her nose. There had to be three dozen. She bent her head and inhaled. "It's gorgeous."

But it didn't prove that he'd changed. He used to bring her flowers before. Just because these were on a plane didn't mean anything was different. But it was hard not to linger over the blooms and wonder.

She took a single seat across from Owen, buckling up and trying to get control of her breathing. Slowly, her Pilates training shone through and her inhalations slowed and steadied, which was more than she could say for the little plane as it bucked out of the water and into the air.

Owen barely waited for it to level out before he undid his own seat belt and came to kneel before her.

"Owen?" What was he doing? Why was he out of his seat? The pilot hadn't said it was safe to move about the cabin yet.

"I can't wait." As she watched, he put a hand in his pocket and slowly produced a black velvet box. "There's something I've been meaning to ask."

She stared at him. At the box. At him. At the box. He flipped the lid to show off a stunning French-set halo diamond band that she was sure would glint and sparkle even in the dimmest light. Awe made her mouth go dry.

"Grace Gaia Monroe. Will you marry me?"

She looked at him and tried to swallow. What was he playing at here? Why now?

"Grace?" His brow furrowed.

She didn't know if she could say yes, but she knew she couldn't say no. So she just looked at him. A small bead of sweat appeared on his brow. "Why?"

"Because I love you. Because I want to

spend the rest of my life with you. Forever. But, Grace—" his throat bobbed "—you're really going to need to give me an answer or this is going to get embarrassing."

Now Grace was confused. Embarrassing? It wasn't as though she hadn't said no before. Of course, he hadn't had a ring nor had they been en route to some likely romantic location, but embarrassing didn't seem the right description. "How so?"

"Well, aside from the fact that I'm down on one knee waiting with bated breath, there's the small issue of our wedding party waiting for us at the other end."

Grace jolted back. Wedding party? "You mean engagement."

"No." A second bead of sweat joined the first. "Wedding. As in our wedding. All our family and friends. Waiting to see us tie the knot."

"Before I even said yes?" She glanced down at the gorgeous ring again.

"Hence the embarrassing part." She saw his throat bob. "I thought it would show you that I've changed, that I'm serious about this, about us. But—" another throat bob "—I see now I might have put you in an awkward situation."

"You might have." Her eyes met his, saw the fear and the hope in them. "If I was going to say no."

"So is that a yes or do I have to ask again?"

"It's a yes." She held her hand toward him, shivered when the cool metal slid along her finger. Even the fit was perfect, tight enough so the weight of the stone didn't make it spin, but not so tight that it felt uncomfortable. She held her hand out so she could look at it properly. The way it picked up light and refracted it back. How good it felt. How Owen looked when he saw it on her. "But maybe you could ask again, now that I'm ready."

"Grace Gaia Monroe. Will you marry me?"

Grace didn't need to think about it this time. "Yes." She threw her arms around him and held on tight. "Even though you called me that horrible name."

"What? Grace?" He kissed the side of her neck as he lifted them both to a standing position.

She laughed, feeling lighter than she had in, well, forever. "I hope you're not poking fun at my name."

"It's just that Gaia has such a nice ring to it."

Grace snickered. "Oh, good. Then you won't be upset if I tell my mother you're considering changing your name to be at one with nature."

She felt the lift of his eyebrow and the curl of his smile. "Would you?" He sank back onto the couch, bringing her with him so she landed on his lap and carefully removing her suit coat. Then he flicked open the top three buttons on her shirt, his fingers trailing across her skin as he did, making her shiver and yearn.

"Yes." Grace let her eyes drift shut to enjoy his attentions. "She'll make you drink her special tea and do a ceremony, too."

He pushed back her shirt to expose her shoulder and upper chest and kissed his way down. "Will she read my tea leaves?"

"Only if you're lucky."

"Well, then I hope my luck holds." He licked the side of her neck.

Grace was distracted by him kissing her again and by her ring when the sun flashed across it. "Owen?" She leaned back. Her suit jacket had been tossed aside and her shirt was completely unbuttoned.

"Yes." He kissed her neck again.

"We're getting married tonight?" What about dress, flowers, invitations? Where was it happening? She hadn't had time to plan it, not any of it. Even an elopement required that she book a wedding officiant, apply for a marriage license and choose the pseudo-altar. "You can't just decide to get married. You have to plan and organize." And she should know.

"Which is why I started planning last month."

"Last month?" Who was this man and what had he done with Owen?

He nodded, looking mighty pleased with himself and awfully handsome. He reminded her of a little boy proudly showing off his schoolwork. Or arts-and-crafts Christmas ornaments. But still. She gestured to her business suit, now rumpled and more than half off. "I can't wear this."

"Give me some credit." But he didn't look upset, more amused. "There are dresses at the venue. And before you panic, Mal took Hayley with her to pick them out."

Hayley was in on this? And she hadn't said a word, or even given a hint. She had to credit her young employee for her ability to keep things quiet. Was she the only one unaware that her wedding was being planned right under her nose?

"But you had some say. You picked the flowers." He grinned when she frowned at him, having no recollection of doing any such thing. "Hayley said you have a favorite that you always try to steer brides toward, but they never choose it. Some sort of waterfall thing? She promised she'd take care of it."

Grace swallowed, both touched and surprised that Hayley had noticed and remembered her favorite bouquet—simple white peonies bundled together with glossy white ribbon and a cascade of small trumpet-shaped white flowers that reached almost to the floor. It seemed she was an even better employee than Grace had realized. "Did she?"

"Hayley was a big help once I convinced her that I was serious. Mal helped with that, and between the two of us, along with some family input, I think we did okay." He reached out to cup her face. "But if there's anything you don't like or you want to change, we'll just call tonight an engagement party and hold our wedding later."

She hadn't seen what he'd done, she had no clue about what was awaiting her, but when she opened her mouth to tell him, all that came out was, "It sounds perfect." Because at the end of the day she'd be married to Owen Ford.

And that was all that mattered.

CHAPTER SEVENTEEN

OWEN STOOD AT the front of the altar, set up on Cedar Sparrow Farm in front of the small pond with the sun just beginning to set. He felt keyed up, but it was anticipation and excitement for the life he was about to start rather than anxiety.

He'd decided against having his brother or anyone stand up with him, though he had asked Donovan to be a witness. Because this moment was about him and Grace and it felt right not to have a traditional bridal party. Nothing else was particularly traditional about the wedding, so he saw no reason for the ceremony to be any different.

Mal and Julia were in the main house with Grace and her parents. The other guests were seated in the simple white chairs set up on the field. His family, her brother and his girlfriend, some of the neighbors who'd watched Grace grow up, her staff and some of his. It wasn't large, not even thirty people in attendance, but it was just right.

Donovan had held the big wedding, the one

that invited all the family's business interests and acquaintances they'd collected over the years. And that had been right, too. Donovan was guiding the company, the one people would look to both now and in future. While Owen was happy to take on a slightly smaller role, one that was more hands-on.

It suited him, like the more intimate wedding suited him. And everyone he wanted here was here. His eyes landed on Travis, who looked uncomfortable in his suit, or with the prospect of seeing Mal. Maybe both.

Owen was distracted from his thoughts and whether he should give Travis an assist in talking to Mal when the musician, a local guitar player Grace's parents had recommended, changed from his low-key strum to a rhythmic pluck. Owen's heart began to race even before he saw Julia and then Mal appear.

They both looked beautiful in their strapless, knee-length white dresses. So did Sparrow, in a flowing white dress that ended midcalf and had crocheted stripes. It was completely Sparrow as was Cedar's white suit, which Sparrow had proudly announced was made from hemp and hand-sewn by a woman who lived on the other side of the island.

Owen had worried about having an all-white wedding. A little too nontraditional, not enough focus on the bride, but then he saw Grace's face, the awe, the wonder, the love shining through, and he knew he'd been right to trust Hayley.

Even surrounded by a sea of white, she stood out. Her pale blond hair down, smooth and sleek like a film star from the forties, and her luscious body hugged by a sheath dress. He wanted to peel her out of it now. Even with her parents standing on either side of her, walking her down the white runner they'd laid to where he and the officiant waited.

He wanted to run toward her in his new, specially purchased white kicks. He'd been worried that he might look too Elvis or too Bieber, but Hayley had assured him he would look great and she'd been right. She'd been right about everything, if the look on Grace's face was anything to go by. And then she was beside him, a secret smile playing over her lips, and the officiant was calling everyone to attention to begin the ceremony.

It passed in a blur. Owen knew he did the right things because no one had to nudge him along or ask him to repeat himself, but he didn't really absorb any of it. All he thought about was Grace and getting her out of that dress later to show her just how much he loved her.

They moved to the backyard of the main house after the ceremony, Grace and Owen holding hands the whole way. Hayley had been busy back here, too, dressing the place up while still maintaining the simple pleasures Owen recalled from his previous visit. He pulled Grace toward one of the amazing wooden chairs and took a seat, tugging her down on his lap. "Have I told you how excited I am to see what you're wearing under that dress?"

She looped her arms around his neck, a casual and familiar gesture, and leaned to whisper in his ear. "Who says I'm wearing anything?"

"Not even married an hour and you're already punishing me in unusual and cruel ways." He grinned when she laughed and grinned harder when she promised she'd make it up to him later.

Their intimate crowd mingled, drinking champagne and wine, beer and soft drinks, and enjoying a mix of food. Canapés and hors d'oeuvres conceived and prepared by Julia and a few of her staff, and down-home, rustic bites from Grace's family and neighbors. Homemade jams spread on crackers made with locally milled flour and topped with cured meats.

Owen sipped his water and watched as Grace moved through the crowd. Her pale hair glowed in the starlit night, as did her eyes when she looked at him.

"Get a room." Travis slapped him on the shoulder and dropped into the wood seat beside him.

"I intend to. Just as soon as it's not considered rude to leave."

"Look at you all well-mannered and responsible." Travis sipped from a bottle of water, too. "I almost don't recognize you."

"That's because you're not looking at me." Owen shot a pointed look in the direction Travis was looking, at his sister. "Have you talked to her?"

Travis ducked his head. "No." He didn't give further explanation.

Owen waited a moment. "So you're just going to sit there and study her from afar?" Because he knew Mal and she wasn't going to approach Travis unless she had to. Travis shrugged. "Fine." Owen pushed himself up. "And once this is over, you remember you owe me."

"Owe you?"

But Owen was already halfway across the patio and less than twenty seconds later, on his way back with his sister in tow. "Owen." She stumbled over a root. "What are you doing? I was talking to those people."

"It's my wedding. I'm allowed to steal you away." But he slowed slightly and navigated a little more carefully until he halted in front of the wooden chairs.

He heard Mal's sharp intake of breath, felt her nails bite into his arm and saw the hungry look in Travis's eyes. "I'd like to see the two of you talk." He gave Mal a small nudge when she tried to take a step back. "You do whatever you want after, but talk now. Consider it my wedding gift."

"I already bought you something," Mal said.

"I'd rather have this. For both of you." He saw the bob of his sister's throat, the way Travis's hand reached up to loosen his collar, and knew he was right. They might not make up. They might not even make nice. But they both needed this for closure. Satisfied, he turned on his heel.

"Where are you going?" Mal called after him.

"I've got a date. With my wife." And he used the line again to pull Grace away from the small crowd of well-wishers gathered around her and lead her around the side of the house.

She clung to him, her scent and body surrounding him. "Where are we going?"

"Sex house?"

She laughed and stopped him with a light touch on his shoulder and a brief kiss on his neck. "With all these guests to entertain? What if they followed us?"

"They wouldn't." He skimmed a hand down her side. Her dress was a cool, silky material.

"Have you met my mother? She would. And very possibly give us a lecture on safe sex." She sighed in his ear and Owen's body responded.

"We're married now." He brushed her hair off her neck for better access.

"Then she'd give us a lecture on prenatal care."

"Okay, no lectures of any sort. They ruin the mood." But he skimmed his hand down her side again, which fixed it. Or maybe that was just Grace. "Thank you."

She leaned back to look at him. "For what?"

He smiled. Believing in him, expecting more of him, challenging him. "Everything." He kissed her and then allowed her to lead him back to the reception. "Sex house later?"

She glanced back over her shoulder, a sweet, sexy glance that made him want to scoop her up and take her there now. "I don't know. You might have to convince me."

He stopped and since she was holding on to him, she stopped, too. Then he turned them so her back was against the house and bracketed her body with his. He saw her chest rise and fall more quickly as her breathing increased. His increased, too, watching her body stretch and strain against the thin material. He licked the length of her neck, the way he knew she liked. Drawing out the movement and then blowing, warm then cool. Her breathing was raspy when he finished. "Like that?"

She smiled. A satisfied, seductive smile. "It's a start."

It most certainly was.

* * * * *

Don't miss Mal's story,
coming from Harlequin Superromance
in September 2015!

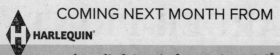

COMING NEXT MONTH FROM

HARLEQUIN®

super romance®

Available June 2, 2015

#1988 ABOUT THAT NIGHT
by Beth Andrews

Texas millionaire C.J. Bartasavich is used to being in control. But when he discovers he's going to be a father after a one-night stand with cocktail waitress Ivy Rutherford, suddenly he feels powerless. If he wants a place in his child's life, he'll have to prove to Ivy that he's honorable, kind and worthy of her and her baby's hearts.

#1989 A FAMILY COME TRUE
by Kris Fletcher

Ian North has always helped Darcy Maguire with her baby daughter, because that's what best friends do. But when an unexpected visit means Ian and Darcy have to pretend to be a couple, suddenly everything is *complicated*. The attraction is definitely there...but can they really be a family?

#1990 HER COP PROTECTOR
by Sharon Hartley

Detective Dean Hammer can't get June Latham out of his mind. The veterinary assistant is beautiful, sexy...and frustrating. Dean is certain she knows more than she's letting on about the murders he's investigating. And when she comes under fire herself, he knows he must protect her. But can he get her to trust him with her heart?

#1991 THE GOOD FATHER
Where Secrets are Safe
by Tara Taylor Quinn

For Brett Ackerman, Ella Chandler is the one who got away. Now she's back, asking for his help with a family crisis. But time together leads to a night of passion— and an unexpected pregnancy! Brett never planned to be a father, but maybe this is his chance to be the man Ella needs.

HSRLPCNM0515

LARGER-PRINT BOOKS!

GET 2 FREE LARGER-PRINT NOVELS PLUS

2 FREE GIFTS!

◆ HARLEQUIN®

Romance

From the Heart, For the Heart

YES! Please send me 2 FREE LARGER-PRINT Harlequin® Romance novels and my 2 FREE gifts (gifts are worth about $10). After receiving them, if I don't wish to receive any more books, I can return the shipping statement marked "cancel." If I don't cancel, I will receive 4 brand-new novels every month and be billed just $5.09 per book in the U.S. or $5.49 per book in Canada. That's a savings of at least 15% off the cover price! It's quite a bargain! Shipping and handling is just 50¢ per book in the U.S. and 75¢ per book in Canada.* I understand that accepting the 2 free books and gifts places me under no obligation to buy anything. I can always return a shipment and cancel at any time. Even if I never buy another book, the two free books and gifts are mine to keep forever.

119/319 HDN GHWC

Name _____
(PLEASE PRINT)

Address _____ Apt. #

City _____ State/Prov. _____ Zip/Postal Code

Signature (if under 18, a parent or guardian must sign)

Mail to the **Reader Service:**
IN U.S.A.: P.O. Box 1867, Buffalo, NY 14240-1867
IN CANADA: P.O. Box 609, Fort Erie, Ontario L2A 5X3

Want to try two free books from another line?
Call 1-800-873-8635 or visit www.ReaderService.com.

* Terms and prices subject to change without notice. Prices do not include applicable taxes. Sales tax applicable in N.Y. Canadian residents will be charged applicable taxes. Offer not valid in Quebec. This offer is limited to one order per household. Not valid for current subscribers to Harlequin Romance Larger-Print books. All orders subject to credit approval. Credit or debit balances in a customer's account(s) may be offset by any other outstanding balance owed by or to the customer. Please allow 4 to 6 weeks for delivery. Offer available while quantities last.

Your Privacy—The Reader Service is committed to protecting your privacy. Our Privacy Policy is available online at www.ReaderService.com or upon request from the Reader Service.

We make a portion of our mailing list available to reputable third parties that offer products we believe may interest you. If you prefer that we not exchange your name with third parties, or if you wish to clarify or modify your communication preferences, please visit us at www.ReaderService.com/consumerschoice or write to us at Reader Service Preference Service, P.O. Box 9062, Buffalo, NY 14240-9062. Include your complete name and address.